DELIVER ME FROM DARKNESS

Wendy,
come join me in
darkness...
...and hug love.
Best
Tes Holarne

P.S. Thanks for being a
Wellion... :)

DELIVER ME FROM DARKNESS

TES HILAIRE

sourcebooks
casablanca

Published by Sourcebooks Casablanca, an imprint of Sourcebooks, Inc.
P.O. Box 4410, Naperville, Illinois 60567-4410
(630) 961-3900
Fax: (630) 961-2168
www.sourcebooks.com

Printed and bound in the United States of America.
QW 10 9 8 7 6 5 4 3 2 1

To those who encouraged me to keep at it when the goal seemed unattainable. To those who put up with me while I reached for the stars. And to those who helped make this dream come true. You know who you are. Thank you.

Chapter 1

SHOULDN'T HAVE OPENED THE DOOR. ROLAND INSTINCTIVELY knew the fragile-looking burden draped over Calhoun's arms was going to wreak all kinds of havoc on his well-ordered life.

To hell with the door; he shouldn't have answered the damn phone. Then he wouldn't have been swayed by the rare frantic tone in Calhoun's voice when he'd called begging for a favor. 'Course, even if Roland hadn't picked up the phone, Calhoun would have assumed Roland to be in at this time of the afternoon and come pounding anyway. And yeah, Roland could have ignored that too, but doing so went against every ingrained fabric of his being. At least the being he'd once been.

This is what I get for remembering my manners.

"Thanks for this." Calhoun brushed by Roland, twisting so as not to bump the head of his precious cargo on the master bedroom door.

Roland grunted and moved into the bathroom in search of a towel. Best to keep his opinion to himself. *Get that scrawny thing and your sorry ass out of here* would not go over well.

Mumbling a string of curses, Roland yanked on the faux-antique glass knob of the teak cabinet and searched the handcrafted shelving for a sacrifice. All his towels were new. Everything in his loft was new. He liked new. Crisp, clean.

Unsoiled.

The tension in his shoulders crept down his back. With senses as heightened as his, any tainting of his personal belongings made relaxing difficult. It was going to take him weeks of cleaning and nighttime airings to remove the urchin's scent: like a friggin' garden…fresh-bloomed lavender, dewy mornings, and dirt. The dirt would only ruin his sheets, but the other smells had him spiraling down toward crazy.

Eyeing his choices, he grabbed one of the pristine white towels that didn't still have a tag on it and headed back to the bedroom. His efforts were wasted. Calhoun had already pulled back the sleep-rumpled blankets and was laying the filthy jumble of scraped elbows and dirty denim on Roland's clean sheets. Roland sighed and tossed the towel on the nearby dresser.

The bed was officially ruined. He hoped the cost of his newfound kindness would be limited to the bed. He hadn't even been here a week and his new sanctuary was being unsanctified. It had taken him months to find a New York City loft without any stains of violence, another to have it remodeled to his exact specifications, and still another to purge it of the stink from the contractors who had redone it. He suspected the lingering presence of this…girl…would take far longer to expunge.

"How long are you going to be?" Roland asked, trying to keep his displeasure from sliding into his tone. Calhoun was right; Roland did owe him a favor—a big one too. Roland just wasn't sure if this qualified. This wasn't big; it was colossal, and not only because of the cost of his Stearns & Foster.

Calhoun glanced up at him absently from where he'd been carefully tucking Roland's new, unwanted guest into the vast California king bed.

Damn. I loved that bed.

Calhoun blinked as if he had to think about what Roland had asked, his concentration obviously still on the woman currently soiling Roland's new silk sheets.

"I hope to finish by dark. If not, soon after," Calhoun finally said when he got his head out of his ass—or maybe that was his head out of his dick.

"Make it dark," Roland said, his breath hissing through clenched teeth in an effort not to inhale anymore of *her* scent. Not that it mattered. All he succeeded in doing was altering the girl's heady pheromones into candied sugar on his tongue.

And this was why he didn't allow humans, especially females, into his home. The seductive scents, the gentle whoosh of blood pumping, and the soft murmurs she'd make as she tossed and turned in *his* sheets. Roland fisted his hands. The call to rut, to feed, was like a rabid animal clawing at his insides. He'd kept that animal carefully caged, would keep it caged. Yet something of his internal trauma must have shown in his eyes. Calhoun's gaze snapped from Roland to the skinny slip of a girl he'd so lovingly tucked in bed, and then back to Roland again, his expression becoming increasingly alarmed.

Calhoun stood to his full height, which at a towering six foot five put him nose to eyebrow with Roland. The air in the room began to tingle. Roland could feel the gathering of power. See the aura shimmering around his supposed friend. That faint light singed Roland's skin.

Roland hissed, hastily giving ground until he was

across the room and practically pressed into the panel that hid his walk-in closet. Fury mounted within him and he had to work hard to suppress the vicious beast from awakening. He would never hurt Calhoun. His best friend, the only one who'd stood by him, the one Paladin who'd seen enough humanity left in Roland to take the chance to try and save him…to let him exist. But even Roland had his limits, and even for Calhoun he would not quiver like some cowed dog in a shadowy corner.

"You're teetering on the edge, Calhoun," he snarled, letting the fire spark in his eyes to emphasize his words. It might burn him, but he could have Calhoun's throat in his hand before the Paladin could draw enough heavenly light to turn him to ash.

Calhoun stopped glowing, but even so, Roland could sense the barely contained power bubbling beneath the surface.

"Is this going to be a problem for you?" Calhoun asked, his eyes flint gray.

"No." Roland rubbed his face. The skin was tender, but no real damage. "But it's been days."

Calhoun took a step forward, a lion ready to lunge into battle. "You won't touch her."

"I never said I would," Roland ground out from between clenched teeth. "She's safe from me."

Calhoun's eyes narrowed to slits.

"Jesus, Calhoun. I haven't taken an innocent since—"

"Since when?"

"Since you came after me," Roland finished. A flash of memory: the red haze of the bloodlust, the loss of self. How many innocents had he taken? He didn't know.

"She's safe with me. Regardless of when you return,"

Roland said, then curled his lip in distaste. "I have some emergency supplies in the freezer."

Pig blood and Red Cross discards. Lucky for him he was immune to illness. Though sometimes he wondered if contracting some horrific disease would have been a better way to go than this interminable hell he lived.

The tension in Calhoun's body eased. He clamped a hand on Roland's shoulder. "Thank you. After this, I'll owe *you* one."

"Get back here by dark and we'll call it even," Roland told him, annoyance making his voice sound as if it were being dragged over gravel.

Calhoun chuckled. Turning back to the bed, he gave the slumbering girl one last long gaze. The softening in his eyes alarmed Roland. Calhoun was tough as nails. Hell, even his dry humor was rusty. What was she to him?

"She's special, Roland," Calhoun stated, his awed tone confirming Roland's fears. Calhoun was already half gone. "Take care of her."

"Special how?" Roland hoped Calhoun meant special in the gifted kind of way, not special in the till-death way. Humans and Paladin didn't mix. It was that whole mortality thing. "You said yourself that she passed out within seconds of showing up on your doorstop."

That's about all he'd gotten from Calhoun. Some woman had shown up at his door and passed out. Moments later the reason for her flight had become apparent as Calhoun's sensors all went off. Rather than face an army of Ganelon's underworld fiends, Calhoun had grabbed his new burden and abandoned ship. And come here.

Why here? Why not to Haven? And who was she that she'd attracted the attention of Ganelon's minions?

All questions for later, after the curly-haired chit woke up and Calhoun had gotten his hard-ass head back on his shoulders.

The sound of a throat being cleared distracted Roland from his unwanted guest. Calhoun glared at him, his face deadly serious.

Shit. Calhoun wasn't the only one whose head seemed to be misplaced. Had Calhoun replied to his question? He didn't even know.

"What?" Roland asked, going for casual over deer-in-headlights.

"I've never regretted not killing you that day," Calhoun said. "Not once. Just—just take care of her."

Roland could feel the shift in his friend's loyalties. Calhoun had stood through Roland's fall from grace and through the Elders' demands that Calhoun terminate his once best friend. But now? And for a stranger?

There were a thousand things Roland wanted to say in the face of Calhoun's silent betrayal. Instead he shrugged. "No problem. She'll be safe and sound when you get back. Not a single hair on her head disturbed."

With a last measured look, Calhoun left the room. A few moments later the outside door snicked shut, leaving Roland and his new roommate alone.

I should leave. It's not like I can't sleep on the damn couch.

Instead he found himself lingering.

What was it about the girl that held Calhoun's interest? Roland's gaze followed the tangled mane of dark chestnut curls spilling down over her neck to where her pulse fluttered erratically.

He frowned, a twinge of concern making him start for

the bed, hand outstretched, before he stopped himself and lowered his arm back to his side.

Tired from her flight, no doubt. She definitely looked worse for the wear. The torn T and dirt-blushed cheeks would not make her a fashion plate. He supposed she'd be pretty enough when she cleaned up. She had the petite build and angular shoulders of youth and a wealth of freckles to go with the illusion, but her fully rounded breasts, emphasized by the tucked blankets, and the slight crease between her eyebrows suggested she was older. Mid-twenties maybe? Still too young. Too innocent. Despite the dirt, this woman was pure as the stark-white, fresh-out-of-the-package sheets she was laying on.

Roland rubbed his hands over his face, noting the resulting sharp sting on the inside corners of his lips. Fuck. His canines had elongated. Calhoun must have known this would be a trial for him—he wasn't an idiot—but Roland doubted Calhoun understood he'd just placed before his fallen friend a feast of pure delight. A human, Paladin or not, wouldn't have been able to smell the scent of a virgin. But Roland could.

This was definitely a problem.

Swearing a litany, Roland forced his feet to move—out of the room.

Karissa was running—and not doing a very good job of it. The toe of her sandals caught in an exposed root and she stumbled forward, barely catching herself on a nearby tree trunk before she performed another face-plant into the rotted leaves covering the unnaturally quiet forest floor.

Chest heaving and fingernails clutching the rough bark, she chanced a glance over her shoulder. Still there, still searching, even if they hadn't spotted her yet.

She scooted on her butt around the tree, knowing that hiding was futile. Her pursuers' senses were too good for her to hope they'd move on past. Two demons and their pet imps. Why had she tried to outrun the bastards on foot?

It was her only option. More than the exhaustion that caused her heart to hammer like a hyperactive bass drummer, thoughts of congealing pools of blood and broken, twisted limbs kept her from finding the calm she needed to flash her way out of this mess. She needed to compose herself. Shut down the memories. Concentrate. If she could lose her trackers in the lengthening afternoon shadows of the park, then maybe she could also get to the top of one of those high-rises where she could see across the city and use the last bit of energy she had to make one final massive jump.

Good plan, right? Or at least it would have been if she could execute part one.

Blinking her eyes against another gruesome flashback, Karissa tentatively craned her neck to the side to peek around the massive oak trunk. The imp she'd spotted should have found her trail by now, but a quick scan of the area showed no visible signs of the beast.

She frowned, gnawing on her lip. Long seconds passed. The eerie silence broke with the first high-C warble of a nearby cricket and was soon joined by a chorus of others. Had she really lost her pursuers?

This would be where I get going while the getting is good.

Yeah, good idea.

Lower lip caught between her teeth, she took the first tentative step to her left…directly into the arms of a chameleon.

Karissa jerked upright, her breath tearing out of her lungs on a long scream. Arms and legs thrashed as she tried to free herself from the snare of the invisible arms entrapping her. The creature hissed, long and low. Had to get free. Had to run.

Oh God, what will they do to me?

Same thing they did to Papa.

On a choked cry of grief and fury, Karissa kicked out again. She might be going to die today, but she'd go down fighting. A door banged open, followed by a gruff "What the hell?"

Karissa stilled, blinking as she took in the dim bedroom. Not Central Park. The arms that had ensnared her? Silk sheets tangled around her limbs. The hiss? She shifted and slippery soft fabric whispered with the movement.

Just a dream. Only…

She zeroed in on the man shadowing the doorway. Broad shouldered, though not bulky. Still, he filled up the space enough to be imposing, especially with his dark hair, black clothing, and eyes that were…Oh, crap! Vampire.

She scrambled up, flipping off the side of the bed. Weapon, she needed a weapon. Her gaze darted around the room. Huge bed with sacrificial white sheets. Long, bare mahogany dresser. Bedside nightstand with cast iron lamp perched atop it. Yes!

With a yank she tore the lamp cord from the wall, brandishing the wrought iron base like a bat. Not much, but it would have to do. Too bad it wasn't wood. Wood she could have worked with.

"It's all right," the vampire said, his arms outstretched and low, palms down.

All right? she scoffed, swallowing the hysterical giggle that threatened to follow. What was he? Stupid? Being trapped in a room with a vamp and a bed and no route of escape was decidedly *not* all right. The question was whether he planned to rape her or feed from her first.

"Perhaps an introduction would set you at ease." The vampire stepped forward, right hand extended. "I'm Roland. And you are my…guest."

Guest? Hardly. Kidnap victim maybe. But of whom? Did this vampire want her for himself, or was he acting on orders from someone higher up? Maybe the same someone who'd sent the posse out after her. The same someone who'd…

She gulped back the lump in her throat. Escape first, grieve later.

A glance down had her blinking at the pale hand he offered. Odd. In her experience, vampires were skinny, malnourished things—unless they were master vampires. Those had more meat to them. This one held the stature and lean muscling to be the latter—not to mention the affluent digs—but the dark circles under his eyes didn't add up.

Disgraced master vamp, perhaps? Maybe he hoped to trade her for a reinstatement of his status.

She jerked her head up and took a step back. The glowing embers in his eyes fixed on her neck. Ditch trading her in; this one may have been a former master vamp, but he was a *hungry* former master vamp.

His lips twitched and he tilted his chin toward the hand that remained outstretched. "It helps if you set the lamp down."

Yeah, as if she'd help him get his hands on her.

She straightened, weighing the lamp with a slight jiggle up and down.

"Okay," she said, then tossed it at him.

The next moment she popped out, her molecules zipping along a plane that wasn't quite there and reforming at the last place she'd fixed her gaze—which was all of ten feet behind the vampire in his own hall, a hall currently tilting on its axis under her unsteady feet.

Darn it. The jump had only been twenty feet or so. Still, her stomach pitched in answer to the dizzying side effects.

Swallowing back the swell of acid threatening to rise, she blinked and scanned her surroundings. Right or left? Left seemed to be a complete dead end so she took the right and stumbled on uncoordinated feet into the room beyond. Before her a large loft stretched out—kitchen, dining area, couch, plasma TV—but no windows and no doors. Of course.

"Well shit," the creature mumbled from behind her in the bedroom. "He was right."

She didn't bother to ask who *he* was or what he was *right* about. Like she gave a crap. The location of a window to teleport out of, heck, a door to the outside would do. That's the only thing she wanted to know. Somehow she didn't think asking her host would procure an answer. Speaking of which…

She glanced over her shoulder. The vamp moved silently but with purpose down the hall toward her. A couple more seconds and he'd be upon her. She cast her gaze around for somewhere to go. There was another room beyond, but it was even darker than this one. Not much chance of windows there. Not like she had many other options available.

A new weapon might be nice though. She scanned the kitchen counters. No knife block. Damn, wasn't it her luck to find the one vamp that didn't indulge in the useless habit of consuming real food? But there on the island atop a stack of slit envelopes lay a small pocketknife. Yes!

In a second she'd winked across the room and had the knife in her grip. Using the counter to steady herself, she spun around to see how close he was. He leaned against the far wall as if he didn't have a care in the world. Not that he should. With no windows and no door in sight, she was effectively trapped.

His brow arched. "You think you can kill me with that piddly thing?"

No, but she could hurt him. "Vampires bleed too."

He sighed, resignation clouding his eyes. "Mind taking this discussion back to the bedroom? You've touched enough things."

Touched enough things? What was this? A hypochondriac vamp?

Not wanting to waste energy, she took a chance and darted for the archway and the room beyond. On her way she dragged her hand over the island to scatter his envelopes, toppled two stools in her wake, jerked the phone off its holder on the wall, and smeared her free hand over the intricate molding of the archway. Who knew—maybe he'd freak out about the spread of germies and collapse in a foaming, raving fit on the floor.

Panting from the short sprint to the threshold, she took in the multitude of obstacles between her and the fireplace. A couch, end table, and the inconveniently placed armchair in front of the empty hearth. Behind the chair would be a basket of wood, right? Wood was good. A nice large splinter and she'd have a stake.

He swore behind her, drawing closer—though it sounded like he'd paused to right the stools.

She gathered her energy, her focus locked on the chair.

"Don't think about it. Not the chair. It's custom-ordered leath—"

She popped out, then moments later jerked back out of the netherplane with a sick twist in her gut—too many hops, too close together—and landed on the chair. It rocked beneath her and she had to plant her hands on the back to steady herself. The knife dug in, slicing a long slit into the leather.

"Fuck."

She glanced over her shoulder. He stood in the archway between her and the kitchen dining area, his hands laced through his shoulder-length black hair and his head tipped toward the high ceiling as if praying to God for patience.

Unlikely. Not only did he have all the time in the world—one of the quirks of being undead—but God wasn't going to answer the prayers of one of those creatures.

But how about spotting one of your daughters a splint of wood? Amen.

Or a flamethrower, she added. She'd settle for one of those.

Prayers said, she scrambled over the arm and looked behind it. No wood. The fireplace was gas. Of course. And since she wasn't MacGyver, chances of rigging an impromptu flamethrower were slim to none.

Thanks for nothing there, big guy.

Karissa expected the vampire to be hot on her heels. She was surprised he hadn't caught her already. But he stood in the same place, arms crossed over his broad chest, a look of long-suffering on his ruggedly handsome face as he watched her flounder around behind the ruined leather chair. *Colin Farrell goes Goth.*

What was she thinking? Handsome? Vampire? He must be trying to enthrall her. Only she didn't feel the things her papa had said she'd feel if she'd been enthralled: no loss of self, no hungry yearning to please her master. No way in heck did she have any inkling to please the bastard studying her from under those dark slash of brows.

She frowned.

He smiled.

Oh no…she didn't like that look.

"Lights off," he said with a devilish gleam in his midnight eyes.

The room went pitch-black.

Chapter 2

ROLAND STALKED THE EDGES OF THE ROOM, CIRCLING closer and closer to the woman stumbling blindly around in the center. No chance her scent would ever be gone now. Not with her hands stretched out, sliding over every piece of furniture he owned. She crashed into the end table, her full-lipped mouth curling around a string of muttered curses. She would know that his vision was all but perfect in the darkened room.

"Lights on! Illuminate," she called out, and when that didn't work, "Turn the effing lights on now, you chicken shit bastard!"

His lips twitched. God, she had sass, and a sexy-as-sin voice too. But it was meant for husky bedroom naughties, not for terror-laced demands.

He hated hearing the fear in her voice. Not because it raised the ugly head of the predator in him, but because it drew out something else. Something he'd thought he might never feel again...protectiveness. The type of protectiveness a male Paladin felt for his woman—or at least the woman he hoped to court.

Get over it, Roland. You're not a Paladin any longer.

Still, a voice screamed in the back of his head, *Mine!*

He stopped by the armrest of the love seat, five feet and two obstacles from his goal, as he tried to regain his composure and push down the unwanted desire. Upon waking, she'd somehow gone from a dirty street urchin to goddess: well-toned shoulders, a small waist, and a nicely flared ass. The pretty, wide-eyed face and pert breasts were merely a bonus. Girl she was not. Though she *was* innocent and scared ten ways past terrified right now.

"I'm not going to hurt you," he said and received the same skepticism he'd gotten back in the bedroom.

"You going to trade me off then? Sell me to the highest bidder?" she asked, retreating to the armchair as she grabbed a book from the coffee table.

He frowned, wondering how much she knew of the inner workings of the creatures that made up the dark underside of the city. Most people were blissfully unaware that they lived side-by-side with a host of predators that would love to either eat them for dinner or steal their eternal souls. How had this woman come by her awareness? More important, how had she come to be? Roland had watched the last female Paladin die ninety-four years ago. And no Paladin male would let a child, half-breed or not, roam the streets unguarded. Yet here she was, undiscovered, alone, and—if Calhoun's report was to be believed—targeted by a horde of soulless beasts...*beasts like me*.

He refocused his attention on the frightened woman. She had flung open the glass doors to the gas fireplace and was crouched before it, trying to light a rolled up piece of paper via the pilot light with unsteady hands.

Shit. Resourceful indeed. And just what he didn't need, more burns.

"Not a good idea, *mon chaton*." He was across the room before the endearment had left his lips. She yelped as he bent down over her shoulder and plucked the singed paper from her hands. He dropped it, stomped the embers out before the flame could flare into existence, and turned back to find that she already had a second glowing paper torch.

Add tenacious to the list.

"We just discussed this, *ma petite peste*. Don't you know that burning books is sacrilegious?"

He didn't go for the paper this time, but grabbed her shoulders and yanked her up.

She screamed, struggling to wave the flaming paper behind her. He let go of one shoulder long enough to swat the offending page of Tolstoy away before it could touch his arm.

The split second was too long. She spun around, her free hand arcing toward him like a claw. He caught it inches from his face—*huh, short stubby nails*—and simultaneously stomped out the second hiccupping flame marring his wood floor.

A clipped snarl rattled through her slight frame, but instead of sounding fierce, it emphasized her fragility and the fact he could crush her if he wasn't careful. Roland softened his grip. A knee came up, barely missing his manly parts as he twisted out of the strike zone. And then she turned into a thrashing, bucking animal in his arms.

So much for fragile. He spun her around, using her arms like ropes to lock her upper body. But not her legs. She kicked, arched, then slammed her heel down on his instep.

"Ow! Fuck, that hurt. What the hell kind of shoes are you wearing anyway?"

She jerked both legs up—strappy sandals with

spiked heels, figures—kicking off the wall. Because he was favoring the injured foot, the abrupt movement put him off balance and he stumbled back, tripped over the misplaced end table, taking them both tumbling to the ground.

Self-preservation had him rolling on top of her. No way was he giving those spikes another chance to sink into his flesh. If he could get those damn legs out of the equation, maybe she'd realize she was whooped, take a breather, and allow him to explain.

For one blessed second she went still beneath him, her sharp intake of breath followed by a delicious little shudder that racked her body. His own throbbed in response. Forget angular; this woman was soft in all the right places—like her ass currently cupping his cock, which was slowly rising to the occasion.

"I'm not going to hurt you," he tried again, then ruined whatever chance of comfort the words might have offered by sniffing at her neck. But what a damn fine neck, long and slim. And her scent? Intoxicating.

She whimpered, squirming beneath him.

Gawd. "Hold still!"

Which just made her struggle more to get free. He tried to shift his weight to force her immobility, but she was a wormy one, and her hips wriggled insistently against his crotch. His reaction was typical and immediate. The iron hard length of his full erection pressing into the cleft of her ass had the desired effect his muttered reassurances and brute strength hadn't. She froze.

"Better," he said, though it was anything but.

She hiccupped a choked sob, her salty tears scenting the air. Something jagged and unpleasant twisted in his gut in response. Damn it. He'd said hold still, not give up.

"For the last time," he ground out, "I promise I'm not going to hurt you."

She sniffled, giving a little jerk of her shoulders. "Why should I believe you?"

There she was, his obstinate little kitten.

"Maybe because I haven't hurt you yet? Maybe because it was Calhoun who left you in my safety?"

She sucked in a breath. "Liar."

"If you behave, you can ask him yourself."

"When? Where is he? What have you done to him?" She bucked beneath him again.

"Stop!" Thickheaded woman. "I've done nothing to Calhoun. Again, you can ask him that in, oh," he twisted his head, letting his senses explore outside the apartment, almost dark, "ten, fifteen minutes. Okay?"

She inclined her head slightly as if she agreed with his logic. About damn time.

"Now. If I agree to turn the lights back on, will you promise to not pop out someplace else?"

She nodded again, more firmly this time. He wasn't a fool. She didn't believe him about Calhoun, probably thought he'd sucked him dry and stuffed him in a closet somewhere. And because of that, Roland knew he couldn't really expect her to keep her word—hell, he wouldn't if he were a woman alone in an apartment with a hungry vampire—but he needed to get her to trust him somehow. He figured she'd eventually tire herself out with all the popping in and out of the other realm. There were no Paladin who could currently pull that trick, but he knew one of the first Paladin had been a teleporter. Written accounts noted how the gift took an immense amount of energy. Worse came to worst, she would pass out.

"Lights on." The dim overheads came on. As always, he had to blink even though the light was faint. And yup, there she went, only…*shit*, he was going with her.

Not cool, not cool. He held onto her with a death grip, feeling his molecules shift and jerk into the other plane. If she knocked him loose here he instinctively knew he'd be trapped—assuming he wasn't eradicated immediately.

Here they had no true body, but he could feel his will, and hers. She wanted him off. He wanted just as powerfully to remain attached. He concentrated on the thought of the soft skin of her wrists beneath his hands, what the velvety slope of her neck and collarbone felt like along his cheek and chin. They only rode the other plane for a split second or two, but it seemed like forever before they popped back into reality—kitchen, if the pile of crinkling envelopes were any indication.

His ears rung like he stumbled out from the last cymbal crash of creation, his vision spun with similar chaotic images, but his hands were still wrapped tight around her wrists and her soft body was still writhing beneath his.

He jerked his hands free of her, scuttling back like she were the sun itself. He'd found someone whose gift was as dangerous to him as Calhoun's. The other plane was a realm of possibility, the workshop of the One God. It was there He formed the likeness of Himself into His children. It was there He gathered together those volunteer angels, sculpted them into Paladin warriors, and delivered to them their mission—protect

His children from His fallen son. As a fallen Paladin, Roland assumed he'd never visit the sacred dimension his grandfather had told him stories about. He doubted he was welcome in that holy dimension now.

The spinning of his senses and the hammering of his dead heart finally slowed. He stood up from his crouch, blinked, and looked around at the empty great room.

He grimaced at his weakness, but reminded himself that she had years of experience recovering from the jolt. Should he try and find her again or let her hide until Calhoun came back? Let Calhoun try to soothe the little troublemaker.

Even as he thought it, Roland's shoulders itched with the need to move, to hunt her down. Why? Not because she was prey. He stopped thinking of her that way the moment she'd opened her big brown eyes.

Because you don't like the idea of Calhoun soothing your woman.

Not my woman, he reminded himself even as he savagely fought the urge to find her and mark her before any other Paladin could.

The door buzzer went off. Too late. It was dark and Calhoun was back. Roland didn't need to look at a clock or a window to know. His body was honed to the comings and goings of the night.

"Shit," he muttered and stalked down the hall to the paneled door that hid the exit.

A word had the locks popping and the door sliding open. Money had its perks, and he'd certainly had enough time to accumulate it.

"Calhoun," Roland greeted curtly, giving his back to his friend with the oh-so-impeccable timing.

"She still asleep?" Calhoun stepped into the hall behind him. The door shut automatically, locking them all in.

Roland grunted and moved the five steps to the bedroom door. Her scent lingered, but the room looked empty.

Calhoun peeked in. Hard gray eyes zeroed in on Roland. "Where is she?"

"Playing hide-and-seek it would seem," Roland cast over his shoulder as he continued down the hall. Probably back in his study, trying to start a blaze with his books.

A creak of floorboards behind him had him spinning around. She ran out of the bedroom, curls flying, and barreled into Calhoun's side.

"Help," she gasped as she tried to tug Calhoun toward the closed exit. Calhoun was about as movable as a brick wall and she was practically all over him trying to push, shove, and pull him to where she wanted him to go.

Roland's blood pounded, jealousy plumping his veins.

Calhoun blinked down at her, then whipped his head back to Roland. "What did you do?"

"No, don't," she pleaded, latching on to his elbow and trying to draw Calhoun back toward the invisible door. "He'll kill you."

Roland folded his arms across his chest. It was either that or flash across the room to rip Calhoun's throat out for touching his woman.

Not my woman. Shit. Why in hell were his Paladin bonding instincts asserting themselves now?

Calhoun flipped his gaze from her to Roland, his brow marred with a deep furrow.

Roland shook his head. No, he hadn't done anything to hurt her. These were simply female hysterics.

"Logan, please!"

And damn. She knew Calhoun's first name. He really didn't like another man's name rolling off those luscious lips.

She let go of Calhoun and ran to the end of the hall where she ran her hands around the handleless door, trying to figure out how to open it.

"Help me," she pleaded again.

Calhoun moved in behind her. His hand closed down around her wrist, turning her back around. He dragged her slim hand up to his chest.

Roland saw red. *Get your hands off my woman.*

Fuck. Shit and damn it all to hell. *Not* his woman!

"It's dark out there, love," Calhoun said. "Safer to stay here."

Roland fisted his hands, working hard to tamp the glow he knew had flared in his eyes with Calhoun's endearment and their entwined fingers.

She started to protest, "But he's—"

"He's a friend."

She shook her head in disbelief. "Do you know what he is?"

Calhoun's grip shifted to her upper arms, his normally harsh features tender as he answered her. "He's a vampire. And my friend."

The blood drained from her face, and she began to tremble, relying on Calhoun to hold her up.

Uh-oh. Here they went again. She was going to wink out at any second.

Roland sighed. "You've done it now."

Calhoun's eyes flashed to his, the question "done what?" visible in his confused gaze.

Before Roland could warn his friend about his little kitten's gift, she crumpled into Calhoun's arms.

Roland crouched, his fingertips touching the heavy black rubber of the roof as he absorbed the shock of the impact. A second focus on the next point, then a press of power, a twist, and he was soaring from this building to the next. Traveling across the city like this wasn't as cool or as unique as his little minx's trick, but it had basically the same effect. He could all but fly from one place to the next in the blink of an eye. Only his movement didn't involve vast amounts of personal energy or traveling in a dangerous realm to do so.

Damn, she was powerful.

His own gifts as a Paladin hadn't been nearly so impressive, at least not to his mind. His sixth sense of knowing certainly hadn't helped on the night his family had been slaughtered. Too late to save them. But too early to save himself.

During the ninety-four years since he'd been turned, he'd come to rely more and more on his vamp-enhanced strength and senses. He figured if he had to deal with the raging lust, the dark craving for blood, and the striking terror of light, he might as well enjoy some of the perks.

He was using a combination of both his old gift and his newer ones now. His Paladin senses exposed for something "off," someone "dark," while his vampire eyes and ears strained to catch the sight or sounds of trouble below. So far nothing had tweaked his radar.

Then again, he was finding it difficult to concentrate. Calhoun had looked pissed when Roland had blown out of the loft with no explanation, but he'd had to get out of there. The mere sight of *her*—he still didn't know her name, damn it—in Calhoun's arms had about snapped his control. When he'd realized that his friend planned to slide into the bed beside her, keeping vigil until she woke again? Roland's canines elongated thinking about it.

He knew he should go by Calhoun's place and check things out. As much as he wanted to twist his hands around his friend's neck right now, he didn't want Calhoun walking back into a trap. Besides, if anyone had the pleasure of killing Calhoun, it would be him. First, though, he needed to hunt, to get the damn bloodlust out of his system. He wouldn't be safe to head back to the loft until he had. The vamp in him demanded blood, fresh blood. Nothing else would sate the need.

Roland closed his eyes, drawing a deep breath: rancid waste, the sting of car exhaust, the cloying scent of alcohol and cigarette wrapped around sex. This area of the city with its tightly packed buildings, eclectic pulse of throbbing rhythms, and flashing neon lights was known for its nightlife. All well and good, humankind had a childlike, self-indulgent streak and needed to play their games somewhere. But areas like this often attracted the unsavory sort as well, those who would prey on the naive moths drawn to the flame of party lights.

Scooting to the edge of the roof, Roland settled down to wait. After a quarter hour, the back door to a nearby club banged open. A man stepped out, half pulling a woman who'd slumped against his side. She was young, college age, obviously toasted, and wore the pink blush of innocence and youth. The man was linebacker broad with graying temples and the beginnings of a beer belly—and his core was dark, edged with violent red. Roland had seen demons with cleaner souls than his.

"I don' feel s' good," the girl slurred, her head rolling on her neck as she tried to cast her gaze around her. "Where are we?"

"Outside. Thought some fresh air might help," the man answered, throwing her a greasy smile.

"Oh." The girl hiccupped. "Good…idea."

"I'm just full of them. In fact…" The man twisted her up against the side of the building, smashing her body between him and the bricks. "I have another good one."

Her eyes clouded with confusion. "Hey. Le' go. I never said—ow!"

The man had wrapped a hand in her hair and was dragging her head back at an awkward angle, abrading the back of her skull against the rough surface.

"You didn't have to say." The man licked the girl's exposed neck, from the tip of her collarbone up across her jaw to the base of her ear. Her pulse pressed against the slick wake on her skin.

Roland's own pulse throbbed in response, his tongue swelling with the need to take his own taste. He clenched his fists, averting his gaze until he could tamp the urge back down.

Innocent. She was innocent. Her only mistake the stupidity of youth.

"You've been flaunting that sweet ass at me all night," the man continued. "And now I'm going to take it."

Alcohol, or drugs, or whatever, made it take a moment

for his words to sink in. Then the girl's eyes widened, her mouth forming a shocked "Oh" as her body began to tremble.

"No, please!" she pleaded, showing her first signs of life. Her hands came up, pressing against the broad chest in front of her as tears leaked from her eyes.

The man laughed, spinning her around with a face plant into the brick as if she were some sort of rag doll and he the puppeteer. He twisted her right arm up behind her in a locking hold. At the same time his other hand dived under the hem of her short dress.

"My, my." He smiled. "Thong. Aren't we a bad girl?"

The heady mix of sweat, fear, and lust filled the alley below. Roland could barely think, so strong was the call of those scents. He hissed, his fangs slicing into his lips. His nails dug into the brick façade of the building. A slick pool of anticipation slid down the back of his throat. The muscles of his legs tightened.

The man would pay, and the girl? Well, a nice scare should put an end to her partying days.

Roland leapt.

Chapter 3

"SEVEN TWENTY. CUTTING IT CLOSE, WEREN'T YOU?"

Calhoun stood at the end of the hall silhouetted by the dim glow of recessed lighting in the great room, a steaming mug of coffee in his hand.

Roland couldn't disagree with his friend. Close didn't begin to cut it. He could still feel the burning kiss of the sun on the back of his neck. Everything had taken longer than expected, and his hope that the heavy cloud cover from last night's storm would buy him extra time had been misplaced.

Taking care of the woman's would-be rapist had proven difficult. The man's mind, though foul, had been strong. It had been tempting to just suck him dry and be done with it. It certainly would have been a much simpler solution to the scum's addiction to blood and fear. It was only because Roland could understand that addiction that he hadn't killed the man outright. Blood, fear, lust—the same cravings Roland had suffered from in those initial months after his turning. Still did. Time, and the thought of Calhoun's disapproval were he to slip, kept Roland in line. The man from the back alley had no such control and, it would appear, no desire or reason to alter his violent ways. Nope, Roland's black-hearted donor du jour was going to require a couple more visits before the new lessons on ethics fully took.

I really should have sucked him dry. Pain in the ass

*is going to be an understatement for the foul-minded
bastard*. Disgusted, Roland stalked down the hall, bur-
rowing deeper into the lead-lined walls of his refuge.

Calhoun lifted an eyebrow, a silent comment on
Roland's dark mood, but wisely offered up the mug
when Roland neared.

Roland grabbed it and, taking a long sip, held the
bitter warmth on his tongue. That vampires didn't have
to eat was a truth, one he was fully aware of when he
indulged and the meal sat solid in his gut before plow-
ing a path through his system. Didn't stop him from
having his morning coffee, though, or the occasional
evening scotch. Liquid wasn't so hard on his system as
the sporadic meal he suffered through for form's sake;
besides, his taste buds hadn't died when his body had
the first time.

"So what kept you?" Calhoun asked.

Roland swallowed, savoring the punch of caffeine.
Another perk: caffeine in the morning and alcohol at
night. His body absorbed what it could from whatever
he ingested almost immediately. The effects were instantaneous and powerful. However, unlike the lasting power
he consumed from the blood, both caffeine and alcohol
faded as quickly as the original punch, making it possible
for him to nod off or fully function minutes later.

"Your place is crawling with vamps," he answered
between sips. "Or was, I should say. The few I missed
would've had to go home for the day, as I did."

"Damn." Calhoun ran his hands through his hair.
"Why do they want her?"

Roland gave Calhoun a hard look. Innocent woman
plus power equaled a feast for the undead. Calhoun

might not have been aware of the first bit, but the latter he probably knew by now.

Calhoun's gaze shifted down the hall toward the closed bedroom panel. "Shit. When I said she was special—"

"You didn't mean that." Roland cut Calhoun off before he could go into detail. He didn't want to hear his friend waxing poetically about the woman who should have been *his* with that wistful tone.

Calhoun stared at the blank wall, the lines in his brow tipped into a V above his nose. The deep crease didn't mar his features in the least, adding character rather than detracting from the harsh planes of his face. Like all Paladin, Calhoun's age was indeterminate. Prime, some might have said, if not for the eyes. The eyes spoke of how old a Paladin really was, and Calhoun's were harder than most—except now.

Roland tried really hard not to obsess about what was making his friend soften. "So you've seen her little trick then," he asked.

Calhoun threw him a dark look—there was the steel. "You could have warned me she was a teleporter before you blew out of here."

"And ruin the surprise?" Roland smirked and ambled over to the study. He frowned as he took in the mess and had to further hide his emotions when the lingering scent of her fear punched him in the gut.

"She was only pretending to have passed out," Calhoun said from the kitchen. Mugs clattered as he grabbed another from the cabinet. "Tried to slip out behind you. Would have made it if not for the double entry. After that I chased her around a good five minutes before she eventually collapsed."

Calhoun sounded perplexed, as if he couldn't fathom why she would have been scared of him. Gee, maybe because the man she'd run to for help had turned her over to a vampire?

Stiffly, Roland sat in the ruined leather armchair. He didn't like the scent of her fear, but he did like her scent in general and it was strongest here…and on the floor where he'd lain upon her. Damn. He jerked his gaze away from the area rug.

"She's a Paladin. Full-blooded, to have such power." Calhoun followed him in, a new mug of steaming coffee in hand, and plopped down on the love seat.

Roland cleared his throat, setting his coffee aside. "Do I need to remind you of the exact day when the last female Paladin died?"

Calhoun looked up at him sharply. No wonder. Roland never brought up that day unless he was forced to. His coffee turned to a pool of acid in his stomach as memories flooded him. The blood. God. All the blood. It had been a massacre, and he'd been helpless to stop it.

"You know as well as I," Calhoun said, drawing Roland out of his true nightmare, "that a Paladin could be two hundred and look like they're twenty."

Roland shook his head. "She doesn't feel that old. She feels…"

"What?"

"Young, innocent."

Calhoun leaned against the back of the love seat, a scowl on his face. Roland could tell Calhoun wanted to argue, but he knew Roland's gift would give him this kind of insight.

"Possibly a half then," Calhoun said after a long moment of consideration.

Roland skewered his friend with a look. "Then who's the father? Unless he died before he knew he'd sired a child…" He trailed off, knowing Calhoun would understand the implications. For whatever reason, there had always been more male Paladin. With nine out of ten births being boys, a female Paladin, even a half, would have been protected and cosseted by the entire council. Not left to flounder in a world full of dangerous creatures bent on her destruction.

Calhoun pounded the arm of the chair. "She's not a merker."

Roland remained silent. That she might be a merker didn't sit right with him either. Merkers were the Paladin's dark brothers. Fathered by Ganelon the betrayer and born of demon mothers, they were a mix of all things evil. Yet they could blend in perfectly with the human race. The only good merker was a dead merker. Which meant that if she was a merker, Calhoun would be required to kill her. There was no way Roland could allow that. No one would touch her.

He pinched the bridge of his nose. He needed to focus on the matter at hand. The woman's heritage was all that mattered now. As soon as they knew who her parents were, they could figure out why she was being hunted and what would happen to her next.

It didn't make sense that she was so damn powerful. There were very few full-blooded Paladin anymore. That's what happened when the pickings were slim. There were fewer offspring in general, and the rest became less powerful as more and more of their blood was diluted by human mothers.

Calhoun tugged at his lip thoughtfully with his thumb and forefinger. "You think her mother could have been a merker-human cross, her father Paladin?"

Now Calhoun was really grasping at straws. A Paladin male would never mate with a creature that held demon blood, no matter how diluted the bloodline. Besides, "Would that matter?"

"Shit, no." Calhoun sighed, running his hands over his face and through his hair. Light played off the paler strands, reminiscent of the otherworldly glow he summoned with his power. Good. Clean. There were other words that could be used to describe Roland's friend, not all of them flattering, but that was Calhoun's essence. Calhoun deserved someone like that too. He deserved a mate who would make him happy. One who could erode the corrosive mantle of responsibility he'd donned in response to the ever-increasing demands upon him as son of the Paladin leader.

The dark part in Roland considered letting his friend struggle with the issue—maybe if Calhoun thought the woman part merker he'd lose interest in her—but the issue of her origin couldn't be ignored. Maybe she could never be Roland's woman, but that didn't change his instinctive urge to protect her. And he didn't relish the idea of killing a friend.

"Her essence is bright," Roland said. "Clean. Pure. And when she teleports, she's traveling through His planes."

Calhoun sat up straighter, his eyes widening. "How do you know?"

"She, uh, kind of dragged me along for the ride."

Calhoun's gaze sharpened. "How was that possible?"

Roland shook his head, still bemused. "I don't know. I had a hold of her at the time, and…"

Calhoun's eyes turned steely, his grip tightening around his mug.

Roland lifted an appeasing hand. "Hey, she was trying to set me on fire. I was just trying to stop her."

"Huh." Calhoun's fingers drummed on the ceramic mug. "And you were able to tolerate it?"

Roland shrugged. "We weren't there long."

"Still…"

Calhoun didn't finish the statement, but Roland knew what he was thinking. It was amazing Roland hadn't been fried on the spot. Only those with pure souls could linger in His planes without discomfort. And since Roland no longer had one…Perhaps that was it. He no longer had a soul.

"So." Roland cleared his throat. "What are you going to do with her?"

Calhoun took his time in answering. "I don't know. She's obviously in trouble. I *should* bring her to Haven."

It was clear the thought of doing so was distasteful to Calhoun. Roland saw it in the rolling muscle of Calhoun's jaw, the tension in his hand as he raised his mug and took a slow, methodic sip.

"Do you think that's such a good idea?" Roland had thought it a good idea before, back when Calhoun was tucking a dirty urchin in his clean sheets, but now?

He brushed aside any thoughts of "mine" before they could rear their ugly head. The presence of her gift was enough cause for concern without factoring in his possessive instincts. The creatures of the underworld wouldn't be the only ones hunting her for her power, though for far different reasons.

"Do you have a better one?" Calhoun asked.

Roland was quiet for a moment before finally saying what they both were thinking. "They'll want her for themselves."

A prize to be possessed. A power to be controlled. Just because the Paladin had once been angels before being commissioned by God didn't mean their tenure on earth hadn't affected them.

"Damn it, I know." Calhoun slapped his cup down so hard that it sloshed, the dark liquid running across the table to seep into the remnants of the Tolstoy.

"You could mark her." Roland's aversion to the thought formed a taste far more bitter than the coffee in his mouth.

The marking was one of the most sacred traditions among the Paladin. It was said that for every Paladin that He created He also created a soul that would perfectly match. It was something every Paladin dreamed of: finding his soul mate. The marking was a signal to all that the mate had been found, accepted, and the irreversible bonding of their souls complete. As time had passed and fewer Paladin females were born, the finding of a true bond mate became rare. Desperation modified the marking, enhancing it with ceremonies and spells to form a bond that was not naturally there. That ceremony was now both a test to see if a pairing was compatible and then, if it was, a seal of intentions. If so, a pair-bond was formed, creating a link between the couple that would grow with time. The strongest of these would eventually mimic that of a true mate-bond in that what one felt, the other felt, what one desired, so did the other. Their minds would be linked, their hearts for one another. But one thing it could never do was link their souls. A pair-bond was a powerful thing, and though it would never be as strong as a true mate-bond, if allowed to form completely, it was irreversible…except in death.

Roland glanced over at his friend, his blood simmering at the thought of another male bonding with the woman that should have been his. It didn't help that Calhoun's eyes had brightened, his finger tapping like a runaway metronome against his lip. Before the urge to leap across the room and claw at the throat of his friend overtook Roland's control, Calhoun shook his head.

"No. Right now she's scared. She doesn't trust me, and I don't doubt that she hates me a little bit. She wouldn't agree to a marking, and I would never do so without her consent."

"They will." *I would*, he added to himself.

Calhoun got up to pace the room, his strides jerky and filled with tension. Roland's own tension burned like a ball of iron in his gut. She couldn't go to Haven. The sense of disaster accompanying the thought was enough to convince him. The question was why did he feel this way? Was this another case of knowing? Or was this another facet of the unwanted pull she had over him?

Didn't matter. Her going to Haven was unacceptable. Some other option would have to be worked out.

"She can stay here," Roland found himself saying, even as his body involuntarily stiffened in the plush leather chair. What the hell was he thinking? He could barely keep his hands, let alone his fangs, off her. And here he was offering to look after her?

Calhoun looked at him carefully, his puzzlement obvious. No wonder, considering Roland had been wanting her gone since the moment she'd arrived. "You think that's wise?"

Roland shrugged. "I sleep during the day. I doubt we'll interact much."

Calhoun stood and nodded. "I have to attend my father's council and see if I can't gather some information of my own, but I will be back by this evening."

Roland followed Calhoun to the door. "Sounds good. We shall breathlessly await your return."

Calhoun shot him a decidedly unamused glare.

Roland smiled, giving the command to open the door. Calhoun paused on its threshold, giving Roland one last measuring look. "You are sure about this?"

"I'm sure."

Calhoun left, and the door gave a deceptively soft snick as it closed and locked behind him. The sound should have been something more ominous, a clang or a creak at least.

Roland turned to stare blankly at the door to his sleeping chambers, but all he could see was the remembered image of what all those mahogany curls looked like spread out over his pillow.

Yes, he was sure. He was sure as hell that none of the bastards at Haven were going to get a chance to claim her. Now he just had to dig in for the duration…and hope that he wasn't making the biggest mistake of his—or her—life.

—◦◦◦—

"You have got to be kidding me." Karissa glowered down at the bright yellow walkie-talkie that held down an equally innocuous-looking note: CALL ME IF YOU WISH ANYTHING.

Ha, as if. What she wished was to find a time machine, go back a week, and smack herself in the head for taking the path that had led her to this moment. Barring that, she'd settle for getting out of here. Somehow she didn't think her kidnappers were going to go for that.

She looked around the room: same four walls, same bed—*really starting to hate that bed*—same dresser, same nightstand with its bedside lamp that spilled light onto the tease of civility and the lie. The walkie-talkie and the note—as if she weren't a prisoner. As if the door weren't barred and locked. Okay. Maybe not barred, but certainly locked. Bastard.

The walkie-talkie crackled to life. "You ready to talk?"

Karissa hissed in a breath through her teeth. Heck no, she didn't want to talk to that thing. She didn't want anything to do with it. He was a vampire. A killer.

She pointedly turned her back on the walkie-talkie, not that he'd know, but it made her feel better. Like ignoring the tingle that raced through her body at the rolling rumble of his voice made her feel better.

What was with her? She should be scared shitless. No, she *was* scared shitless. She distinctly remembered being scared shitless when he'd been lying on top of her grinding his erection into her butt.

For a second. A very *brief* second before her body had betrayed her, fear melting into a delicious tingle across her skin. God! What was wrong with her? Twenty-four years and never had she had any serious lust pangs. Yet one glance from this vampire and she was practically hyperventilating.

Huh…Maybe he really did enthrall me.

Well, she was aware now, could throw the enthrall-ment off as easily as she cast off clothes. She'd do her damndest to resist any further attempts too. It was only a matter of willpower, after all.

The thing crackled again. "Fine. You can listen then. But you know…you should really cut me a break. It's not every day I agree to having a guest."

Guest? She snorted. "Prisoner more like," she muttered.

The walkie-talkie hummed to life again. "At least cut Logan a break. He's only trying to help."

Yup. Logan was helping, all right. The aiding-and-abetting kind of "helping" that the police would charge a criminal with.

The little yellow Motorola was quiet for a while. She thought perhaps her "host" had decided to give up, but then it crackled again. "Don't suppose you want to tell me your name."

Nope. She remained silent.

"So…I guess I'll call you Freckles."

Freckles? Her hand flew up to the bridge of her nose. She hated being teased about her freckles. Another point against him as far as she was concerned.

"What were you doing on Logan's doorstep?"

Running—duh—from the likes of you. And didn't that prove what an idiot she was. Trusting Logan had to be up there with all-time stupidest moves of the century. But she'd needed help, and she'd clung to her papa's belief that Logan would help her, with a desperation born of need. Too bad Papa hadn't known about the "friends" Logan Calhoun kept.

"Okay. Don't want to talk to me? Fine. Logan will be back tonight. You can tell him."

As if she'd talk to that traitor either. She wondered how much money he'd gotten for her. Or, he and Choppers *were* friends. Maybe they shared. She shuddered.

"Just so you know, here is how things are going to work."

If he thought she was going to do anything but possibly tear off his balls and shove them—

"There is only one bathroom and one bed here. And I intend to use both."

Sticky sour fear pooled in her mouth. Her gaze flew to the locked door. A door he could unlock at any time based on his whim. In an apartment she couldn't get out of. With a light system that he could control with a mere word.

As if on cue, the door opened. Roland stood on the other side of the threshold, his scowling face illuminated by the dim lamp beside the bed, the dark shadows from the pitch-black hall behind him caressing his figure like the creature of the night he was.

Oh, God.

"...so, you can either come out and spend your day out here while I sleep in there, or..." his scowling lips curved up, exposing sharp canines, "...you can share the bed with me."

Chapter 4

ROLAND HAD NEVER SEEN A HUMAN MOVE SO FAST. SHE was off the bed and flat against the far wall of the room in a split second, her gaze falling longingly at the dark hall beyond his shoulder.

Guess it was no contest. The dark trumped sharing space with him. The logical part of him understood this—woman plus vampire, *hello*—but another part, that which had awoken unexpectedly as of last night, wanted to stomp and scream and tear up a few things...and then pin her down and force her to accept him because, God damn it, she *was* his mate.

He shook his head violently to the side, as if he could dislodge the urge to claim her by doing so. *Don't go there, Roland. Doesn't matter if she* could *have been your bond mate. She can't be.*

Bond mate. He rolled his shoulders, the tension in them running down his back. He'd been purposefully avoiding thinking about her in those terms. Yet now that he had, he knew it was true, and with that came a confusing mix of anger and confusion.

Why her? Why now and not before...before he'd become a monster?

The unfairness of it caused a growl to rise in his throat. He just barely managed to cut it off. A quick glance showed her still plastered like wallpaper against the wall, her eyes watching him warily. Monster indeed.

Moving carefully so as to not totally freak her out, he crossed the room to his bed. He peeled off his T-shirt—she gasped—and stepped out of his jeans—a shocked cry. Normally he would have dropped his boxers too, but the sight of her, her body held perfectly rigid, like some damn bunny trying to avoid notice, stayed his hands.

He flopped down onto the bed instead, lacing his hands behind his head, and closed his eyes. He supposed he could have pulled up the covers, hide the erection tenting out his boxers, but he'd be damned if he would hide his desire for her. She was just going to have to get used to it—and him.

Damn it, Roland. When are you going to get this through your thick head? She cannot be your woman!

And because she couldn't, he needed to drive her away before his vampire instincts took over and he did something incredibly stupid—like open his eyes and try to enthrall her.

"Coming to bed, *mon chaton*?" he asked, purposefully lowering his voice into a husky drawl.

His answer was a rapid beat of her feet as she ran from the room and down the dark hall.

———

Hours later Karissa's heart was pounding with fear, her body tingling. She shook her head, trying to dispel the image of the vampire's evident desire. She told herself if he'd been planning on following her, dragging her back to the bed, and having his way with her, he'd have done it by now. Therefore, she was safe.

But for how long? Why hadn't he bitten her yet? Why

hadn't he taken advantage of the enthrallment and had his wicked way with her? It was his nature to do so, yet he hadn't. She immediately rejected the idea that it could be because he was an *honorable* vampire. She didn't need to remember her papa's teachings to know there wasn't such a thing, not when just yesterday the proof had been shown to her in the most brutal of ways.

Nope, there must have been some reason her host hadn't sucked her dry yet. And the weird gut-level pull he seemed to have on her must be something he was doing to keep her quiet, or more likely keep her off-kilter. She could not actually be attracted to that thing. Just like he couldn't be good.

She stretched her legs out in front of her. They were tingly and numb from being curled to her body, just as her arms were tired and sore.

Not to mention my backside. She shifted from hip to hip. The floor was hard and her flight in the darkness hadn't been graceful either. She'd bumped into more than one object before she'd found a corner to curl up in. Bastard hadn't left any lights on for her. Probably found it amusing to think of her blindly stumbling around out here.

There had to be a way to get the lights on. If nothing else there was the fireplace in the study. She should be able to get that going—unless he'd cut the gas to it.

She crawled through the great room toward the study, where she encountered the corner of the sectional with her head, bumped an end table with her shoulder, then finally rubbed up against the archway. From here she knew her way a bit better, the imprint of the love seat, coffee table, and leather chair burned in her mind.

She circled around them, crawling around the far side of the area rug, until her searching hands encountered the change from drywall to metal that suggested she'd found the fireplace.

The fact that there was no dim light from the pilot told her he'd at least turned it off. She found the knob and through pure guesswork twisted it until it started clicking.

Ignite, ignite, ignite.

Nothing.

Had to be a valve for the gas here somewhere. But try as she might, she couldn't find it. Five frustrating minutes later she still hadn't gotten any flame.

"Argh!" She stood, drew her leg back, and let loose a vicious kick. The metal edging on the bottom banged and gave a fraction where her heel struck—*hope I dented it*—she only wished it had been his face.

With nothing to do but wait, she made her way to the leather chair and plopped down. The stuffing from the damage she'd done padded the back of her head, making her smile slightly. She may not be able to get out of here, but she could certainly make her displeasure known.

"Why are you sitting in the dark? Not to hide from me I hope." Logan's smooth voice slipped around Karissa, waking her from a half doze. She blinked, her eyes stinging against the glowing ball of light that bounced over the palm of his hand.

Cool trick. She wished she could do that. Beyond Logan's glowing orb, the room, like the rest of the apartment, was indeed pitch-black, a fact that continued to irk her to no end and had lent to the violence of her fury during the last few hours. She'd searched every stinking inch of the place—other than the bedroom—looking for some sort of controls. Nothing. In fact, other than some basic furniture, the apartment didn't have much of anything in it. Decidedly annoying, since it had made expressing her displeasure difficult, but she'd done her best.

She stretched her legs out in front of her—good, at least they hadn't fallen asleep—and shifted into a more ready position perched on the edge of the leather chair.

"No. I'm sitting in the damn dark because I can't figure out how to turn on any lights."

And just like that the room was bathed in light.

"What did you do?" She glared at Logan.

Logan was too busy taking in the disaster to answer. The damage was minimal in here, really. If he thought a few strewn cushions and a torn up book was bad, wait until he saw the bathroom.

"How did you get the lights on?" she demanded again.

The corners of both his eyes and mouth were crinkled, as if he were fighting a smile. He quickly banked the expression, lifting and dropping his shoulder. "Nothing," he said, twisting his hand and extinguishing the light orb. "Roland must have tweaked the command codes to allow you to turn them on and off."

And didn't that sting the pride. She hadn't even bothered to try and turn them on via voice commands.

He took a step into the room. Karissa scrambled off the chair, putting it between her and him. His flint gray eyes narrowed as if trying to decide what his next move should be. She was struck again that his eyes didn't quite match the face. The face itself had a handsome, well-defined bone structure with devil-may-care dimples that could daze even the most feministic woman's mind, but the eyes spoke of a hardness derived from a wealth of life experience. If she'd had to judge him on his eyes alone, she'd have thought him honorable. In this case, actions—bringing her to a vampire's den—spoke louder than words.

"I'm not going to hurt you."

"No?" Oh yeah, witty come back, that.

"No." He took another tentative step.

She tensed and shifted her weight to the balls of her feet, ready to spring.

He stopped again, sighing. "I want to help you. And by God, you do seem to need help." There was that curve of the lip again as he glanced at the massacred cushion on the floor. "Roland's going to be pissed."

"Then help me," she ground through gritted teeth, "by letting me out of here."

"Every underworld creature known to man is hunting you out there." He cast his hand out, gesturing to the blank wall—as if the outside world was right behind it. Probably was—*now if I could just get to it*. "Getting out of here wouldn't be very smart," he continued. "And since you came to me for help, I have to assume there are some brains to go with the gorgeous face."

Yeah, as if that were going to work. With big brown eyes, mud-splattered freckles, and what could be best described as a cherub face, she was more the she's-so-cute, pinch-her-cheeks kind of pretty. Not gorgeous. "Don't try to flatter me."

"I'm not. I'm simply telling you the truth. Just as I'm telling you the truth about the dangers waiting for you outside. Just as I'm telling you the truth when I say you have nothing to fear from me. I want to help you."

Karissa tipped her head to the side, her eyes narrowed as she tried to read his sincerity. She'd always considered herself a decent judge of character, not the best, but decent. Papa had been the best—it helped to be empathic. Karissa hadn't inherited the full extent of his talent, but occasionally she could get a read on a person's true intentions. Especially if she were touching them and the emotions behind their intent were strong.

She couldn't get a read on Logan right now. No contact. And he was holding himself carefully under control, his features blank. Still, she was alive and unharmed, so that had to stand for something.

And, even if it doesn't, pretending to believe him is certainly a better way to find out what his plans for me are.

He must have seen some of her tension ease because he smiled, those dimples flashing. "Do you think we could sit down and talk about this like reasonable people?"

Her chin came up, not liking the implication that she hadn't been reasonable thus far. Maybe true—she glanced at the destroyed cover of *Redemption*—but still. "Okay. Where shall we sit? Around the cozy little island in a kitchen that has no real food, or in here, chatting around the nonexistent fire? Because, you know, the owner is a vamp and doesn't eat, and for some reason," her gaze drifted to the curled bits of burnt paper on the floor by the fireplace, "he doesn't trust me not to burn his apartment down around him."

"Yeah, Roland has a thing about fire."

"And light. And, oh, human blood."

Logan's eyes shuttered, the light of amusement dimming. "He's not like that."

"Really," she drawled.

"I'd trust him with my life."

He spoke with solemn conviction, his steel-blue eyes deep with emotion. It was enough to convince her that it wasn't an act.

She gnawed her lip, feeling even more uncertain than before. Could she have read this entire situation all wrong? Had she truly spent the last who knew how many hours running from and fighting a threat that didn't exist? She couldn't believe that. Yet Logan obviously did. There must have been a lot of history between them, enough to account for his misplaced trust. It made her curious to know what that history was, if not for the fact that she had more important things she needed to know. Besides, she got the impression that Roland was a closed topic with Logan.

"All right. I'll take your word on that…for now."

"Thank you." He gestured toward the archway and the room beyond. "I brought some food. How about I fix you something to eat?"

At the mention of food, her stomach rumbled. She gave a chagrined smile and nodded. "Sounds good."

She followed him to the kitchen, relieved that he didn't say anything about the overturned chairs and slashed furniture. He simply detoured to pick up two stools that seemed salvageable, gave them a quick test for strength, and placed them on opposite sides of the island. She tentatively settled on the farthest one—rickety, but it would hold her—while he began to take out groceries from a large brown bag. Bread, lettuce, cheese, sliced ham, tomato, instant tea, and a bag of chips.

"I know I'm ravenous after I drain myself in the use of my gifts." He gave her a quick look from under long, dark lashes. When she didn't respond, he turned his attention back to the preparation of the meal. She found herself studying him anew. With her tentative decision to trust him made, his imposing mass seemed strong rather than scary, and those eyes…an astute woman could read a lot in those eyes, if she didn't get side-tracked by those dimples first. Which brought to mind the question, why wasn't she? Logan was the type of man who many women would drool after, but she didn't feel any sort of pull.

No, only blood-sucking vampires turned her on. *Brilliant, Kari.*

"So. Can I be so bold as to ask your name?"

She drew her gaze up from where she'd been watching his hands deftly slice and stack the makings of two gigantic sandwiches. Competent hands, wide palmed with long, tapered fingers and calloused pads. He watched her carefully, his eyes no less intent than when he'd asked for her trust five minutes ago. Despite the intensity, she found nothing menacing in his gaze. Still…

Better safe than sorry.

She reached across the island, laying the tips of her fingers on his hand. He stilled, his pupils dilating. Shock zipped through the pathway the simple touch had opened, followed by a warming that turned into a sense of satisfaction and gratitude. Because he took her touch for trust? His lips curled into a smile, and just like that, his decision to do whatever it took to protect her, with his life if need be, became his fore-most purpose.

Karissa jerked her hand back, not liking the thought at all. Sure, she'd come to him for help. Yes, she'd been hoping he would protect her. But with his life? The responsibility of that didn't sit well on her shoulders. He didn't know anything about her, other than that she'd been nothing but trouble and a pain in the ass so far—oh, and she had a nice face. Couldn't forget that.

The abrupt removal of her hand had his smile reversing into a full-blown scowl.

"Sorry, it's just…" She waved her hand limply, then tucked it in her lap with her other. She raised her gaze to his, hoping she hadn't blown this totally. "Karissa. Karissa, um, Donovan."

"Well, Karissa, it is nice to make your acquaintance."

With purpose he set down the knife he'd used to slice the tomato, the same hand she'd touched, and held it out to her. A test. Did she trust him? Could he trust her? Knowing she'd be a fool to fail this one, she placed her much smaller hand in his, offering up a faint smile in an effort to ease the tension that had descended. She also made sure to keep her internal shields closed and *didn't* try and read anything this time.

"Same goes, Mr. Calhoun."

He gave her a nod, his lips turning up in an amused smile at the formal title.

Warmth heated her cheeks. She looked at their joined hands. He loosened his grip and she carefully extracted her fingers, glad he'd let her go without making any sort of production of it.

"Now, Karissa," he settled on the stool across from

her, scooting a paper towel with one of the ham and cheese sandwiches on it toward her, "can you tell me how it is that you know my name and how you ended up on my doorstep?"

Picking at her sandwich, she told him about how after a morning full of trivial irritations she'd cut out early and arrived home to find her grandfather slaughtered on the kitchen floor. She didn't tell him about all the blood, or how his blank eyes had seemed to stare at her accusingly. Nor did she tell him how they'd argued the night before because she'd enrolled in a set of evening classes at the university despite his long-standing insistence she not be out after sunset. Twenty-four years old and never had she been out past dusk. She merely told Logan how the moment she'd seen Papa's body, she'd immediately known that it was nothing human that had attacked him.

"So I ran," she finished, her voice sounding eerily numb to her own ears.

"And happened to land on my doorstep?"

She shook her head. "Papa said I should go to you if something were to happen to him."

"And your grandfather's name?"

She swallowed hard, barely able to get the name out. "Joseph."

His brow creased. "And you share the same last name?"

She nodded.

He remained silent while he took another bite of his sandwich, chewed, took another. His careful consideration drove her crazy, and after he finished the second half and still hadn't said anything she'd had enough.

"What are you thinking?"

He wiped his hands on the empty paper towel, then tossed it in a nearby trash bin. "I'm wondering not only how he knew of me, but why your grandfather sent you to me."

She blew out a breath, sending an errant curl dancing in front of her eyes. "I was kind of hoping you could tell me that."

"What, exactly, did he say?"

"That if anything happened to him I should find Logan Calhoun, that you'd help me."

He leaned his elbows on the counter, lowering his head so his gaze was on par with hers. "Find...so he didn't tell you where to find me?"

She shook her head.

"And how did you find me? I'm not exactly listed in the phone book."

She twisted her hands, running one thumb across the palm of the other. "I, uh, actually work for the phone company. I was curious one day and went into the unlisted numbers."

He shook his head. "Well that explains it."

"Explains what?"

"I'm Logan Calhoun Jr. Your grandfather probably meant for you to find my father—who, by the way, does not have a phone, either listed or unlisted. He's head of the Paladin council, so it would make sense for you to seek his protection."

"Paladin?"

Logan's eyes narrowed. "How much do you know about us?"

She pushed away the messy remains of her uneaten sandwich in exasperation, folding her arms across her chest. "I have no idea what you are talking about. I thought Paladin were some sort of elite warrior back during the Crusades or something."

He shook his head. "The name was hijacked. The first Paladin came into being centuries before the Crusades started."

"Came into being?"

"Created, by the one God. Each Paladin warrior was chosen from volunteers who stepped forward from the ranks of His angels. They were given various gifts and sent to earth to protect His children from the evils seeping into the world."

Whoa. God? Angels? Karissa fidgeted on her stool, unable to make eye contact. He was waiting for some sort of answer though, so she gave him the only one she could. "That's…I don't know."

"Hard to take in?"

She gave a nod. Overwhelming, unbelievable, even for a believer. Yet, she did believe. She couldn't have seen the things she'd seen in her life and not be prepared to accept what, to others, would seem surreal. She took another set of deep breaths, making sure her voice was steady when she finally spoke. "So, um, what happened? I mean, evil is present now more than ever."

The corner of his mouth quirked up. "Seems like it, doesn't it?"

"You don't agree?"

"I do, to a certain extent. Man will always be challenged to stay on the path of Right."

"But that wasn't really the Paladin purpose, was it? To be guiding shepherds." He'd called the Paladin warriors, not priests, after all.

"No. We were meant to fight Lucifer's minions."

"You don't still?"

"Oh, we do. But there are some complications now."

She urged him to go on. Belief had kicked aside shock and she realized she sat across from a man descended from angels. It should've been reassuring, yet she couldn't seem to ease the fear still knotting her gut.

"We were making headway there for a while. Then, in the late eighth century, the Paladin were given the task of protecting an artifact that could open a gate between the different dimensions of heaven, hell, and earth. It was a simple mission, to transport the piece from Spain to France through a pass in the Pyrenees Mountains under the cover of Charlemagne's army. One of their brothers betrayed them."

"The battle of Roncevaux Pass?"

His brows rose. "You know your history."

"Papa was a history teacher." She was surprised at how strong and steady her voice sounded. How could it when her entire insides felt iced over? Papa *was* a history teacher. Papa *was* an avid reader. Papa *was*. She shuddered.

"Have you also heard of *The Song of Roland*?" Logan asked, evidently oblivious to her pain. It took a moment for what he asked to sink in, but when it did…

She jerked, her gaze darting toward the hallway. Roland was a Paladin? But how? When he was…

"No, not that Roland. Though he is his descendent."

She turned back to Logan and licked her dry lips. "Okay, we can go into that later. But that song is just a—"

"Story? A myth?" He nodded his head. "True. And without knowing the full extent of all the forces at work, so is the historical account of a battle that I'm sure you've heard."

"All right. I can accept that." Divine warriors and gates between heaven and hell, history might acknowledge that religion played a part, but they wouldn't admit to anything mythical or unexplainable. "So. The Paladin were betrayed by one of their brothers?"

"Ganelon. In *The Song* he was Roland's stepfather and was angered because he thought Roland was trying to set him up by volunteering him for the dangerous mission. In real life he was one of our elders, part of the original council of twelve, and thought himself the inherent leader. When God put Roland in charge instead—"

"Ganelon was pissed. Got it."

"Ganelon was so infused with jealousy, a human condition none of the Paladin had ever known before taking on their earthly forms, that he made a bargain with the hordes of evil beings sent by Lucifer to steal the artifact. With the pact made, he helped set up an ambush. As Charlemagne's army made their way through the pass, the rearguard was set upon by hordes of Basques, their ranks swelled with Lucifer's fiends, and they were separated from the main force. What occurred after was a massacre."

"So all the Paladin died?"

"Of those that were involved in that battle? All but one."

"And the artifact?"

"The one who survived took it and hid it. His descendants are the only ones who know where it is kept and are always head of the council."

"Like your father is head of the council."

Logan gave a nod of acknowledgement.

She tilted her head, studying him. Believing that he was a warrior was no hardship. His finely honed body and his steel eyes told her that. But to think of him as a descendent of an angel? That was harder. "So, um, your gifts are inherited and make you a Paladin too?"

His brow creased as he tapped the island. "There is a bit more to it than that. We're born with the gifts and are raised and trained to follow in our elders' footsteps. When we're old enough, our parents present us to the one God where He approves us as His warriors."

"Does He ever disapprove?"

His mouth thinned, his eyes shadowing as he looked down. "Yeah."

Wow. She got the distinct impression she didn't want to know what happened when He didn't approve so she asked something else instead. "And does He ever make new Paladin from His ranks of angels to send down?"

"Not in over a thousand years."

A thousand years. And it sounded like the Paladin had taken some pretty large hits along the way. "How many Paladin are there now?"

"Not nearly enough," he replied solemnly, his head lifting so that his gaze bore into her, as if she were supposed to read some secret message there. A shiver ran up and down her spine, and not a good shiver. She shrugged it off. She was being silly. Despite the whole kidnapping thing, which, perhaps, wasn't so much a kidnapping but for her protection, he had been nothing but a gentleman.

"There are always twelve on the council," Logan said, flicking his gaze away as if only now realizing how intensely he'd been staring at her. "Right now we have perhaps another fifty whose duties span the entire globe."

"Oh my God." Talk about outnumbered. There were hundreds, no thousands, of vampires in New York City alone. She'd played by Papa's rules. Never going out at night, always staying in the crowd, but that didn't mean she hadn't sensed their presence hanging in the shadows on rainy days, or stalking the subway's underground network. She couldn't even begin to guess how many other creatures walked the streets in search of human souls. Those that could come out during the day were harder to pick out, their ability to glamour only broken if she made contact and had her inner shields open. Something she didn't dare do for fear of showing her hand.

"How do you survive?"

He took her hand, his eyes dark as wet slate as he held her gaze. "Our survival hangs very much in the balance right now. But perhaps you can help change that."

His thumb rubbed over the back of her hand. She didn't like the intimacy of the contact and pulled her hand free, folding both back in her lap.

"I don't know how I could—"

"No. I suppose you don't." He straightened abruptly. "And that isn't the main concern right now either."

"What is the main concern?"

"Keeping you safe."

Now *that* was something she could get behind.

Roland inched down the hall on silent feet. The near constant murmur of voices had drawn him out of a sleep that had been far from the usual sleep of the dead. Truth was he never slept well. Too many memories. Too many regrets. Not to mention he'd been doomed to a day of tossing and turning with *her* so near. He might have been able to resist the pull of her presence, but her voice, feminine and sweet, mixing in with the rougher baritone of his best friend had been nothing but another nightmare upon the many others that haunted him.

Coming to a halt at the end of the hall, he leaned an arm against the end cabinet and waited for his presence to be noted. As much as he wanted to rush in and break up the happy little scene around his kitchen island, he didn't want to scare her again.

It didn't take more than a couple seconds. Calhoun straightened from where he'd been leaning across the island, spun on his stool, and gave Roland a nod of greeting. *Her* gaze followed. After a quick intake of breath that had her spine going as rigid as rebar, she settled her elbows back on the counter, picking at her half-eaten sandwich in what he considered a sad attempt at apathy. Did she really think she could convince him that some wilted lettuce was more interesting than an apartment with a Paladin and a vampire in it? Especially given her earlier reaction.

"Calhoun." Roland folded his arms. Better that than lunging at Calhoun and tossing him across the room into the—upended?—end table. He took in the chaos that had once been his living room. Seems she'd been redecorating while he'd tangled with old nightmares. A few mangled pillows didn't concern him though. Calhoun had been *touching* her. And it didn't sit well with Roland at all. "Thought you weren't coming back until this evening."

"Thought you slept all day," she snapped at him, her eyes narrowed. Ah, she wasn't unaware of him. And wasn't it good to know she hadn't lost all her spunk. Just for Logan. With him she appeared to be all chummy. And didn't that just rub raw.

He shrugged. "Normally I do. But what with all the racket out here…"

Her cheeks reddened, even her freckles. Funny, he never realized freckles could do that.

"Roland, you've met Karissa Donovan," Calhoun said.

Her name coming off another man's lips scraped like coarse salt over his new wounds. He'd thought nothing could ever make him willing to do harm to his best friend and brother of his heart, but it seemed there was one thing. And her name was Karissa.

Should be me introducing her by name.

"Well, since you two seem to have hit it off so splendidly, I have to get back," Calhoun said after another minute of silence. Even managed not to sound too sarcastic. "I figured Karissa might appreciate some real food since all you have is coffee, scotch, and a bag of stale Doritos."

More silence. She sure seemed to find that lettuce interesting.

Calhoun tapped the counter, drawing Karissa's attention. "You have my card. Call me if you need anything," he jerked his head toward Roland, "or if this one gives you any trouble."

She stiffened, her head swiveling toward Roland as her face paled.

Shit. Was Calhoun trying to sabotage his chances of getting along with her? Did he actually want her to be terrified of him? *Possibly*.

"I thought you said I'd be safe." Her tone said that she didn't believe it.

Calhoun casually swiped up his crumbs and tossed his wadded up paper towel into the garbage. "He growls, but rarely does he bite."

"Logan," she squeaked.

At the same time Roland let loose a string of swear words, ending with, "You're an idiot, Calhoun."

Calhoun looked back at her, finally noticing he'd been scaring the shit out of her, and swore. He rounded the island, bending down so he was level with her. "I wouldn't leave you here if I didn't think you'd be perfectly safe. Trust me, Karissa."

Roland watched, fists clenched, as her brown eyes settled on Calhoun's slate ones, as if drawing strength from the steady gaze.

Should be me she looks at like that.

After a last, uncertain glance at Roland, she looked back to Calhoun and nodded in acceptance.

Should be me she gives her trust to.

Calhoun straightened, tucked a loose curl behind her ear, then cupped her delicate chin.

Yup, a dead man.

"I'll be back in a few hours," Calhoun said.

Her lips parted, a furrow in her brow, then another jerky nod. "Okay."

With a reassuring smile and a tip of his head, Calhoun left the apartment.

Roland waited until Calhoun's presence had not only left the inner door of his windowless prison, but had traveled through the outer barriers and into the elevator to travel down to the lobby forty-eight stories below. Then, and only then, did he step farther into the kitchen and, with measured control, open the cabinet over the refrigerator—the one cabinet door not ajar, completely missing, or hanging by a sole hinge—to dig out the much needed scotch.

"Scotch and Doritos?" she asked, surprising him. He'd expected her to run the moment his back was turned.

He shrugged, setting the scotch and the crystal glass on the island to pour out a measured two fingers. "If you're going to eat or drink, might as well make it worth it."

"But Doritos?"

Maybe he was wrong. That was definitely not fear. Her nose was wrinkled up in disgust, the sprinkle of freckles making the expression positively effing adorable. He wanted to kiss the wrinkle away. Instead he smiled, hoping it would further break the ice. Who knew? Maybe they could even make it up to cordial animosity by the time Logan returned. "Everyone's entitled to their vices."

The wrinkles straightened, her posture turning stiff. "I thought yours was blood."

Hell, who was he kidding? As much as he might have wanted otherwise, there would be no reciprocation of feelings on her part.

"Touché." He tossed back the scotch, poured two more fingers, and swallowed them too.

"And you're an alcoholic as well," she snorted in disgust.

He wished. If he were, then maybe he could toss the scotch down fast enough to drown the voice that was still screaming *mine* in his head.

He gave her a feral smile, making sure to expose his canines. She practically jumped off the stool, her hands clutching the rounded seat as if she were ready to grab it up, smash it, and use the wooden legs as a shield of stakes if he dared so much as to breathe. He took a step back, giving her room as he leaned against the counter by the sink.

"You seem to know much about vampires, I would think you'd know that we can't become drunks."

"You don't have to be drunk all the time to be an alcoholic. It's a matter of addiction," she said, eying him warily.

"And you are a woman of technicalities." And in her limited view he could never be anything more than a monster. He was inclined to agree, but he was also a stubborn bastard. He wouldn't let himself be a monster, nor would he allow himself to be pegged so neatly into that hole.

He rolled the mostly empty glass in his hand, the dollop of liquid sliding up then down the side of the cut crystal. "Let's go with this theory of yours, shall we?"

"What theory?"

"Why do people become alcoholics?"

She didn't look inclined to answer, and made herself busy by scooping up her half-eaten sandwich and bringing it to the trash.

"Escapism, yes? They like how the drink makes them feel. They like that it can make them forget. They have forgotten what life is like without it. A vampire, as you may, or may not, know processes the alcohol almost immediately. Ergo we can't suffer from the same chemical dependency that an unturned human would. Ergo no addiction." He looked at her curiously. She hadn't fled after depositing her trash and now leaned against the island less than a yard away. Brave…and foolish, given her obvious distrust of him; a simple reach and snatch and she could be in his arms. And then…then…his gaze dipped to her mouth.

"So, you drink it for the taste."

"Of course." He straightened, heroically keeping his one hand in his pocket and the other wrapped around the glass. "Why else?"

She stepped forward, her brown eyes locking on his as she stared him down. "Oh, I don't know. Maybe you drink because at one point in time you were human. Maybe you still remember the sweet sting of the alcohol hitting the back of your mouth, the spreading warmth as it burned in your belly, and the lazy waves of indifference that rolled in with it, demolishing all cares or worries. Maybe you were an alcoholic, or had the propensity to be one at least, and now, being what you are, and not being able to escape from it, you are instinctively succumbing to the addiction. In short, you are weak."

"Weak." The vile word rolled like a jagged stone in his mouth.

"That's right." Her mouth curled up in a saccharine smile, small white teeth flashing as she leaned closer into his personal space. "Weak."

Weak indeed. If he had been a weak man, then every time he went on the hunt he'd let instincts overtake him and succumb to the call of blood pumping through the veins of his prey. Just like a weak man, when faced with a friend's request to harbor a young innocent that would tempt every aspect of his being, both vampire and Paladin, would have turned his back. If he were weak, he would have continued to deny what he already knew in his heart, in the hollow place that once held his soul: She was his mate. And if he were weak, he would have used that as an excuse to take what he wanted from her, to claim something he had no right to claim.

He was not weak. At least, not completely. Though there were times when he faltered. Like now, looking down into those beautiful brown eyes that were trying to bore a hole in his head. Melted chocolate. He wanted to drink them in, the same as he wanted to taste the full strawberry pink lips that were currently pursed in smug challenge.

She probably didn't even realize she had thrown down the gauntlet, probably thought she was being defiant, showing her strength by daring to get so close. Stupid woman. Hadn't anyone ever told her not to play with fire? If her brown eyes were an addiction he could drown in and her lips an edible fruit, then her smooth skin was the fuel of his desire, her crisp floral scent the accelerant. An inch closer and they were both going to go up in flames.

One kiss. One taste. One moment.

He shouldn't. She was too pure for him. She deserved more than a mate who could only offer her pain. More than a monster who would crave her blood as much as her companionship. He should turn his back on her now and get the hell away from here before he did something they'd both regret.

He shifted into her space.

Her head tipped back, hair slipping down her back, exposing her long neck and the pulse that flitted there. A hand came up as if to ward him off, but she stopped partway, hovering as if with indecision. He watched self-preservation war with something else…something that caused her lips to slacken into an openmouthed "oh" and the hand wavering between them to fall lightly upon his chest, curling into the soft material of his shirt.

A pulse of red fire licked at the soft whites, pinks, purples, and yellows of her essence. Roland's nostrils flared, scenting the concurrent change in her body chemistry: crisp lavender spiked with spicy musk.

She might not want to be, but she was aroused.

Hell.

Straws. Camels. Backs. Everyone had a point when they broke. Turns out his was his mate's desire.

He closed the distance between them, lacing one hand behind her head in her curls as the other reached to set the empty glass down. It landed with a plunk on the butcher block. At the same time a small gasp of indrawn breath left her lips. Sweet full lips. One taste. Just one.

As he lowered his head, he told himself that if she fought him, if she pushed him back, if she so much as turned her head, he'd stop. He told himself this, but the truth was the desire for *this once* had become a howling torrent of need racing through his body. He couldn't stop if he wanted. So it was a damn good thing she didn't ask him to.

His hand, now free, settled on her lower back, holding her steady as the other dug farther into the silken locks and tipped her head back farther for his attack. He bent closer. Their mouths met. The lingering burn of the scotch mingled with the sweet nectar of her blood that pulsed and plumped up that full, rosy mouth. He thought a simple taste would be enough to quench his thirst, to calm the wild beast of need. He was wrong.

With a growl he tightened his hold on her, pulling her closer, increasing the pressure of his mouth as his tongue stroked a path along the crease of her lips, demanding entrance. As soon as she yielded, her lips parting to allow him in, he knew: One kiss would never be enough. He wanted a lifetime of them with her. No, he wanted forever.

Chapter 5

ROLAND DEEPENED THE KISS, TAKING EVERYTHING, soaking up her essence, and giving in return the only thing he could ever offer her: mind-blowing pleasure. He had nothing else. The man he'd been, the Paladin, had been lost long ago. Long before she was born. Long before she was even a thought in her parents' minds. She must have been in His, though. The One God chose the soul that would perfectly match that of the Paladin during the ceremony that initiated them into the order. Sometimes the bond mate would be revealed soon thereafter, but often it was decades, sometimes centuries, before the mate was sent down to earth for them. Only when the time was right, when the mate was most needed.

But Roland had needed his mate ninety-four years ago. Not now. Talk about a major FUBAR. The Big Man wasn't known for His mistakes, but as far as mistakes went, this one was colossal.

Anger roiled through him, overshadowing his continuing need. Roland rallied against it, burning through it with the intensity of the kiss. So sweetly she yielded, how hot her tongue was against his, how erotic the little murmurs and gasps that rose in her throat. If he could be addicted to something, it was her.

Mine.

Only she would never be his. A vampire and a Paladin?

No one would allow it. The council would do everything in its power to keep him from completing the bond. Like, say, calling *again* for the end of his existence.

Remember this, remember me when you're taken from me and the others are fighting over you. Remember and know that none of them can be to you what I am.

She jerked away, her hand flying up to her mouth.

He expected her to run now. Damn. She should run. All he wanted to do was drag her to him again. Instead she stood there, perfectly still but for the slim fingers that traced her swollen lips, as if she couldn't bear the loss of sensation her abrupt withdrawal had caused. If hers burned with the same need as his did, then she probably couldn't.

Her chest heaved. Her pupils were wide, their focus flickering between his own eyes and the mouth that had been crushing hers moments before. A pink tongue slipped out, tasted the bow of her top lip, then retreated with a guilty flush to her cheeks.

He couldn't help but enjoy her obvious discomfort. If the colors swirling in her essence were any indication, she still didn't know whether to run or throw herself into his arms again.

Her chin came up, her eyes narrowing dangerously. "What was that?"

God she was beautiful when she was angry.

He was unable to tamp down the smile that curved his lips. "That, my dear Karissa, was me being weak."

"How dare you."

Yes, how dare he? It was a good question. He dared because she'd been made for him and him alone. And now that he'd had a taste of the paradise she offered, God help—yup, Him too—anyone who said otherwise. He couldn't tell her that, though, and she expected an answer. Besides, sometimes the simplest answers were best.

He arched an eyebrow in retort. "You didn't seem to mind so much."

Her cheeks went from baby girl pink to lobster red, and she folded her arms across her chest defensively. "I thought we had a deal."

"Really...I don't recall making any sort of deal with you." No. There had been no deal. The only deal he was willing to make was to enjoy as much of each other as possible before he was forced to let her go, which, interestingly enough, he'd decided would be when he was dead.

She took a step back, as if deciding the three feet of space wasn't enough. She was right.

"With the rooms." She made a back and forth swishing motion with her hand. "Ships passing in the night and all that."

He closed the distance, reaching out to finger a curl that had drifted down across her shoulder. Soft, silky. She drew in a quick breath. There was desire in her eyes hidden under the embarrassment, anger, and uncertainty. She couldn't quite hide the want that made her drink in every plane and angle of his features.

He looped the curl around his index and middle fingers, leaned in, and brought his mouth down so it was mere millimeters from hers. "I think I like it better when our ships meet."

She yanked her head back, pulling the curl from his fingers with a wince. "I don't."

He managed to tamp down his amusement, barely. He could smell her arousal. Whether she wanted it or not, her essence recognized that he was her mate. But he figured it was better not to give her a reason to attack him right now, not when the result would be them rolling around naked on the floor. She deserved a better initiation into the bonding process. Tender kisses, flowers, wine, and silk sheets. He wanted to court her.

If he stayed here, that wasn't going to happen. Cold shower. Best idea of the hour.

Making a fist with his right hand, he brought his arm up across his body to cover his heart, giving her a formal little bow. She didn't know what it meant, but he did. The promise of a bonded male to his mate: my heart, my body, my soul, for yours. "Then I shall give you a reprieve…for now."

With a string of muttered insults and curses following him down the hall, he retreated to the bathroom. The door whooshed open at the touch of his palm, and he stopped short of the threshold. Seemed her tantrum of earlier had extended here.

He stepped gingerly into the bathroom and began to clean the mess. It was with amusement that he gathered up the tossed towels and shredded toilet paper and a wide smile that he began to wipe down the walls. It was there, among the many inventive insults scrawled in soap and shaving cream on the mirror above the sink, that one particular word popped out at him: Killer.

The significance of it and what it would mean to his sweet Karissa ripped him apart, reaching for the place where his soul should have been. Heart, body, soul. A man could not give what he did not have.

Tom signaled the bartender for another round. It was his fifth of the evening. The bartender—Greg, wasn't it?—grabbed the Gentleman Jack from the shelving unit against the wall and with expert ease, he leveled off the shot glass without spilling a drop.

"Should I leave the bottle?"

Tom stared at the remaining four inches of amber liquid. At least five or six more shots left. Better not.

"Nah."

Greg nodded, grabbed a twenty from the wad of bills Tom had placed before him on the polished oak, made quick change of it, and tossed back down a ten and four ones. Without so much as a nod, the three-quarters empty bottle was returned to the shelf and Tom was left alone with his dwindling pile of cash, the soon-to-be empty shot glass, and his dour mood.

Lifting the glass, he contemplated what it was that had his craw misaligned. The day had been like any other. He got up that morning out of the same too-big-for-one-person king-sized bed, brushed his teeth and took his shower in the same deco-modern master bath, took the same route to work in his souped up Mustang GT500, and pushed some papers around at the same boring white-collar job at the bank.

It was the bar, he decided, that was not the same. Normally he made a quick stop by his townhouse to change then headed downtown to where the streets were lit not by streetlamps so much as the glowing neon freak-show signs. Tattoo parlors, dance clubs, adult stores…This little sports den was like flat soda compared to the pop and sizzle of the places he was used to frequenting.

There was nothing going on here. No thumping music to show his moves to, no strobing lights to play off his cuff links, no shuffle of Benjamins for little white packets of pure king-of-the-world Xstacy…no pretty coeds to fuck. He should be there. Not here. But he hadn't felt up to going out to his usual haunts tonight.

And why the hell not?

Because of those eyes. Glowing red eyes that still stared at him from his nightmares. It had to be nightmares. What he'd dreamed had gone down last night was too fucking weirded-out to be real. Sure, there had been a coed and a back alley. And before that there had been some liquor and some powder. But no way in hell had there been a fucking vampire. That shit wasn't real.

And if it wasn't real, then why the hell was he in here cowering rather than out doing what he normally did? Was he such a friggin' pansy ass that he was going to let some impure X put him off his game? And that's what it had been. Bad X. He should find the dealer who sold it to him and off the branded fucker. Better yet, spread the word that Tattoo Guy was selling inferior products and let someone else off him. Fewer repercussions that way. He needed to put the nightmare behind him, find a new dealer, and get on with his shit. Life was waiting, after all, and at thirty-nine he wasn't getting any younger.

The sense of eyes boring into the side of his head had him looking down the bar to the right. The barkeep was staring at him uneasily, his hands drying and re-drying the same glass over and over again. WTF?

What was the asshole staring at? He was a goddamn paying patron, after all. Tom's anger bubbled, his hand clenching the shot glass. Some of the precious top-shelf splashed over the rim. The waste of the expensive shit pissed him off further.

Shit. The shot was half-empty but not because he'd drunk any. A quick review of the last couple minutes told him he'd probably been nodding and gesturing to himself like a fucking crazy person. And now Greg thought him the next candidate for the loony bin.

Well, he wasn't. He wasn't crazy. Crazy was seeing things that weren't there. Crazy was thinking the fucked up dreams that came after an evening of binging were real. Crazy was letting said dreams fuck you over the next night too. Well, that wasn't happening here. Nope. Tom was going to finish his shot, grab up his money—no tip for busybody Greg—get into his GT500, and do what a real man would do, which was do what he always did. He had at least another decade before his looks went to total shit, and his money couldn't lure out the pretty coeds. He was a former all-star college athlete, a successful banker with a good crib and a better car. Yeah, he was still a player to be reckoned with. Red eyes or not, nothing was going to keep him from living life to the fullest.

With the decision made, Tom tossed back the shot—there was a reason they called it liquid courage— slammed down the glass, and pushed up off his barstool. Then, with a jaunty swagger, he made his way out the door into the parking lot where he stopped and took a deep breath of night air.

A smile cracked on his face, his body thrumming

with purpose as he began to whistle on the way to his
Mustang. The night was young yet and all his. Carpe
diem and all that crap.

—⁓⁓—

Roland examined the peeling linoleum floor, the pads
of his fingers brushing over the dark brown stains that
were layered over what must have been decades of other
stains. Karissa's home. Her sanctuary. The place where
she should have felt safe, yet murder had occurred here.
Recently. The blood was old enough to oxygenate but
not so old as to leave no clues.

Killer. The accusation, and the fear that he might let
loose his frustration and rage on his best friend when
Calhoun returned for his shift, had driven Roland into
the night. He'd been able to trace the faint taint of death
that still clung to her back to her Brooklyn home.

Karissa was right. He *was* a killer. And for this he
would be again. Whoever had taken the life of the man
who had fallen here would pay in kind. An eye for an
eye. Death for death. So it would be.

Whoever the man was, he was a relation to Karissa.
He could pick up enough lingering scent to know that.
Someone had removed the body. Not the police either,
for there was no blatant yellow tape, despite the obvious
crime scene. Whoever this man was to Karissa—father,
brother, uncle—his absence had only been noted by one.

Was Karissa here when he died? Did she watch? Or
did she return home to find a loved one's dead body
sprawled out on the floor?

Another memory of bloodstained tiles flooded Roland,
overlapping his vision so that it wasn't this kitchen floor

he stared at, but a grand hall, pristinely kept and polished except for the awkward splashes of red that splattered the damask silk on the walls and streaked wavering lines across the cool-white marble floors.

His nails dug into the floor, it dimpled, then gave way. Not marble. Cheap 1980s linoleum. Roland shook off the memory, concentrating again on the present. Whatever had happened, it had been violent. He wondered if Karissa was now, like him, plagued with nightmares.

"I wondered who would show up. You or Logan."

Roland spun around on the balls of his feet, remaining crouched. A girl sat casually on top of the washing machine stuffed into the short hall attached to the room. A mudroom of sorts. She must've slipped in through the broken window. Plain and simple, he was distracted and she sneaked up from downwind.

"Who would you have preferred?" He straightened casually. Gabriella was not a true danger. Not unless her maker was close enough to control her. A quick opening of his other senses showed no dark and oily essences in the area. Well, other than her. But she wasn't all dark, only around her edges.

"Logan, of course. That man is positively delicious." She bared her fangs as she slid down off the washer, strutting across the room. Her hips performed a shimmy that was far too erotic for her gangly, adolescent angles.

"How's Mom?" he asked, knowing it would annoy her.

She wrinkled her nose, dropping the seductive swagger with an equally skilled foot plant and thrust of the hip. "Still six feet under. Where you left her, I believe."

His lip curled up. "Too bad. I would have liked to kill her again."

She shook her head, red locks bouncing. "No way. If somehow Christos finally manages to convince Lucifer to waste enough stolen souls to resurrect her, *I* get to kill her."

Roland chuckled. Gabriella had been trying to kill her birth mother off long before she'd been made vampire. It was probably what got the poor girl turned. Glena had, most likely, hoped she could get her daughter under control with the help of a master vampire. Speaking of which…

"So, where is your maker? He doesn't normally give you too much leash."

"He's your maker too."

"Yes, but he doesn't control me."

That earned him a dirty look. Not that he had expected anything less. The fact that Gabriella couldn't quite manage to break the blood bond Christos had over her was the proverbial thorn in her side. She still had the rebellious nature of the fourteen-year-old she'd been when she was turned and hadn't lost the you-can't-tell-me-what-to-do edge that got her in so much trouble.

She continued to ignore his question, stalking around the room as she did her own study of the blood splatter patterns. He watched her carefully, looking for any signs of guilt, satisfaction, or outright pleasure. All he saw was disgust. Good.

"Must have been messy," she said.

"You weren't part of this, I take it."

She peeled her lips back. "Vegan, remember? I don't do anything that is, or might have been, alive."

He believed her. There was a rumor that she'd been trying to kill herself since the day she'd been turned. Her master, of course, wouldn't have that. Christos couldn't get Gabriella to feed, no matter how desperate the bloodlust was, but he could give her transfusions when she was too sick from starvation to object. Judging by the healthy glow of her creamy skin, Roland suspected she'd been given a few pints rather recently.

Roland glanced back at the bloodstained linoleum, wondering if the body of the victim here had gone on to be a donor. If it was fresh enough, the blood would have still been good. His jaw tightened at the thought.

"So, how is Christos?" he asked, hoping the answer was miserable. The bastard deserved to rot in a fiery pit in hell—right beside Glena.

"Awful as ever."

"You not giving him what he wants?"

She curled back her lips in a feral smile.

Roland chuckled, letting a spark of amusement flash in his eyes. "Good girl."

Gabriella gave him her first true smile of the night before clamping down on the genuine emotion. She looked at her nails, pursing her lips over a chip on her pinkie. "Christos isn't my biggest problem right now, though."

"Oh? Who?"

"Ganelon." Her lips turned into a distinct pout. "He has the whole gang on orders to bring him this girl— alive. What's so special about her anyway?"

His eyes narrowed. "What girl?"

She rolled her eyes, giving him a my-you're-dense kind of look.

His jaw clenched. Answer enough. Ganelon himself was after Karissa. Shit. "What's his interest in her?"

"You mean other than the fact that she's the first female Paladin in almost a century?"

Roland grunted. "Doesn't explain why he wants her alive."

Yeah, alive should have been reassuring, but it wasn't. A Paladin alive and in Ganelon's hands brought with it a whole new meaning to the term suffering.

Not Karissa. Roland would not let that happen.

Gabriella shrugged. "All I know is that Ganelon thinks she's going to be the weak chink in the Paladin's armor."

"And how is that?"

"He's convinced she is the key to their downfall," she said, her words sending a chill of knowing down Roland's spine.

———

Foreboding flashes of a future he couldn't quite see chased Roland all the way back to his loft: *His Karissa, strapped down. Crimson blood spilling from her vein. Vampires. Paladin. Death in the light of day.*

He shook the images off, concentrating on Gabriella's words instead, knowing that they were the key to unlocking the why and how behind the broken vision and thus preventing it from coming true.

The weak chink in the Paladin's armor was understandable. There wasn't a Paladin out there who wouldn't lay down their life for Karissa. With the distinct lack of female offspring in the Paladin lines, more often than not, male Paladin were forced to turn to human women, some gifted, some not, to find a compatible partner. The problem was that Paladin genes became diluted with each subsequent generation, their gifts fading. A Paladin-Paladin pairing was more valuable than all the treasures of the world. Karissa didn't realize it yet, but she was the last hope the current Paladin generation had of rejuvenating their line.

And if Ganelon finds a way to get to her, he'll use her as bait.

It was the only explanation. The only reason to keep her alive. Her death would bring down upon Ganelon the brunt of the Paladin fury, but that fury would be over ice. Vengeance *was* a dish best served cold.

If she was alive though…Well, men did foolish things when they were desperate. And given how diluted the Paladin lines were with human blood, there wasn't a man among them who wasn't a bit of a fool.

The muscles in Roland's legs coiled, he pushed off, leaping over the last block of clogged traffic. He landed with a grunt, knees bent, arms splayed for balance—*getting too old for this shit*—then was up and running toward the rooftop door. His senses were already telling him he was too late, but he had to check, just in case Calhoun had decided to shield her for some asinine reason. Like, maybe, she was in danger?

Thirty seconds later, he was barreling through the empty rooms of his loft. Hall, bedroom, kitchen, great room, study…Karissa wasn't here. Panic squeezed his lungs while, conversely, adrenaline forced his veins and arteries to open wider.

"There's no sign of a struggle," he told himself. "No scent of fear."

Well, other than the lingering fear from when she'd run from first him, then Calhoun.

"Shit." He spun around, his hand smashing through the drywall beside the fireplace.

Where the hell were they? Calhoun wouldn't have been stupid enough to bring her to his place; that left…Ah, fuck.

Chapter 6

ROLAND ENTERED THE ANTEROOM TO THE HALL OF Haven, slipping in with a curl of shadow from the adjoining servant hall. Keeping his sights on his quarry, he drifted across the deep recess behind the line of statues that rimmed the room and melted into the far corner. The risk he was taking by coming here was great. Any of his former peers, if they were to see him, would take it upon themselves to eradicate his presence—and not just from Haven. And then they'd go after Calhoun, because Calhoun was supposed to have eliminated his fallen friend long ago. And if Roland still existed, then it meant Calhoun had lied about doing so.

Of course, right now Roland didn't give a shit about Calhoun. Bastard had brought Karissa here.

From his shadow, Roland watched Karissa pace. His entire body tingled from the mere proximity of his mate. Karissa, however, appeared to be too busy wearing down the wool on the Persian rug to have noticed that she was no longer alone. A fact that sent a wave of unease coursing through his system. She was alone, unaware, and completely vulnerable. What if it hadn't been him who'd sneaked into these hallowed halls? Sure, the chances of that were slim, but still, what the hell was Calhoun thinking?

Didn't matter. As soon as Roland got Calhoun alone and wrapped his hands around the pretty Paladin's throat, the answer wouldn't matter anymore. Wouldn't matter because the stupid fuck would be dead.

Ah, hell. Roland closed his eyes and concentrated hard on taking a few deep breaths, forcing his anger to dissipate, the red haze to clear from his vision. It was the bond calling. The need to protect was sending his sensibilities into a tailspin. Calhoun wouldn't have dared bring Karissa into Haven's Hall without gaining permission first, and he wouldn't have trusted another here to watch her while he asked for that permission.

Probably smart, actually. The chances of a breech of Haven's defenses were next to infinitessimal, and another Paladin might take the opportunity to try to put his mark upon her. Not that it wouldn't happen the moment she walked through those massive, carved doors, but at least then there would be witnesses to keep some of the less scrupulous among them in line. Unlike claiming a mate, which was more of an acknowledgement of a bond than a creation of one, forming a pairing was a long, drawn out procedure. Petitions submitted, permissions granted, marking, courting, then the bonding ceremony. Finally, the presentation before the One God to sanctify the pairing.

There'd been times when one, if not all of the preliminary crap had been skipped, but never the last. And since Karissa was *his* bond mate, there would be no sanctifying of any bond to anyone but him.

That wouldn't keep them from trying to claim her, though. When no mate became immediately apparent, every Paladin in there would go by the rule that possession was nine-tenths of the law. Some might try to court her first, but eventually it would become a free-for-all to see who could mark her and see if it stuck.

Over my dead body.

Roland stood up from his half-crouch, stepping into the light cast by one of the dim globes that soared a good two stories above them. Karissa was so anxious she almost paced by him again, but just as she was about to pass, she yelped and stumbled back, her foot catching on the rug.

Roland's superior speed saved her. He was immediately beside her, grasping her elbow and pulling her upright.

"You scared the crap out of me!" she accused, her pulse skittering under his grip. Fear laced her scent, causing him to cringe.

"I'm sorry. That was not my intent." He released her, thinking it might reassure her that his intentions were honorable—or, at least, not dishonorable.

She glanced over her shoulder, worry furrowing her brow as they landed on the entry to the room, which currently contained at least half the Paladin force. Not just the elders. Calhoun must have requested an emergency session. Damn, what was the fool thinking?

Karissa took a step closer to them, away from him, but then stopped. As if torn.

When, after a few more moments, the doors to the hall didn't bang open—and she didn't race to them—she turned her attention back to him. "What are you doing here? I wouldn't think it was exactly, um, safe for you here."

Her big brown eyes, filled with concern—for his welfare—warmed him to the core, driving away the chill that had seeped into his bones upon finding her gone from his loft.

"No, not exactly," he drawled.

Her gaze fell on his mouth, her lips parting slightly as if remembering what his had felt like upon hers.

He arched a brow, giving her an amused smile. "You going to scream and bring them racing in here?"

There was a brief moment of hesitation. "No. I just didn't expect for you to show up here. Why did you?"

"Because of you, my dear Karissa." He let the name slide off his tongue like a caress, enjoying the way it sounded. More enjoyable was the shiver that ran through her slight frame.

She edged back another step, drawing farther away from him and closer to the hall. He didn't like it but could understand how she might be torn between the pull of the mate-bond and what she felt was logical.

"You, my dear, are the most popular girl in the city right now." And whether she realized it or not, she was about to become even more so. Unless he could talk her into leaving with him now.

"They're, um, still looking for me?"

He gave a nod. After he'd run into Gabriella, he'd had to sneak his way back through a half-dozen demons, two dozen vamps, and three merkers, all of whom had come out to prowl the rundown neighborhood where she'd lived. The demons were there to scent her out, of course. The vamps on the street were fishing for information—even managing to keep their canines hidden long enough to ask questions of the neighbors. And the merkers, well, they were there to make sure no one got any ideas about keeping Ganelon's prize for themselves.

She shuddered, her gaze going back to the heavy wood doors. "I guess coming here *was* the best option then."

He could sense the apprehension behind her words.

Logically, she might think her words were true, but she too seemed to sense that there was danger here. But then, why had she come? He knew he made her nervous, but he thought she'd gotten past outright scared.

That so, Roland? Then why did she just inch back another step toward a room filled with unknown men?

He frowned. "Did Calhoun talk you into coming here? Did he say something to make you think the loft was unsafe?"

She hesitated, then shook her head. "I can't live my life locked in your apartment. You said yourself that those creatures are still looking for me. I need help. Logan and the other Paladin can provide that."

The underlying message was that he couldn't... because he was one of *them*. And thus, in her eyes, one of the people she needed protection from. Even now she was slowly edging toward the door again. His jaw clenched as he fought the urge to move across the distance and place himself between her and it.

"If you go in there," he nodded toward the hall she'd just glanced at longingly, "there is no going back."

Her head jerked back around to him. He had her full attention now.

"What do you mean?"

"Once you walk through those doors and make your existence known, they won't ever let you leave again."

She paused. He took the opportunity to close some of the distance that had cropped up between them. Her eyes widened. She started to step back, but after a worried glance over her shoulder, she jutted her chin and held her ground instead. "I don't understand. Why would they do that?"

"Because they'll want you," he explained. Was he so vile that she'd risk the false security of the unknown over his protection? "Every man in there will want to claim you for himself."

Her eyebrows flew up. "Claim me? As in grunt, grunt, pound their chest, 'she's mine,' claim me?"

He had to fight hard to keep his lip from quirking up. She had no idea how close she was, at least in analogy. "Something like that."

She shook her head. "I don't believe that. Those men were once angels, for crying out loud; they wouldn't do that."

"They're not angels. Not any longer. They're men with special powers, egos, and one too-busy and often-absent God to keep them in line."

He watched her contemplate his words, indecision shifting uncomfortably with unease across her face. He reclaimed another foot of distance. "There isn't a man here who won't fight to have you. And there isn't a man here who will give a damn if you care to be the spoils of their war or not."

She shot him a skeptical look. "And you will? Care, that is."

"I care very much."

He reached up. She tensed but didn't move away as he wrapped a tendril of her mahogany curls around his hand. Her chest was lifting and falling; her gaze zeroed in on his mouth as it drew closer and closer. He saw the moment the bond won. She swayed toward him, her head tipping back, her lips parting slightly.

God, what he wouldn't do to kiss her now. But here was not the time or place. He needed to get her home, away from the immediate danger. And right now she looked ready to follow him anywhere.

With a smile he lifted his other hand, pressing it gently against her waiting lips. "Come back home with me, Karissa. I promise not to cross any lines or break any more...deals."

Her head jerked back as if he'd slapped her. With a yank, she was out of his hold and had scurried back a half-dozen feet.

"Karissa?"

He started to step forward, but she thrust out her hand toward him, palm out.

"Stop."

He did. Not because he wanted to, but because he was afraid she'd take another three steps back and bump into the door. And if she alerted a room full of Paladin that there was a vampire in the house? Well, he might be seeing his death sooner rather than later.

"Stop trying to enthrall me," she hissed.

Enthrall her? "I'm not—"

She cut him off with a glare just as, behind her, the door started to creak open.

Karissa spun around, her arms flying out as she hastily backed up against Roland. Why had he come here? Why had he stayed? It had been Logan's one condition for bringing her here: Don't mention Roland. Karissa hadn't needed to ask why to know the results of such a slip wouldn't be good. And now Roland was here.

If the Paladin saw him...

A man slipped out of the crack in the door, the lights playing off the golden highlights in his hair as he quickly shut it behind him.

"What are you doing here?" he hissed in low tones.

Just Logan, thank God. Karissa's arms fell, and she sagged into the solid mass of Roland behind her. Large arms closed around her, offering support.

A close call, much too close. If that had been anyone but Logan, or if they'd sent someone out with him to retrieve their visitor…

Why do you care, Karissa? You were ready to run into that hall and beg their protection just a few minutes ago.

Logan's gaze zeroed in on Roland's arms wrapped around her rib cage, drawing attention to the lingering embrace.

She blushed but couldn't seem to bring herself to straighten up and pull away. Too weak, too tired… too…what?

Eventually Logan dragged his line of sight up over her head to Roland's face. "Are you an idiot? You need to get the hell out of here, now."

"Who's the idiot that brought her here?"

Logan's eyes narrowed dangerously at Roland. "She's safe here at Haven."

"Is she?"

"Yes," Logan said, but there had been a moment of hesitation. A split second as his eyes flickered to hers and away. Which meant: lie.

Karissa's nails dug into Roland's arms. She hadn't taken his warnings all that seriously, but in the face of Logan's doubt?

"I'm not leaving without her," Roland said, his voice firm.

Logan took a step forward. "Like hell."

"You are a fool if you believe no harm will come from bringing her through those doors."

Logan glanced uneasily over his shoulder, then back at Roland. "Is this...is your gift telling you this?"

"No. Simple logic is telling me this. The same logic that had you bring her to my place rather than here originally."

Logan's mouth thinned, giving her a glimpse of the hardened warrior she suspected he truly was. One who, once committed, believed wholeheartedly in his cause. One who would do anything to achieve the end regardless of the means. "Things have changed."

"What? What's changed?"

"It's too complicated," Logan hedged, casting a glance at Karissa.

Karissa shifted uneasily in Roland's arms. The thing that had changed was her. After Roland had blown out of the apartment for the evening, she'd tried to erase the memory of his kiss with a long, hot shower. When that hadn't worked, she'd tried sleeping, and when that hadn't worked, she'd gone into the study to ask Logan to tell her more of the Paladin. After listening to numerous tales, she'd come to the conclusion that she had to get to know these men who were constantly putting their necks out for humanity. They might be able to help her too. Besides, it had been as good an excuse as any to get Logan to bring her here at this ungodly hour of the night.

It was Roland's fault. If he could have left things as ships passing in the night...

"Listen, Roland," Logan went on, his voice somewhat moderated but no less firm than before, "I will protect her. But I can't protect you if someone comes out and finds you. Which, if I don't go back through those doors with her in the next thirty seconds or so, could be real soon."

"It's not your right to protect her," Roland growled.

"Not my right? And what? You think it's yours?"

Roland stiffened, his arms tightening around her. Karissa squeaked a bit and they just as quickly gentled again, though not as loose as before.

"You can't be serious." This from Logan.

Serious? About what? Maybe it was her exhaustion-fried mind, but she was having a real hard time making sense of this conversation. There were hidden meanings and underscored points that she was just not capable of deciphering after all the trauma of the last forty-eight hours, not to mention the night she'd had of tossing and turning. Which too was all Roland's fault. That damn kiss again. It was like a phantom lover had slipped into the bed next to her, and every time exhaustion had finally taken over and she'd started to drift off it was to the memory of how her lips had burned under his, the feeling of his arms around her.

Like they are now.

Her body trembled, savoring the strength and the heat that wrapped around her. Though his embrace was a tad constricting, Karissa didn't get the impression he meant her harm. Quite the opposite, in fact. If anything she felt…safe.

Before she could sort the thought out, Roland leaned down, his breath caressing her ear. "Let's go, Karissa."

The whispered words had a hoarse edge. She tipped her head back, blinking up at him. His eyes were red and fixated on Logan.

An overpowering urge to reassure him overcame her. Karissa twisted around in his arms, her hand splaying over his chest. Those red eyes shifted to her, a low rumbling rising in his throat. Funny, even that didn't scare her. Nope, the kick of lust that pierced through her body, spreading warmth right down to her core, was definitely not an indication of terror.

"What the hell are you doing?"

Logan's voice broke whatever spell she was under. She managed to drag her gaze away from Roland's hypnotic eyes and look over her shoulder. Logan's eyes weren't hypnotic, or red. They were heated, though, with fury as they sliced into his friend.

"Get out of here, Roland. Now. Or I might open these doors myself."

And he meant it. There was no doubt about that. Roland seemed to know it too. He'd become as tense as steel as he shifted her behind him.

Her heart hammered, torn between worry and disbelief. Was the idiot actually thinking of fighting a hall full of Paladin over her?

Nuh-uh. No way. She slipped back around him, stubbornly placing herself between the two men. She was an independent woman perfectly capable of making up her own mind. And she'd already decided that she needed to meet the men who were, day in and day out, holding the line against the creatures responsible for her papa's death.

"I'll be fine," she said, giving Roland an awkward pat on his pectoral.

"Of course you will, you're coming with me," Roland said.

She shook her head, not sure if she was denying Roland or her stupid alter ego that seemed to be all in favor of her leaping into the vampire's arms and letting him bring her back to his lair.

"Karissa."

She looked up—bad move—and immediately fell back under the spell of his fiery gaze.

Logan made a sound like a growl from behind her, his voice rising as he drew closer. "So help me God, Roland, if you don't stop trying to enthrall her—"

Enthrall me. Karissa jerked away, using one of the defensive moves Papa had taught her to break Roland's grip and then scuttled back until Logan grabbed her arm and dragged her against his side.

She looked down at the floor, positively crushed by her own obvious gullibility. Oh God, what an idiot. So much for willpower. Obviously she had none.

"Karissa…I swear. I'm not trying to enthrall you."

Roland's voice sounded rough and guttural, as if it pained him to be speaking the words. Why? Because he wasn't used to someone breaking his enthrallment? Or could the vampire actually have a conscience about lying? But if that were the case, then why did she doubt herself?

"I only want to protect you."

His words struck a chord deep below her breast. It's what she felt when he held her. Besides the lust, he wanted to protect her, cherish her…love her.

Love? Vampire? *It's official, Karissa, you're certifiable*.

Pointedly averting her eyes, she said, "Please go, Roland."

"Karissa…"

"No. I'd be the biggest fool in this room if I put my trust in you. Not with what you are."

She thought she needed to touch someone to tap into the gift her papa had passed down to her, but she swore, just then, that she could feel the ripping of Roland's heart. If hurt could be measured in silence, then the heavy hush that fell on the room after her words could have drowned her in pain.

She blinked back the unwanted moisture in her eyes, at the same time biting her bottom lip that threatened to quiver. *I'm sorry, I'm sorry. I can't…I can't trust myself around you.*

She wrapped her arms tighter around her ribs, concentrating on the centering presence of Logan beside her. Only it didn't help. Logan seemed as confused and torn as she was right now. He was, however, determined to keep her from going with Roland.

"Don't leave her alone," Roland warned, then spun around, melting back into the shadows of the dim room.

Chapter 7

No sooner had the shadows closed around Roland when the door opened again.

"Yo, Logan, what's the holdup?"

With one last furtive look at the place where Roland had disappeared, Karissa followed Logan's firm tug on her arm and turned to face the Paladin who'd come out of the hall to retrieve them. The man had come to a halt inside the anteroom, his hand still on the handle of the massive door as he sized her up.

Karissa was so used to looking up at men that it was a bit of a surprise to come almost even with the Paladin's bourbon-colored gaze. He was lean, his skin dusky, with dark hair that fell haphazardly over his eyes, down across his prominent cheekbones. His features could almost be considered effeminate, only there was something decidedly male about him.

The Black Knight.

As soon as the thought popped into her mind, Karissa knew it to be true. She wasn't sure how. It felt almost like someone had reached in and planted the knowledge in her mind. But her shields were shut tight again and, in general, her psychic ability was limited to impressions rather than another person's exact thoughts or emotions, and never outright details. Weird.

The Paladin let go of the door, letting it click shut

behind him. He then folded his arms across his chest, letting out a long whistle.

"So, this is your little psychic, huh?" His grin split wide. "Little young, isn't she?" His gaze skirted across the bridge of her nose. "What is she? Sixteen?"

Karissa drew herself up. "I'm twenty-four, thank you very much."

"Really…" He assessed her anew, his voice laden with meaning.

Logan went taut, his fingers all but bruising the soft flesh of her upper arm. "Enough, Valin. I believe you were sent to bring us into the hall, not delay us further."

Valin turned his gaze on Logan. "Ah, yes. Further delay. Makes one wonder what the cause of the first delay was…"

Karissa realized that Logan's firm grip on her looked like she had second thoughts and Logan had to bring her back in line. Not quite the truth, but damn close. Bad thing was now, having met Valin, she was more inclined, not less, to try and run away.

She resisted the urge to look over her shoulder at the shadows again. If Roland was gone, it would make her look more reluctant than she already was. If Roland was there…God, would the idiot try to come to her rescue?

Probably, she answered her own question. The man seemed to have a touch of suicidal in him.

Determined to smooth things over, she put on a false smile and looked to Logan. "It's okay, I'm ready now." She turned the smile on Valin. "Just a case of the jitters, meeting all of Logan's brothers all at once like this."

"Brothers, huh…" Valin turned a hard stare on Logan. "And what *have* you shared with her about your brothers?"

Oh, crap. Had she totally screwed this up? Logan
hadn't said anything about her needing to play dumb on
the things he'd told her thus far. Karissa had to bite her
lip to keep from opening her mouth and trying to cover.
When in doubt, say nothing.

"I believe that is some of what needs to be discussed
with the others, don't you?" Logan asked, gesturing to
the door.

"Indeed." Valin pulled the door open and, with a
dramatic wave of his hand and a tip of his head, ushered
them inside.

Not even two steps in and Karissa had to fight a
sudden loss of mobility. She'd been uncertain of leaving the relative—and she did mean relative—safety of
Roland's apartment. She'd been awestruck, and yes, a
bit intimidated by the sprawling Gothic mansion Logan
had driven her to. She'd been positively jumpy in the
anteroom with its dim lighting, barely enough to illuminate the grave features of its silent marble sentries.
But nothing had prepared her for this. The hall was vast.
And reminiscent of a huge church or something. High
arched ceilings supported by thick, marble columns,
exquisite carvings, ornate chandeliers, the prerequisite
saintly figures…only thing missing was the huge stained
glass windows.

Karissa fell into step with Logan, and again almost
tripped to a stop when her legs threatened to collapse.
Wow. These Paladin sure knew how to pack a punch.
Sheer power. Absolute confidence. It sat on the shoulders of every man in the room. Most of them were
packed into the front rows of the hall, but in the very
front, instead of an altar, was a long carved table, and

behind it sat seven men, which left five spaces empty. These must have been the council of elders that Logan had mentioned. Not one among them was old, at least not to her eyes, but they did all bear an air of maturity, and compared to the other couple dozen prime males in the room, they seemed perhaps a tad deflated. No, not deflated. Just not *as* physically imposing.

It was work not to squirm under the many sets of eyes that seemed intent on assessing her, but she managed, concentrating on keeping her stride long and unhurried. She didn't need to *appear* to be as nervous as she felt.

She curled closer to Logan's side, thankful for his rock-steady presence. He squeezed her arm closer to his body, his thumb continuing to stroke the back of her hand reassuringly.

"You have nothing to fear as long as I'm nearby," he said softly.

She wished his words brought something more than the gratefulness she felt. Logan was a good man. He was the one she should be attracted to.

But I'm not. Nope, only one man seemed to have the ability to turn her brain to mush.

Silence stretched, making their walk down the aisle seem longer than it should have been. It was the right thing, coming here. She'd obviously needed to get away from Roland and whatever it was that he did to make her so scatterbrained. Here she could get some answers. These men were God's warriors. They'd help her…though if they didn't stop staring at her, she was going to scream.

"Which one is your father?" she asked, leaning in close to whisper the words. Logan had said only a handful of men, and a couple of the elders, would be able to respond to his request for this late night—or early morning, as the case may be—session, but there were at least twenty men here, plus seven elders, none of which had a familial resemblance to Logan.

"None. He was detained but will be joining us as soon as possible."

"And the other four empty chairs?" Karissa wondered if at some point the vast hall had been filled with Paladin. If so, then the glaring empty space was a real testament to the losing battle they were facing and the toll it had taken on them.

"Three elders are not available at this time, and the last seat is currently…unfilled."

Karissa looked up at him sharply. The pained tone in his voice made her believe there was something special about that unfilled seat, but his face gave nothing away.

Poker face. Get one of your own, Karissa. Because right now, you're an open book.

She schooled her face into impassiveness, turning her attention forward once more.

Finally, after what seemed an eon, they reached the front rows. As they passed, the curious gazes followed until she stood at the front before the long table, with seven sets of eyes studying her unabashedly and two dozen sets boring into her from behind.

These men needed to get a life if the sight of a woman in their midst was cause for such unwavering attention.

One of the elders sitting in the middle of the table, next to the other empty seat, cleared his throat. "Logan, Son of Logan, despite the fact that you have offered little explanation, we have granted your request to bring an outsider into our midst. Now it is time to divulge the reasoning behind this break from protocol and tradition."

Ah, maybe that was it then. The attention wasn't because she was female, but because she didn't know the secret handshake to the club.

"Forgive me, Gerar. I thought it best to present Miss Donovan before the whole council."

"And why is that?"

"She needs our protection. Ganelon's fiends have taken an unwholesome interest in her," Logan said, his body still, but his words filled with power and conviction. "They not only attacked her home, killing her grandfather, but continued to chase her through the city. Even now they search for her."

Gerar shifted in his seat, as if this news made him uncomfortable. Well good. Being wanted by hordes of demons and a coven of vampires made her damn uncomfortable too.

"And how do you know this?" Gerar asked.

"Because she came to me for protection, and even now both her house and my own are swarming with minions from Ganelon's army."

There was a swell of mumbling from behind them. The seven council members were quieter, bowing their heads together as they discussed Logan's words. After what seemed like forever Gerar straightened, clearing his throat to restore order. The hall immediately quieted.

"Is this true, young lady? That your home was attacked and that you were then chased to young Logan's door?"

"Karissa, sir. And yes, it is."

The man leaned forward, his eyes piercing as he

asked, "And how did you know to flee to *his*," he jerked his head toward Logan, "door?"

"Because my papa told me to go to him if ever I was in trouble."

"Your papa."

"My, uh, grandfather. He raised me."

"And how would your grandfather know of Logan?"

Logan's hand tightened on Karissa's arm, effectively shushing her. "Karissa's grandfather was a psychic."

Karissa sucked in a breath. Logan also knew her grandfather's abilities lay more in empathy, not in any sort of clairvoyance. Yet, he was purposefully misleading the elders. Why?

"Ah." Dark eyes, practically black, turned back on her. "And did you inherit your grandfather's clairvoyant gift?"

"No, I ah…" She looked desperately at Logan, wondering what she should say.

"Lie," intoned a nondescript, brown-haired gentleman on the end.

Seven sets of eyes narrowed on her.

"You didn't inherit your grandfather's gift?" Gerar asked. His tone hadn't exactly been warm and fuzzy before, but to Karissa it sounded decidedly menacing now.

"No. I did. Just a bit."

"Truth," the nondescript man spoke again.

Seven sets of eyebrows raised.

"But you said you didn't inherit your grandfather's gift a moment ago. Why?" Gerar asked.

"I said I didn't inherit a gift of clairvoyance. Not that I hadn't inherited some of Papa's gift."

"Truth."

Gerar looked back to Logan. If those eyes had been

directed at her, Karissa would have fainted…or at least tried to pop the hell out of here. But they weren't, and she was amazed at how well Logan held up under that gaze.

"Care to explain, Logan?"

"Miss Donovan's talents are for her to divulge, not me."

"But you brought her here."

"Because she needs help, protection, and she has nowhere else to go."

"That's right. Because Ganelon is so interested in one little psychic human that he'd waste his resources on hunting her down. Interesting."

Karissa could feel the attention shift back to her. It didn't take a genius to know every man in the room, even Logan, damn him, was staring at her again.

"Well, Miss Donovan, care to explain the gift you inherited?" Gerar said.

And this was how a two-year-old felt, only she was too old to squirm. "A touch of empathy."

"Empathy." He glanced at Nondescript, who shrugged.

"Though not exactly," she hurried on.

Gerar folded his hands on the table before him, probably to keep from reaching out and snapping her neck. She so wasn't doing this well.

"I sense intent, not anything concrete."

"And the intent of the beings that followed you?"

"To capture me."

"Not to kill you?"

"I didn't get that impression, no."

"I find that hard to believe. Ganelon would have no purpose in a low-level, gifted human. And his minions would look at you as nothing more than a light snack. Berin?"

Logan shifted uncomfortably beside her, his first outward sign of unease.

"Still truth. She believes it, at least."

Gerar's long fingers tapped the table. With a final drum, he slapped his hand down, looking over her shoulder at one of the men behind her. "Alexander, I believe we could use your talents here."

Karissa spun around to see a large man approaching from three rows back. Other than his size, he didn't look overly threatening. In fact, if the slight curve of his lips were any indication, he seemed sympathetic to her discomfort. It didn't matter. She didn't want to be the subject on which his talents, whatever they might be, were used.

Her gaze went past him to the door at the back of the hall. One jump and she'd be well ahead of them…if only she knew where the heck she could run.

Logan's hands closed on her shoulders. "You're scaring her, Gerar."

"If she has nothing to hide, then there is no reason to be scared."

"And there is no reason to put her through the inquisition either. She is innocent in this and came to us for help."

"Maybe," Gerar leaned forward on his elbows, "but you have to ask yourself, Logan, why?"

"Not to mention how her grandfather knew of us, and how he knew to send her to Logan, specifically," a familiar voice piped up from the rows of Paladin.

Karissa snapped her head back around, zeroing in on Valin, who'd taken up position in the front row. While most of the other men looked curious, he looked downright suspicious.

"Good point, Master Valin."

Great. Just great. Ice-heart Gerar and Black Knight Boy were in accord.

Alexander the Giant had about reached her. She cringed away from his outstretched hand. "Don't touch me!"

Alexander hesitated, his gaze going questioningly to the elders.

"Alexander's gift is to measure the strength of a person's gift, nothing more. He will not harm you, child."

Karissa looked back to the table of elders, her eyes honing in on an older gentleman who sat at the far end smiling at her encouragingly. Okay, maybe they weren't all coldhearted bastards. Still…

"What does it matter how powerful my gift is?" she demanded.

"Because if you hold enough power, even if untapped, it might explain why Ganelon was interested in you for himself. Or, at least, it *might* be the reason…" This came from Valin. Asshole. And it was that dislike, and the steel it put in her back, that had her snapping back without thinking.

Her chin lifted, eyes narrowing as she stared down the arrogant bastard in the front row. "Oh, my gift is powerful enough. Powerful enough to stay one step ahead of two demons and their imps."

"That's impossible," someone scoffed from the middle of the pack. "No human, no matter their gift, would be able to get away against those odds."

"Unless they purposely let her go so Logan would bring her here," someone else suggested. "She could be leading them straight to our door."

Karissa bristled, scanning the crowd for support…and

found none. Even Alexander, who seemed sympathetic
a moment before, looked at her guardedly. The only
one who didn't seem to have decided she might be an
enemy in their midst was...oh, crap. Valin. He had
dropped his folded arms and was looking at her with
unabashed interest.

Eyes narrowed, Valin took a step forward. Logan
drew her in front of him, placing his body firmly
between her and the twenty-one—yup, she'd had a
chance to count them now—men behind them.

"Gerar, I demand the council of elders place Miss
Donovan under their protection."

"You think you have the right to demand this?" Gerar
sounded incredulous, insulted even.

"Possibly not," Logan replied sharply. "But she does."

Karissa jerked her head up and saw nothing but
Logan's jaw muscle ticking in the corner.

"And who, and I don't mean her name, is she to do so?"

More ticking. A long pause. "She's a teleporter."

Karissa didn't know that one label could cause the
reaction it did. Every single one of the elders paled,
Gerar jerked upright in his seat, and behind them fell an
ominous blanket of shocked silence. And then? Well,
then the room exploded.

Chapter 8

ROLAND COULDN'T GET FAR ENOUGH AWAY FAST enough, the instinct for blood drawing him deeper into the flashy downtown nightlife. No matter how far he fled, how much he tried to shut his mind down, Karissa's words echoed in his head like some sort of war drum pounding out the beat of his flight.

Not with what you are…

There was no escaping what he was. No, the only thing he could do was try to control and direct the animalistic instincts within him. Lately, he wondered if it was a losing battle. Blood. Fear. Power. Tonight, when everything else seemed to be spiraling out of control, he needed these things more than ever.

His mate. Rejecting him.

He hadn't left until Valin had pulled the massive wood doors closed behind them, effectively shutting him off from Karissa. He had to have faith that Calhoun would protect her. There was no doubt that was Logan's intention, even if it wasn't his right to do so.

You think it's yours? Calhoun's question had been another lash across Roland's bared heart.

It was. Karissa was his to protect. How or why the One God had failed to deliver her in time to save Roland's soul, he didn't understand, but one thing he did know: She was his mate. Calhoun wouldn't believe him. As much as he still considered Roland a brother, he also considered him fallen. And in Calhoun's eyes, a fallen Paladin could never have a Paladin mate.

Karissa thought he was trying to enthrall her. He could plead his case for an eon and she probably wouldn't believe him. Shit. It didn't matter. Regardless of how right it had felt to kiss her, he shouldn't have done so. She might be his mate, but she couldn't be his. He was no longer a Paladin and had no right to claim her. The best gift he could give her was his absence. Maybe, in time, the bond that begged to be forged between them would ease, allowing her to pair with someone else. A deserving partner. Like Calhoun.

And if that bastard dares to touch her I'm going to rip his throat out.

Shit. Roland spun around on the roof he landed on, clasping his hands, knuckles popping as he cracked them. He stared up at the sparkling night sky, sucking down the crisp air in hopes of banking the unwarranted fury. He had to calm down. Calhoun wasn't the one he should be worried about. Honorable and Trustworthy could have been Logan's middle name. His friend might desire Karissa, but he'd never act on that without encouragement. The others, though…

A bank of red clouds hazed out the clear night, warning Roland that he was losing control again. He jerked his head down, pacing the length of the roof to work off some of his fear-induced violence. What he really needed was a distraction. He stopped to study the street below. And wouldn't you know…there, like some sort of bloody steak offering for the hungry lion, was a certain red mustang swinging into a nearby parking garage.

Roland tisked, shaking his head. "Tommy, Tommy…
You really have a thick head, don't you?"

—⁓—

Damn. Logan hated when Roland was right. He never
should have brought Karissa here.

He shifted Karissa farther behind him, making sure to
keep between her and his twenty-one brothers who were
inching closer and closer with each passing moment.
Behind them the elders were all in an uproar, demanding he turn to face them and answer their questions. Not
going to happen. He didn't exactly trust the elders either,
but right now they were the lesser of two evils. At least
they were bound by their station and its traditions. The
men staring out of those forty-two eyes? Not so much.
They wanted her, and Logan didn't doubt most would be
willing to risk retribution if it meant they had first dibs
on marking her.

"Logan? What is going on?" Karissa's voice, barely
louder than a whisper, broke over the general roar of the
other men. Her fragile hands gripped his shoulders, her
slim body tense against his back.

Yeah, um, how to answer that: *Don't worry, Karissa,
these men all just want to rip you away from me and
force their mark on you*. Well, it wasn't going to happen. He was going to protect her. Shielding her wouldn't
work; there were at least three men here who could walk
through Logan's shields and another two who had the
ability to tear them down. And if he allowed her to flee,
Valin, who had the ability to dissolve into darkness and
travel by air, would be hot on her tail. That left…

Turning his back on the advancing threat, he drew

Karissa close into his body and began to mutter the
beginning of the ceremony in the ancient language.
There was a collective pause behind them, then a roar
of outrage as feet shuffled behind them.

Not enough time.

Just then the doors at the back of the hall slammed
open, and a deep baritone voice rang out over the ensu-
ing scuffle. "Christ, Gerar, can't you maintain order for
the twenty minutes it took me to get here?"

The sound of his father's voice should have been a
relief. It wasn't. If anything, it gave Logan a new sense
of urgency.

Finish it, his inner voice commanded with such force
he was required to obey.

"What is going on here?"

Logan dimly heard the heavy footfalls as his father
stalked down the aisle, but the power throbbing within
him was like a rising storm roaring in his ears, obliterating anything but the words crossing his lips and the
woman curled protectively in his arms.

There was more shuffling as the others moved out of
their leader's way, then, "Who is this?"

Karissa shifted in his grip, straining on her tiptoes to
peer around him. Logan's father sucked in a shocked
breath. His reaction did nothing to quell Logan's
determination. His father's concern over the Paladin's
diluted bloodlines was legendary. He'd been searching
for a compatible female with enough Paladin blood in
hopes of rejuvenating their endangered gene pool. And
wouldn't Karissa look like a godsend?

"Karissa, look at me," Logan commanded, his one
hand cradling the back of her neck as he placed the

other over the base of her throat. The power rolling and expanding within him collected in that hand, warming her skin. Karissa's gaze flew up to his, her pupils dilating in surprise.

He finished the last of the ancient words, translating the final part of the marking ceremony aloud as he released the caged energy within him into her slim body. "So that I shall know thee, as thou shall know me: body, heart, soul."

What happened then was completely unexpected. There was no opening of a pathway between their minds, nor was there a birthing of his mark upon her. Instead she stiffened, her eyes rolling up beneath her long lashes just before she collapsed. Logan barely caught her, and wouldn't have if his father hadn't reached out at that moment and offered his own arms as support.

There was a collective intake of breath from the men surrounding them, then absolute silence as father met son's gaze over the still form in their arms.

"By God…Logan, what have you done?"

Easy as pie. A couple fancy drinks, a quick flash of the diamond cuff links as he paid the bill with his Visa black card, along with that charming trust-me smile he was famous for, and she was all his. The blond coed he'd separated out from her friends was so easily impressed—not to mention drunk—that Tom bet he could have had her pinned against the leather steering wheel of his mustang five minutes after her gaggle had skipped off to the next bar. But what would have been the fun in that?

"So. Investment banking, huh?" The blond popped the cherry from her drink into her mouth, her tongue working the stem. "With the current economy, you must be exceptionally good at your job."

Her eyes traveled over Tom. Tom chose not to notice the fact that she was taking in the lines of his expensive suit rather than the slightly less straight lines of his physique. He wasn't a total couch potato, but six-pack abs and bulging biceps were things of his football past. At least he still had his hair. Basically.

He leaned in closer, returning her appraisal look for look, his eyes dipping over her rounded breasts and equally round hips that were snugged into the red dress. "I do well enough. How 'bout you? What do you do?"

She smiled, producing the tied off cherry stem between her teeth. Oh yeah. He could imagine what he would make her do with that tongue. He chuckled, plucking the stem from the perfectly straight pearly whites. Her parents must have had money to pay for that set of choppers.

"Besides that." He winked. "Though that is impressive."

She shifted on her stool, seeming suddenly uneasy as she picked at the knotted cherry stem. "Oh, I'm pre-law. At least I hope I am. The last test I had was a killer."

Came from money, but bombing out in college. Perfect. Tom played at wary, shifting back a few inches and toning back the charming smile. "Ah."

"Ah, what?" the blond asked, tipping her head to the side.

"You don't look like an undergrad. How many years you have left?" ie, How young are you? He'd learned long ago that the best way to lure the coeds into trusting him was to seem a bit uneasy with the obvious age gap.

"I'm a junior," she said, then frowned. He tipped his head in question. She shrugged sheepishly. "Actually, I should have graduated by now but I took a few years off to travel across Europe with some friends. That's why I look older. In fact, today's my birthday. Twenty-four."

"Well then, happy birthday!" he said, raising his drink.

"Oh yes, happy birthday to me," she said a bit hollowly as she stared at her glass. Concentrating, she lifted it and carefully tapped the fruity concoction against his then downing the last third of the glass. He noticed she had to concentrate to place it perfectly center on the square napkin.

"Looks like you're empty. Want another?"

Her brow dimpled as she stared at the tall tumbler, probably debating if she could handle it and whether she'd look less mature if she couldn't. Which she would. Two drinks plus a cheap drunk equaled inexperienced. Fine by him. He liked slutty and dumb well enough, but sheltered and innocent led to the biggest high when he plowed into them with that first punishing thrust.

He put an expression of great concern on his face. "Hey, you don't have to."

She looked up at him, her bottom lip pulled tight between those perfect teeth.

"Really, it's no biggy. If you've had too much I'll walk you out and make sure you get a cab."

"Oh no. I definitely don't want to go home yet." She gave him a reassuring smile, tapping the bar. "Order me another."

"You sure?"

She nodded. "I just need to hit the restroom first."

"I'll be waiting."

With a last flash of her smile, she sashayed—a bit unsteadily—through the crowded club toward the restrooms. Tom waited until she'd entered the dim hall before turning back and signaling the bartender. The man was quick—good tips always equaled good service—and had the next round in front of him in under a minute.

"Anything else I can get you?" he asked.

"Nope." Tom slid him a twenty and a ten. "Keep the change."

"Thanks, man."

Tom waited another minute, and when he was sure no one was looking, slipped a pill into the fruity drink and stirred. It would take a minute to dissolve completely, but he wasn't worried.

Five minutes later Tom was beginning to get impatient. He was tapping his foot on the barstool rung and craning his head over his shoulder toward the bathroom when someone sat down beside him.

He took in the broad-shouldered man in black and frowned. "Hey. That spot's taken."

The man nodded. "Is now. Oh, and thanks for the drink."

Who the hell did this guy think he was? Tom made a reach for the drink, but the man shoved it away.

"Hey, asshole. That seat there is oc-cu-pi-doed, get it? And the drink is for my girl. If your ass isn't outta here in three seconds, I'm going to kick it."

"That so?" the man drawled, lifting the glass to his mouth and sucking it down a good inch.

Tom was too shocked to react. The guy must think he

was some tough shit, but the joke was on him. What was in that glass would have him tripping so bad he wouldn't even know his name in a few.

"Not bad," the man said, studying the peachy liquid. "Would be better without the Rufie though. Don't you think, Tom?"

Tom's heart stuttered, then skipped ahead at high speed. "How the fuck do you know my name?"

The man's gaze swung to him. Tom practically fell off his stool. He scrambled back, a vise clamping around his lungs as he tried to draw in air. No way. This was not happening. The man's eyes were *not* red.

Tom bumped into another occupied stool, got a "hey, watch it" from the fellow he'd jostled. He blinked, rubbing his chest. When he opened his eyes again it was to find the man staring at him, *black* eyes filled with mock concern.

"You okay, Tom? You look like you've seen a ghost or something."

Before he could respond, the blond returned from the ladies' room. Tom scoffed. "You know what? Fuck it. Take the lady's seat, have her drink. We were getting out of here anyway."

He held his hand out for Blondie. She hesitated but had just reached out to take it when Goth swiveled on the stool, putting his knees in the way as he took another sip from the fruity drink. "But if I drink this one, how are you going to drug her? Or did you spike her last drink too?"

Blondie gasped, snatching her pretty French-manicured fingers out of Tom's reach. Goth boy slipped off his stool, leaning down to sniff near her throat. He straightened, his black eyes going soft as he gave her a reassuring smile. "Don't worry, love. The others weren't drugged. Why don't you get a cab and go home. You're definitely over the legal limit."

"Who are you?" Blondie asked. She was looking up at Goth as if he was some sort of fucking savior or something. Tom would see about that.

"Ready to go settle this, Tom?" Goth asked, ignoring the girl's question.

"After you." Tom gestured toward the back doors. With any luck Blondie would be so intrigued by her new hero that she'd wait around a bit to see if the guy came back. By then Tom would have taken care of the matter, grabbed his car, and would be back out front waiting for her. It wouldn't be the first time he'd had to tail a cab to follow his prey home.

The man turned and sauntered toward the back hall. Tom followed, trying not to be unnerved by the fact that the guy, although not any taller, was definitely in much better shape. Didn't matter, though. All Tom had to do was avoid the man's fists until the drug caught up with him.

They stepped out into the rank alley. It was empty but for a half-dozen sewer rats and a plastic grocery bag caught on the corner of the dumpster and flapping in the light breeze.

"You know, you really disappoint me, Tom. I thought we had an understanding."

"Oh? And what's that?" Tom took up position with the open alley at his back, settling down into a defensive crouch.

He didn't even get a chance to blink before Goth was

on him, spinning him around and slamming him into the dumpster. "That you don't rape women and I don't kill you."

That voice…fuck, that voice. It was the one from his nightmare, the one coming from the mouth of the vampire just before he'd sunk his fangs into his throat. *Before I'm through with you, you're going to wish you'd been born without that dick of yours.*

No, oh God no. This couldn't be happening. This wasn't real.

Sharp teeth skimmed over the collar of his suit jacket, dragging across the clammy flesh of Tom's neck. A sharp sting and…

"Don't kill me. Oh, please don't kill me."

The sting abated, twin trails of sticky blood dripping down into his collar.

"Why not? You reneged on our deal."

"I won't do it again! I swear!"

"You swear?"

The man's weight was removed from his back. Strong hands turned him around. Tom kept his eyes clamped shut. He didn't want to see those eyes. Didn't want to see his blood on those fangs.

Not a dream. Not a dream. *Real.*

"Look at me, Tom. Look at me and tell me why I should trust you this time?"

Tom obeyed and found himself staring into glowing red eyes. "I promise, I promise, I promise—"

"You see, Tom, for me, your promise just isn't good enough." The vampire smiled, exposing those impossibly long fangs. "And you know what that means…"

Tom tried to struggle but couldn't; he was frozen

in place as those fangs lowered down toward his neck. All he could do was force out a whispered "No! No…nooooo" before even that was cut off by the burning pressure at his throat.

Chapter 9

"You idiot!" Logan Calhoun Sr. screamed, yanking Karissa out of Logan's arms. His hands, still strong and calloused from fighting, brushed over her slim form, chasing the swirling energy that should have branded Logan's mark into her skin.

Logan was only dimly aware that the entire Paladin presence had crowded close, their bodies thrumming with violence as the instinctive urge to protect a fallen Paladin female rose within them. Even Logan, who'd caused her fall, was pulled to defend.

What have I done? Why didn't the marking work? He quickly reviewed the spell and could find nothing wrong with either the words or the physical press of energy upon her. It should have worked. She should have been marked as his, not laid unconscious, the energy he'd put into the ceremonial marking encircling her like some evil net.

Logan's father grunted a curse. "I can't draw it off."

By God. If his father couldn't, no chance any of the others could break the shield or net, or whatever the hell it was either. Something in his chest fluttered, probably in result to the press of guilt squeezing his torso.

"Alexander!" his father bellowed. "I need you over here."

Alexander looked shocked, but the huge warrior quickly pushed over to the elder's side, dropping to his knees.

"What happened to her? What is going on?" Gerar demanded from the dais, anxiety making his voice ride high.

Logan's father ignored him and gave his orders to Alexander. "You need to draw some of the excess energy from her."

Alexander glanced at Logan—a silent *I don't understand what's going on here* and *what the hell did you do* all rolled into one—then lowered his hands to the reddened skin at the base of Karissa's throat. Immediately his eyes flared wide, then narrowed with concentration as he began to do what he did best—steal a person's energy.

Logan had a million questions he wanted to ask, but none more important than "will she recover?" which would, most likely, be answered with a few moments of patience. *Please, let her be okay.*

It was so quiet time seemed to stand still. The entire hall was breathless as they waited to see if Calhoun Sr.'s gamble worked. The danger of Alexander's gift was that it was not specific. Once it latched on to an energy source, it could suck it and all energy in the area away. Given how pale and fragile Karissa looked right now, it seemed in opposition to what they should do. But leaving her to fend off the energy attacking her didn't seem a viable option either. His energy. Fuck.

Logan raked his hands through his hair, muscles tense as he watched and waited. The air around him began to chill, and he started to tremble. He should move back farther. Alexander was starting to sap his energy too. And after casting the binding spell, his reserves were already low.

Still he didn't, his gaze fixed on the inert body laid

out upon the ornate tile floor, cherry-cola curls spread like a halo around her snowy white face. Even her freckles had paled and her lips, God, her lips had turned that lifeless shade of blue.

Logan started to step forward. "He's going to kill her! He's taking too much energy!"

A hand clamped down on his upper arm, jerking him back. "Don't be more of an idiot," his father growled. "She's a teleporter. She has far more energy than even you."

How had his father known she was a teleporter? He hadn't been in the room when that revelation had been made. More questions for later. Right now…

"I've done all I can," Alexander announced, pushing off the floor. He stood, staggered, then planted his feet wide to balance himself, arms on knees, his chest heaving, sweat pouring off his brow. Anyone who didn't know him would have assumed he was exhausted. He wasn't. Logan had seen him after draining a half-dozen merkers before. Alexander was so pumped full of energy now he was having trouble containing it.

Almost immediately there was a push of bodies as the other men in the room tried to get a closer look at Karissa.

"Back off!"

His father's command came in the nick of time. Logan's gift of pulling heavenly light might not have hurt any one of these men, but he wasn't beneath fighting dirty if the need arose.

It was his father's authority, and that alone, that had the men stepping back again. Anyone else would have been ignored. "Is the east wing suitable for visitors?" he asked Gerar.

The east wing, of course—his father would want to keep her far from where the other Paladin resided.

Gerar looked a bit taken aback but nodded. "It should be. The caretakers are ordered to keep it up."

Logan stepped forward, ready to offer his aid.

"No," his father rebuked. "Alexander will carry her. I think you've caused enough trouble for one night."

Feeling like a scolded puppy, Logan stepped back. He gritted his teeth as Alexander bent down again, and then fisted his hands as the brute lifted her, cradling her head against his chest so it didn't loll over his arm like a rag doll's.

Frustrated with his inability to help, Logan followed them out of the hall, meeting the accusing gaze of every Paladin as he did. Of course they would accuse him. Even though every one of them had been ready and willing to do the same.

"Are you done posturing yet?" his father asked in a hushed whisper filled with disapproval.

Guilt and agitation, sizzling through Logan's veins and prickling at his nerves, went hot. So hot it burned white. It was all he could do to keep the fire from erupting in a brilliant flare of light.

"Wasn't it you who taught me that face is everything?" he asked softly. On this one thing his father and he agreed. Family politics should be kept among family.

His father grunted but didn't say anything further until they were well out of the hall, the heavy doors closing behind them. Then it was simply a directional command to Alexander.

"This way."

They crossed the dimly lit expanse, heading for the

rarely used east wing. Once, the entire complex had been filled with Paladin. Now the roman arches framing the long hall, the Gothic columns, the exquisite marble inlay of the floor seemed but a cold show to an absent audience. Less than fifty Paladin were left and only half of them resided at Haven. Logan preferred his small row house to the vast, lonely corridors, the endless supply of unused rooms at Haven.

His father pushed open a set of ironbound, wood doors. Simultaneously Logan and his father cast a pair of glowing orbs to light the way.

Logan started forward, but his father raised his hand. "Wait here. Make sure no one else comes in."

"If she wakes she will feel safer if someone she knows is there."

"The same someone who attacked her?"

Logan clenched his jaw but wisely kept his mouth shut. His father had a point. He folded his arms, pointedly turning his back so he didn't have to watch Karissa being taken from him. Regardless of his father's logic, he still felt like he was abandoning the woman he'd promised to keep safe.

"You will stand guard at the entrance to the connecting hall," Logan's father told Alexander when he returned from settling Karissa in her room.

Alexander nodded and pushed through the heavy wood door. The doors had no sooner closed when Logan's father lifted up a large block of heavy-duty wood, sliding it into the iron grooves, and effectively bracing the door shut.

"Hold on while I put a shield on this," his father said. The task was simple, a gathering of power, then build it into a spinning illusion of energy using the doorframe to mark its edges. It wouldn't last forever and there were some who could break through, but it was another barrier at least, and as long as Alexander kept the rest of his brothers at a reasonable distance, it was one that shouldn't be needed.

"You are putting a lot of faith in Alexander. He could absorb the energy of the shield if he wanted," Logan said when his father was done.

His father flicked his hand expansively in the air. "Alexander wouldn't be interested in the likes of her."

Why the hell not? Now that it was obvious to every single man present tonight that she had power...

A horrible thought cropped up: Maybe she *was* part merker. Maybe that's why he hadn't been able to mark her. A Paladin's mark would be like an attack on a merker's essence. The inherent opposition of their purpose morphing the purpose of the bond.

"Why..." He cleared his throat. "Why did my attempt to mark her not work?"

"Not here." Calhoun Sr. spun on his heels, forcing Logan to follow if he wanted to get answers. They ascended the stairs to the main hall of the wing, traversed another short hall past endless doors before they entered into an old study of some sort, dusty books lining the shelves and groups of seating arrangements with various lamps and tables between them, each draped in ghostly sheets.

The door hadn't even latched behind them before his father had spun back around. "Damn it, Logan. What possessed you to try to mark her?"

"Did you see what was happening in that hall? Every

single one of those men was getting ready to take a shot at doing what I did."

"So it should be you?"

"I know her. She knows me. Besides, I didn't do it to force a pairing. I did it to protect her."

"Some protection."

Logan stilled. The painful truth of that statement was enough to reopen the floodgates of guilt. He shouldn't have brought her. At the very least he should have better explained what would likely happen once her powers were revealed. The way things had gone down, it had been all but a virtual ambush.

But Karissa had seemed so absolutely sure about her need to leave Roland's apartment. Practically terrified, really. He'd been swayed by her wide-eyed pleas and the trembling hands clutching his arm.

Logan frowned. It didn't fit. Nothing about this fit. Which brought up the question, what the hell had happened between her and Roland?

She's not a merker. Don't tell me she's a merker.

"Why," his voice came out hoarse, so he cleared his throat and tried again, "why didn't the marking ceremony work? Did I do something wrong?"

His father sighed, settling down in the cotton draped chair behind the desk. He fidgeted, leaning forward, then back, crossing then uncrossing his arms. "You didn't do anything wrong. You can gift energy, yes, if she is accepting and has the room to take it in, but you cannot use your energy to injure or mark one of your own blood. The Father will not allow such an abomination."

Ice chilled Logan's veins. "What do you mean of my own blood?"

His father sighed, raking his hands through his hair. "I'm sorry, son. I should have told you before now. I just never thought…No, I hoped…"

"Hoped what?" Logan stepped around the desk, demanding his father's full attention.

His father dropped his hands, lifting his gaze to that of his son. "I'd hoped she would remain hidden, safe, for years yet to come."

"You knew of her?"

"Of course. She's my daughter."

Chapter 10

KARISSA'S HEAD HAD BEEN SPLIT OPEN. NO OTHER explanation. She sat up, clutching at her throbbing temples as if by doing so she could somehow hold her brain inside. She hadn't had a headache this bad since...since, well, never. And given that she was prone to migraines after using her gift, that was saying a lot.

"Oh, God, kill me now," she moaned as another spike of agony pierced her skull, then immediately bit her tongue. She'd been taught not to waste her prayers on those things that were not important, or self-serving, or in this case fallacious. The headache would fade. She just had to survive until then. A better thing to pray for would be a way out of this mess.

First step: Sit up.

Careful of her movements, she planted her palms on the musty sheets and pushed. Her head throbbed so bad she swore that gray matter was about to ooze out of her ears. Yet somehow she made it to upright.

Good. Now to figure out where the heck I am.

Karissa carefully pried her eyes open and met a vision of hazy brown-red. If she hadn't experienced this sort of thing before, she would have panicked. Migraines had a tendency to affect her vision. So she waited, until finally the red started to recede and the brown morphed into shapes and outlines.

Wow. Talk about archaic. The furniture was massive,

heavy, and decorated with intricate carvings and gold gilding. The floors were stone and had three separate area rugs that she supposed were meant to take away the chill. The walls were a deep mahogany paneling covered by saintly paintings and faded tapestries. And over there…holy crap, was that a washbasin?

Monks. These men lived liked Middle Age monks.

Not quite, Karissa. Monks don't go barbaric over a scrawny woman like you.

Her hands flew to her throat. Tender, but not warm or swollen. Not like you'd expect after being practically strangled.

No, not strangled. Branded. Roland had warned her, and he'd been right. There was no doubt in her mind now that every man here wanted to "claim her." And it looked like Logan had decided to stake his territory from the get-go.

Heck no. Not even if the world was coming to an end.

Blood pumping, she flung back the covers and thrust her legs off the edge of the bed. A knife twisted in the back of her skull, sending shooting pains down her spine and out into her extremities.

Okay then. A little slower.

More conscious of her limitations, she eased to the edge of the mattress until her feet sunk into the plush area rug below. Step two: Get to the door.

Using every available piece of furniture she could reach for support, she whimper-walked across the room. The last few steps were more of a stumble as she plunged across the gap from dresser to door, but then her hand closed around the knob and she sagged into the welcoming warmth of solid wood. Victory.

Maybe.

With eyes closed and a prayer on her lips she twisted the handle. Unlocked. Was this for real? Were her newest set of captors such idiots that they were going to let her waltz right out of here?

Her excitement fizzled the moment she pushed the door open. Pitch dark. Figures. It was not her captors who were stupid, but the person who dared to go bumbling around in the dark.

Karissa squared her shoulders, facing down the oppressive darkness. Stupid or not, she was going to get out of here.

Gabriella's heels clicked on the crumbling sidewalk, a measured beat to the sway of her hips. As disguises went, this one worked as well as any. Maybe better, given the genes she'd inherited from Mommy Dearest. *May she rot in hell.*

It was because of that witch that Gabriella was here at all, strutting in her five-inch stilettos down these dark streets that positively reeked of drugs and despair. Okay, maybe placing tonight's exact activities on her list of it's-all-Mommy's-fault indiscretions was a tad much, but Gabriella didn't really see it that way. Gabriella wasn't like some girls who believed every painful milestone or unfairness of life was her parents' fault, but she did believe in placing blame where it belonged. And the fact that Gabriella was out here, on Christos's orders, *was* her mother's fault. The greedy, power-hungry whore had been willing to trade anything—including her daughter's immortal soul—for a chance to rise in the ranks. Didn't matter what ranks, as long as there was power and prestige at the top.

The sharp sting against the base of her throat. A scream lodged beneath her budding breasts. Arms pinned. Hot tears. An elegant hand brushes them away, a murmur offering false reassurances. "Mommy, no! Don't let him do this, Mommy!"

Gabriella's body jerked. She stumbled a few steps before she managed to catch balance both physically and mentally. It was over. Done with. In the past.

She looked down at her shaking hand, clenched it into a ball, and forced herself to start walking again. At least neither Mommy Dearest nor Christos had gotten what they wanted from the deal. Mommy had enjoyed a brief span of increased prestige, but that had been fleeting, ending in her death. And Christos? Christos liked the power he got from controlling a half-blood like her, sure, but that's not why he'd turned her.

It was no secret that the one who found a way to eradicate the Paladin would be raised to right-hand man status. Christos had probably figured that even with a siren mother, the daughter of one those do-gooder Paladin would be precious enough to use as bait. Idiot hadn't calculated things right, though. Nope, he'd been naïve to think her mother's genes could be so easily overlooked and then he'd royally screwed it all up when he'd turned her. The Paladin were a snobby sort, only concerned with "light" vs. "dark" and pureness of soul. Well, there was nothing pure about Gabriella, nothing "light" either. She was bad through and through. Bad enough to dream of blood and death. Bad enough to crave the hot, thick liquid until her stomach twisted and her fangs etched grooves in her own gums. Bad enough to want to drive a stake in Stepdaddy's chest, lop off his head, lap up the gushing life-fluid, and then burn his body to ash to make sure he could never come back.

Oh, yeah. That would be the bomb.

<<Gabriella…really, after all I've done for you?>>

"Argh!" God damn, Christos! With a growl Gabriella pushed away the presence that had slipped in under her defenses. It soon became a test of wills: her determination to kick her maker out verses his indomitable need to prove that she couldn't.

She stumbled to a stop. Beads of sweat broke out over her skin, making her clammy cold in the pre-dawn air. Christos tried to slick around her wall of determination, but she countered, filling her mind with imagery of a bright golden sun, filling all the dark spaces where Christos could hide to spy on her. It burned her, scorched her right to her core, but not as much as it burned him. He would relent first. He had to.

Her body began to vibrate with the need to prove that she could do this. Just when she thought she'd managed to illuminate every shadowy recess within her, a dark curtain of evil slammed down upon her, smothering her image of light.

Gabriella cried out, her knees buckling. She was going to die. He was going to snuff out her essence.

With a laugh, Christos suddenly disappeared, the oppressive weight of his will lifting and leaving her adrift. She stood there, gasping with her eyes closed, back pressed against a lamppost, and fingers curled into the chipped iron paint in an attempt to tether herself to her surroundings.

Damn. She panted. She should have known Christos would be checking up on her routinely. Should have been prepared. Or at least kept her homicidal thoughts tucked away for a time when she knew he'd be preoccupied with something else. Like after he had found the woman they were searching for. Everyone—Christos, Ganelon, even Lucifer himself—was hankering after the girl who got away. Well, they could look all they wanted. Gabriella had a feeling about where the woman was, and she wasn't telling.

And if you're smart, you won't even think about that, Gabby.

Yeah, good idea. Though it was hard not to when she'd been sent out to prowl the streets for signs of the girl. She wasn't stupid enough to disobey Christos. Christos was on a bender. Screw up and you better hope your will was in order.

That suited Gabriella just fine. She was sick of this life anyway. Still, there were worse things than death. And if she didn't want to become intimately aware of them—she pushed off the lamppost, heading back down the street—she should probably get back to work.

Chapter 11

IT WAS THE WHISPERING THAT STOPPED HER—THE hushed sound of two angry men who were both trying to gain the upper hand while not raising their voices. Karissa had managed to make it down what seemed a never-ending staircase and had been following the wall around, searching for another set of stairs going down—or a door, a big wide this-is-the-way-out door—when she was scared shitless by the sound of others…close by.

Go, Karissa, ignore them. For God's sake, don't stand here like a fear-paralyzed mouse.

Only she wasn't the mouse. She was the cat. And undone by her curiosity—had she really heard them say her name?—she found herself trying to peer down the black hall before her. It, like the rest of the building, refused to give up any secrets. Previously, she relied on the vague memory of the outside of the building. Which was not much. She'd been blindfolded for secrecy's sake, and when Logan finally announced they were there, she pulled off the blindfold to find they drove deep into the warehouse section of the city and were idling beside a chain-link fence behind which stood a graveyard of shipping boxes. He punched in a code, drove through…and whamo, gone were the boxes. In their place a cobbled yard filled with fountains and statues appeared, each monument highlighted by spotlights in the dark.

She was so engrossed by what had to have been some

sort of protective illusion that she hadn't zeroed in on the massive structure behind them until Logan had stopped the car. By then they were so close to the building that her gaze had immediately been drawn to the gargantuan center structure. With its multiple peaked roofs, turrets, and carved marble, she was positively awestruck. Vaguely, in a shadowy, knew-it-was-there kind of way, she recalled that there were long wings stretching out to each side, rising perhaps to half the height of the tallest peak. Baring the top floor, she could be anywhere in one of those two wings.

Skimming her hand along the wall, she made her way down the dark hall. This hall was riddled with crevasses, recesses where cool, marble statues resided, other doors that led to God knew where, and…what was that?

Fighting the urge to whoop in celebration at her first sight of light in who knew how long—okay, maybe it had only been a couple minutes—she forced her forward progress to miniscule. Finally, she made it to the door bathed in a slim halo of light and squatted down to stare through the glowing beacon of the keyhole.

As soon as she got a good look at the occupants of the room, she sucked in a breath. Logan, and a man who resembled him too much to be anyone but a blood relative, were facing off behind the expanse of an old oak desk. Neither looked happy, their eyes boring into each other as they both refused to back down from whatever argument they'd been participating in.

I should go. Now. She started to straighten but stopped when the other man dropped his gaze, his eyes seeming to hone in on the keyhole. Oh damn. Damn. Damn. Damn. Was she found out?

The man sighed, looking back to Logan. "Your only job is to keep her safe in that room until it's decided. That is all I'm asking."

Logan's hands fisted at his sides, the only tell that he seemed ready to go for the other man's throat. "I won't let you do it. I promised my protection."

"I am sorry, Logan. But it's a bond mate's right to protect her. Not yours." The man laid his hand on Logan's shoulder, giving it a squeeze as if to temper the words. The action was that of a father to son, though this man looked nowhere near old enough to be anything more than a brother, or perhaps a young uncle. It made her wonder. Logan had never mentioned anyone else but his dad, at least not within the ranks of Paladin.

"She has no bond mate." The way Logan said this sounded almost bitter. "You said a minute ago that you sensed no possible bonds between her and any who were present in that room."

"That is why we have to choose for her. They won't wait for her to choose. They're going to choose one for her unless we pick one first."

"An elder could claim the right to protect her."

The man tapped the desk beside him, his brow creased into a sharp V that aged him considerably. "Times are desperate. I'm not sure even a father could protect her."

"Coward."

The man jerked away, his head snapping back as if Logan had physically slapped him.

Logan went on. "I can't believe you didn't tell me about her. If I knew who she was I wouldn't have—"

"Wouldn't have what? Cozied up to her like a dog sniffing out a bitch in heat?"

Karissa stiffened, heat suffusing her cheeks. Had he just called her a slut? Of all the nerve, he didn't know anything about her!

"That was beneath even you, Father." Logan's tone was low, deadly.

"But true nonetheless," Logan's father—his freaking father!—snapped back, his fists slamming down on the desk. "Damn. How is it that she's in heat?"

In heat? What *were* they talking about?

Logan started to shake his head, then hesitated, drawing his father's sharp gaze. Logan shook his head again, more adamantly this time. "I don't know."

His father sighed. "I guess it doesn't really matter. Though it does make it more vital that we choose an acceptable partner as quickly as possible."

"You cannot force a bond."

"No." The man lifted his gaze, looking back to his son. "But one can force a pairing."

Oh God, Roland was right. No one here could be trusted. Not even the man her grandfather had said she could trust.

"Who, Papa?" the little girl in her memory asked. "Who would take me away?"

Papa's brown eyes became shadowed and he shook his head. "Any of them, all of them. Something happens to me, you go to Logan Calhoun."

"He'll protect me?"

"God, I hope so, child. I hope so."

Her vision blurred, and that woozy she'd-spun-on-the-merry-go-round-too-much feeling spiraled down through her body. She fell forward, her hand slapping against hard wood.

"What was that?"

The barrier holding her up disappeared. Karissa did an elegant hand plant onto the floor. Light spilled from the room, shadowed only by the tall figure standing before her. Karissa raised her head and rapidly blinked away the memory of Papa's rounded face and tickly, white beard. In his place were the hard planes of Logan's aristocratic face as he stared down at her.

"Karissa?" His face twisted into a look mixed with confusion and horror.

"I trusted you," she managed past the tightening in her throat.

If he said anything in his own defense she didn't know; she was already scuttling backward into the hall's offering of darkness.

—⁂—

Roland lifted his tumbler, swirling the amber liquid so it ran up and around the sides of the cut crystal. He wasn't sure whether it was his forth or fifth. Didn't matter. The point was to keep drinking. Maybe if he consumed the alcohol fast enough he could drink himself into oblivion.

Karissa was right. Somewhere in his gene pool was the propensity to become an alcoholic. Now, if only his vampire physiology would take a backseat to his real heritage.

He took another sip of the room-temperature scotch, frowning down at the amber liquid. Too clear. And though it was filled with layers, it was still too…contrived.

Blood. Thick, warm, bursting with flavor. Nothing less would do.

—◦◦◦—

"Karissa!" Her name echoed through the maze of halls, farther away this time. Faint, barely a pin drop in the oppressive blackness she had escaped into.

From the moment she'd gained her footing she'd been running. Had to get away. Couldn't let them catch her.

But it was dark as shit in here.

She stubbed her toe on something, slipped on a patch of floor that had been polished to deadly levels, and barely managed to stay upright by grabbing onto what turned out to be an armless statue. Behind her, she could hear Logan calling for her still, zeroing in on the sounds she was making. And somewhere, she knew, his father would be stalking her too. Too bad for them. She'd jump to the netherplanes and stay there before she let them catch her.

That was a last resort. She was a fighter, not a lamb. Even if fighting in this case meant getting the hell away from them.

She skidded around the corner, nails digging into the molding that lined every corner on this level. To the right was another dark hall, and to the left…There. A light in the distance, a tease of temptation in the dark. Only it wasn't safe there either. There were other Paladin. Other men who would "claim" her.

She turned down the dark hall instead.

—◦◦◦—

The doors to the sanctuary swung open, revealing a woman in flowing cherry-red robes. The rich robes clashed ostentatiously with her eye-popping, pumpkin-orange curls. Still, the velvet was sinful rubbing up against the creamy skin of her nicely muscled arms.

A warrior. A queen. A woman men should lower themselves to their knees for.

She shouldn't be here. *The thought was like a distant buzz tone in the back of Roland's mind, spreading a slick sensation of unease along his spine. Then she dropped her shoulders back, breasts pressing forward against the blue silk gown as a wide smile formed on her luscious burgundy lips. The slick unease turned into a shudder.*

Damn. Switch roles. With a mouth like that, she should be the one kneeling.

"Well, well, well." *The words rumbled up like a purr from beneath her perfect bust to drip like silken honey from that perfect mouth in a husky and full cadence that was…Mon Dieu! Perfect for fucking.* "Christos said you'd be the one to come. I didn't believe him."

Christos. He should know that name. But damn, names seemed inconsequential compared to the stunning woman who was currently running her fingers across the top of her low-cut gown. He'd never seen a more beautiful woman. Something about her…the seductive elegance of that slight movement of hand, the drowning quality of her heavy-lidded, ocean-green eyes.

"You want to come in?" *She stepped back, gesturing with her head over her shoulder at the grand foyer beyond.*

He looked at the checkered marble, the opulent crystal chandelier. Both were inexplicably familiar. Yes. He wanted to come in. He'd come for a reason. He needed to…why was he here?

"Come on," she said when he hesitated. "I won't bite."

The last was delivered with a punctuated lick of her front incisors. Roland practically shivered imagining what it would be like to have those straight white teeth raking over his skin. She'd start at his throat, then work her way down, those red-tipped fingers slowly undressing him so her tongue could find more skin.

She laughed. A full-bodied laugh that had her breasts jiggling pleasingly. A slender hand snaked out, latching on to his arm. "Come on, big boy. I promise this will be a night to remember."

God he hoped so. Roland let her drag him into the foyer. Behind him the door closed with a solid boom. The manor house was quiet. More so than typical, but before the thought could fully penetrate, the redhead had her arms around his neck and her lush lips pressed up against his own. After that it was blurs of images, punctuations of sensation. His shirt was gone before he could blink, tossed to the wayside with her cloak. Her mouth was all over him, exploring every inch of his torso as her deft fingers went to work on his pants.

Out of the corner of his eye he caught movement. A figure, male, skimming the edge of the room.

"Who?" Even though the question came from his own mouth, the voice sounded foreign. Distant. Strange.

And then she was kissing him again. Her tongue plunged between his lips and demanded he taste what the combination of her and him could be like. Oh hell yes. That was good.

He needed her. Now!

He half dragged, half tumbled her to the floor, his hands as determined to press her into the polished black-and-white marble as to push down the already dangerously low bust line of her gown.

A sharp prick pierced the back of his shoulder. He yelled, trying to twist his head to look at his attacker. A long-nailed hand grasped his jaw, forcing him to keep his head forward.

"Never mind him. Concentrate on me."

His gaze dropped to the plump offerings heaving up and down against his chest. Oh yes. Gladly.

His head lowered.

Almost there.

A wrist, dripping blood, was rudely shoved in the way between him and his goal.

He growled out a protest. He wanted her. Needed her. And that bloody mess was in his way.

"Drink. Drink, my love. For me."

Her voice commanded that he drag his gaze up. Her mesmerizing eyes locked onto his, her needs becoming his. Her desire became the force of his will. She wanted him to drink.

Yes. Yes. He'd do anything for her. Holding her gaze, he lowered his head, running his tongue languidly over the dripping red liquid. The taste...exquisite. Sweet, coppery, slick, warm. Addictive.

He opened his mouth and drank further. Couldn't get enough. Would never get enough.

His eyes rolled back, a euphoric darkness overcoming his vision.

Chapter 12

KARISSA'S BLOOD-PUMPING URGE TO FIND A WAY OUT started to fade with a new kind of alarm, the kind that told her she was going to kill herself if she didn't stop. Until then she'd encountered only heavy obstacles—walls, statues, and furniture alike—which did nothing more than leave a collection of bumps and bruises on her already battered body, but it was only a matter of time before she happened upon another stairwell. If she blindly fell down one of those? Well, broken limbs were certainly not conducive to escape.

Karissa slowed, toeing the fine line of making too much noise and progressing forward at a rate more than a crawl. She'd stopped hearing her name a while back. Not that that meant Logan and his father no longer hunted her, just that they were being stealthier about it. Which meant she was going to have to become stealthy too. Forget unseen staircases; she could run right into her predator's arms.

Her hand, which had been hop-skip-jumping along the wall, evened out to a steady drag. The walls were different here. Simple plaster. No wallpaper or paneling or breaks for ornate columns of molding or recesses with statues hidden within. There was a chill in the air, punctuated with the occasional toe-curling cold spot that seemed to want to leach all of her heat. As if this area, even more so than the rest of what she'd decided was an unused wing in the Paladin's grand castle, hadn't seen any use in decades, perhaps even a century. And those cold spots? *Ghosts*.

And wasn't that a freaky thought.

Her fingers hit a tapestry. The threadbare weaving tore from its tether at the top, falling with a muffled flop onto the floor. She halted in her tracks, muscles tense, ears pricked for any sound beyond her own hitching breath. Nothing.

She reached her hand back out, expecting plaster, and met—nothing. An alcove?

Carefully she nudged the fallen tapestry aside with her foot, following the line of the baseboard molding to the open gap in the wall. She slid her foot forward. Her toe dropped over the edge.

A hidden stairwell.

She followed the steps down, her hand running across the uneven walls. Not plaster. Stone. Deeper she went. Fifty steps. A hundred. Always curving to the left. Twice she hesitated, almost turned back, but her determination to find a way out kept her taking the next step, rounding the next curve.

Eventually the steps ended, depositing her in some sort of servants' hall, though it might as well have been a tunnel, or cave. Not one damn window in the place. And the décor was decidedly uninviting. It was dark, cramped, and cold. The stone walls pressed in on her from all sides.

She was made for light. Craved it. And to be confined to hiding in shadows?

Karissa blew out a breath, taking a moment to screw her head on straight. She admitted it. She was afraid of the dark. She'd been raised to be terrified of the things that went bump in the night.

"But you said that evil can sometimes walk in the light of day too, Papa."

Papa leaned forward, his wrinkled face no longer soft and inviting, but stern. "Yes. But at night, you can't see the evil coming."

"Oh, Papa. How right you were." On so many things.

It was her fault he was dead. That stupid night class. She'd led the monsters home to her ailing papa. He'd warned her, and she hadn't listened.

She dashed away a tear. She could cry later. After she got away. After she was safe.

Safe where?

She had no idea. There was no place to go, no one she could trust. Except…

She shook her head, pushing away the thought weaving itself into what passed for logic in her current messed up state. Running to Roland was not an option. It wasn't even that she was worried over whether he had or had not tried to enthrall her. He'd risked his life to warn her about what could happen at Haven. And she couldn't deny the hurt she'd felt from him when she refused him. He wouldn't have been hurt if he didn't care about her.

Which meant everything that happened before had to be taken in a new light. Roland had never kidnapped her. Never planned to sell her or rape her. And, God help her and her treacherous body, she was beginning to suspect he'd never tried to enthrall her either. Nope, everything he'd done—except, perhaps, that damn kiss—now stunk of self-sacrifice and concern for her—not his own—well-being.

She would not be responsible for someone else dying because of her foolishness.

She rubbed her arms, attempting to ward off a chill that came with the thought of going it alone. She'd figure things out. As soon as she made it outside. It must have been getting close to dawn, depending on how long she'd been unconscious earlier. As long as she was able to see well enough to use her gift, she could outrun most of the monsters that were capable of withstanding the sun's rays. Imps, chameleons, the occasional succubus. Yeah, she was able to keep ahead of those.

Karissa pushed off the wall, resuming her tentative progress through the tunnel. She could have sworn that she felt a breeze. And a breeze meant a door, or a window. A few feet later, she felt it again. A definite breeze!

Her heart bobbled beneath her breast. She pushed forward at a pace that she knew was edging on dangerous but couldn't seem to help herself. The air, tinged with car exhaust, was the sweetest thing she encountered since she arrived at the pretty prison.

She was so excited at the prospect of escape that when her outstretched arm rammed up against something solid and steel, sending a vibrating lance of pain up into her shoulder, she didn't even flinch. A door! And beyond, freedom.

She muffled a happy cheer and fumbled around for the latch. It seemed sticky, or maybe just rusted and old, but the door gave way behind the shove and grunt of her stubborn shoulders.

Karissa burst into the street beyond, gulping down the city air and basking in the glowing pool of the streetlamp as if she were a lizard and it the morning sun. Only, it

wasn't morning. Beyond the streetlamp's glow the dark
shadows that bathed the deserted street confirmed one
of her worst fears: It was still night. Either she wasn't
unconscious very long, or she'd slept a really long time.
Damn. She really didn't want to be out here at night.
Maybe she should go back inside, wait an hour or two.

Behind her the door clamored back into its casing.
She pivoted, head shaking as she stared at the closed
escape route.

"Shit!"

She lunged forward, gave a futile tug at the handle,
the muscles of her shoulders straining against the mocking resistance of the metal and steel. Locked. Of course.
What good was a secret escape route that your enemies
could get in? She'd made it beyond the intricate illusion that hid Haven from the rest of New York City's
unsuspecting population and was now back on the litter
strewn streets of the warehouse area of the great city that
never slept. Except here. Not a single soul dared to show
their faces here at night. Karissa didn't need to wonder
too long why that was.

"Already sick of our hospitality?" a familiar voice
drawled.

Karissa spun around.

Chapter 13

IT TOOK A MOMENT FOR HER EYES TO ADJUST, TO PICK out the trim figure standing in the shadows, arms folded, under the awning of the building across the street. But when they did, her lungs caught her breath in a suffocating choke hold. Valin. Of all the Paladin who could have been waiting for her to pop out of the back entrance, Valin was the one she least wanted to deal with. There was something about him that made her think of darkness and shadows, thievery and…yup, murder.

Karissa gulped down a golf ball sized lump of unease and tried to squeeze closer to the steel door at her back even as she desperately sought a way to escape. There were enough streetlamps—even if they were far spaced—that she could manage a sizable jump. The question was, which way?

"It's dangerous out here at night," he said, as if he read her mind and knew she was about to bolt.

"I'll take my chances, thanks anyway," she said, slipping a half-step to the left.

He chuckled, then began to saunter across the empty street toward her. Stalking, really, like he was the predator and she the prey.

Left it is, she thought and shifted into the netherplane.

A flash of brilliant white and a split second later she was smashing back into reality, her feet stumbling on the pitted pavement beneath the streetlight she'd targeted.

She tried to right herself, couldn't seem to stop the slant of the road under her legs, and went down, her palms smashing into the unforgiving asphalt. Damn, that hurt.

She wasted precious seconds as she tried to heave herself up, fighting the nausea that ripped at her stomach, twisting against the spinning world that seemed determined to play havoc on her balance. She felt like she'd just stumbled away from one of those crazy twirling teacup rides at the firemen's field days. And that wasn't even mentioning the anvil that must have fallen on her head. She didn't have many more jumps left in her. Not after the night she'd had.

Still on her hands and knees, Karissa glanced over her shoulder. Maybe Valin didn't see where she'd popped off to. But there he was, a half block away and striding down the faded center line of the road.

She needed to put more distance between them. Fast.

Battling back the brain-ripping headache, she forced her gaze forward. There. A jerk, a gut-wrenching twist, and she was another hundred yards away under another flickering streetlamp. Karissa didn't even give herself time to register the tsunami rolling around in her stomach, didn't pay any homage to the deafening dial tone ringing in her ears, just looked down the street, picked her point, and popped.

That's it. I can't go any farther.

Karissa half staggered, half fell to the mouth of a nearby alley where she leaned against the wall of a brick building badly in need of repointing. By her estimation, she managed to gain a good mile or more on her pursuer.

Unless he could fly—fat chance—then she should be safe…from him.

South Bronx. Her gut said she was in the Bronx. There was something in the way the buildings seemed to sag against each other, the desperation in the air she was sucking down. Now, if only she knew where in the Bronx. She was more of a Brooklyn girl. Still, if she could figure out approximately where she was, she should be able to make her way from here. The question was, to where?

She looked to where the alley spilled out onto the main street, if the narrow two-way road could be called a main street, that is. A street sign would have been too much to ask for, it seemed.

She took a couple sagging steps forward, her hand braced against the brick as if it were her lifeline. It very well might be. She'd probably collapse if it wasn't there.

Her sight distance was limited to the small pools of light cast by towering overhead streetlamps. At least she seemed to be out of the warehouse district. The area had turned into a highly commercialized zone, even if it was struggling. The good news was that the typical night sounds of the city were starting to reinsert themselves, just not here. Here, it seemed, most people were too smart to wander around at this time of night. Except, yeah, that hooker on the next corner.

Karissa took a couple jerky steps toward her. Karissa didn't have any money, but maybe she could play the girl-to-girl card and extract a location out of her. The girl absently glanced over her shoulder, then looked away, obviously writing Karissa off as unprofitable. Karissa hesitated, not because she cared a wit about her inability to barter, but because of the glimpse she'd gotten of the girl's face, and she did mean girl. The redhead strutting her stuff in those five-inch stilettos barely looked old enough to wear a training bra, let alone the skimpy tube top she had on. Karissa's muscles tensed to the point of vibrating. Whatever the circumstances, whoever the a-hole was who'd dragged that poor girl out on the streets deserved to have—

A shadow wafted in front of Karissa, obscuring her vision. She waved her hand over her eyes. Must be tired. The dark cloud of particles coalesced, funneling in around her and settling toward the ground.

Oh crap. What the hell kind of monster was this?

And there was no way she could pull another jump, not so soon.

She scrambled back, her gaze darting around for a weapon. A glass bottle she could break or maybe even a discarded hubcap she could throw at the thing. A thing that looked suspiciously like...

"Valin?" She blinked, trying to make sense of the man who'd formed in the spot previously occupied by writhing darkness. It was Valin. No doubt. But, "Oh God! You're naked."

His lip curled up in a sly grin. "You flatter me. Though it's Valin, not God. He might object to such presumption."

"Why are you naked?" There was a hysterical quality to her voice that she couldn't seem to control. This was too much. Positively too much.

Valin continued to smile, as if that were answer enough.

Who the hell cared why he was naked? What she should be worrying about was getting the heck out of here. She couldn't jump. Not without collapsing at the end, and if he'd managed to follow her here—how the hell had he followed her here?—then it was a futile move anyway.

"What do you want from me?" she asked as she started to edge around him. The hooker probably wouldn't help her, but maybe if her pimp was nearby...

"I thought that obvious."

A curl of horror slid through her system. Naked man chasing woman. Obvious indeed.

"Not going to happen."

"You certainly have spirit. I shall enjoy looking into that head of yours."

"My head?" Okay, that was a far cry from what she'd been thinking.

She didn't blink, knew she hadn't, but the next instant he was on top of her, his left arm braced around her back, clamping her right arm to her side, and circling around to hold her left wrist immobile.

"Your mind." His free hand caressed her sore throat, circling the base in the same way Logan had back in the hall. His gaze lifted, dark brown pools of midnight sliding over her like an oil slick, threatening to suffocate. "Once my mark is upon you, I can not only find you wherever you are, but I will have great insight into your mind."

"You can read my mind?" The question, coupled with the skin-to-skin contact, brought with it a flash of intent. No, he couldn't read her yet, but he would be able to soon. First to mark her. Then...

Hell..."No."

"Relax, Karissa. This won't hurt a bit."

For the second time that night, she was held against

her will as he muttered some sort of foreign tongue like a madman. She tried to jerk away but got nowhere. She made a feeble attempt at raising her knee, but her legs were so weak all she managed to do was graze his knee with hers.

"Hush," he murmured then picked back up the tumbling chant.

She squeaked, squirming in his surprisingly powerful grip. This was wrong. She wasn't meant for him. He was not her mate.

Wha—? Mate? Karissa didn't know where that strange thought had come from, but it didn't matter. She couldn't let this happen. She shook her head; she was not beneath pleading. "Please. Don't do this. This isn't right."

He seemed to hesitate, as if he too knew it was wrong. But then he shook his head, his eyes shuttering, the lines of his face etched by his determination. "You're wrong. This is right. I am the dark, you are my complement."

"I don't understand."

"Yes you do. I need your light," he said, and beneath his hand her neck began to tingle.

Karissa winced as her throat began to burn. No way in hell. Nuh-uh. She wasn't going to go through this again. Scream, head butt, then pop out. She'd take her chances in that white slate of nothingness than remain here and become a victim.

"I can't believe this. Idiots, all of you," a voice, feminine, said just before Karissa could let loose the scream. There was an audible huff, then, "Don't you guys know better than to let your women out at night?"

Must be the hooker.

The burning hand lifted from her throat. Valin spun Karissa around behind him, but not before she got a good look at the girl standing beyond him. Hip thrust out, hair flipped back over her shoulder, she looked to be thirteen or fourteen at most. Except she wasn't. She was far, far older. The proof wasn't in the detached coldness of the eyes, nor in the husky timber of her voice. It was the fangs.

Roland tossed back the last of his scotch, then glared at the bottle sitting on the coffee table. Empty. There wasn't enough liquor to burn away the taste of the blood he'd spilled.

Ninety-four years of bloodlust. Ninety-four years of trying to hold onto his humanity. The first few had been a lesson in abject failure, the bloodlust overriding everything else. Possibly if he'd been turned by a master who cared, one who would help his new charge past the cravings and teach him how to temper his needs…but Christos was not that sort of master. He'd encouraged the mindless violence, had egged Roland on, and Roland had been more than pleased to oblige.

Until Logan. Logan had brought him back. Helped Roland to sever the master-slave bond that Christos had held over him for five seemingly eternal years. It had been eighty-nine years since Roland had killed. Yet he'd almost killed a man tonight. The blond had looked like Angeline. And in his mind it was Angeline, his sister, that Don Juan Tom had been planning to rape. Roland's rage had been so great he'd kept drinking. Wanting to punish. Wanting to lose himself to his nature. When the bloodlust was over him there was no pain, no emotion. Empty. Void. Thoughtless creature of the night. God, the blood had tasted so good.

The phone rang.

Teeth sinking into flesh.

Another chiming burr.

Warm sweet liquid pooling on his tongue.

Brrrriiinnnggg.

Coppery taste sliding across the back of his mouth and down his throat.

With an inhuman growl, Roland grabbed up the phone, punching the talk button. "What do you want?"

"It's Karissa. She's run away."

Roland's hand tightened around the tumbler, the cut glass leaving grooves in his palm. "Are you telling me she's outside? Alone? Before dawn?"

There was an audible swallow on the other end. "They've sent Valin after her."

Roland stood, carefully clicking the off button on the phone, and dropped it in the chair. He raised the tumbler—no scotch left. He started to lower it, then, with an enraged roar, he threw the tumbler across the room where it smashed against the mantel.

Chapter 14

"You're going the wrong way."

Roland spun about, his feet slipping on slate tile before his hand caught purchase on one of the decorative copper finials at the top of the peak he was currently perched upon. Gabriella, the little redheaded minx, was about fifteen feet below him, lounging on the back of a gargoyle as if she didn't have a care in the world. Below them the dizzying lights of the pre-rush-hour traffic whizzed by, intent on their destinations and uncaring of the two vampires who hung precariously to the Jefferson Market Library clock tower a hundred and seventy-one feet above them.

"Why do you say that?" he asked, trying to keep panic out of his voice. Karissa was out there somewhere. In the dark. With Valin. Roland knew that as long as Valin was close enough he would protect Karissa from the likes of Christos, Ganelon, and Lucifer, but who in the hell would protect her from Valin? Regardless, Roland didn't need to share his problems with Gabriella. In fact, it was better he didn't. He thought he knew by now that Gabriella would never purposefully betray him—she hated Christos as much as he—but that didn't mean anything he told her would remain secret. There was nothing sacred between master and slave.

He expected Gabriella to pull one of her quippy comebacks, or flip her hair and act haughty and all knowing.

The girl had perfected her teenage mask. Instead she looked down at the weathered granite, letting her red hair cover her eyes. "She's in the Bronx. South."

He narrowed his eyes, trying to bore through her skull to see what was going on behind those pretty waves. The Bronx was where Haven was hidden, but Karissa would have naturally gravitated toward the area of the city she'd grown up in, which was Brooklyn. He'd headed south because he'd been sincerely hoping she would use her gift to hop and skip on home. Where he again hoped he could find her before Valin, or someone else, did. Was Gabriella telling the truth? Or had Christos hitched a ride and was using his pawn to try and deceive Roland?

"How do you know?" he asked, watching her reaction for deception.

She lifted her gaze, the bridge of her nose pinched with emotion. He saw nothing there but truth and remorse. He was about to ask what was wrong when she opened her mouth and then delivered from between quivering lips, "I saw her there, with Valin." She dropped her gaze again, and he knew the next bit would be the killing blow. "Only, I wasn't alone when I did."

"Oh shit." Valin's arm snapped out, catching Karissa across the chest. Her gaze settled on the three figures that had just landed in front of them. Two were obviously vampires, but the man they flanked, with his black abysses for eyes and the bloodred cloak that flowed out behind him, was something else…something more.

Valin and the redheaded vampire had both been right. Tonight was not a good night to be out.

"Run, Karissa!" Valin hissed, pushing her behind him.

He didn't have to ask her twice. She ran. Well, she tried. Problem was she and Valin had been running since the moment the girl had disappeared. Karissa still didn't understand why the adolescent vamp had told them trouble was on the way, or why she'd then let them go, but she supposed it didn't matter much. The warning had been too little too late; the enemy was too close and Haven too far. Karissa wished she could have jumped—if she could have they would have been safe by now—but the truth was she could barely stand, let alone run. So there they were, five or six blocks away from help.

She made it a pitiful fifteen feet when she hit an invisible wall. The impact burned and she fell back on her butt with a yelp of pain, landing on something sharp.

Her eyes locked longingly on the tease of an escape route beyond the invisible barrier.

"Isn't that something," a seductively low voice said from behind her. The hairs on the back of her neck prickled with each grinding step he took toward her. "Looks like Christos was right. Man, he's going to be pissed at Gabby dearest for trying to hide this."

Karissa didn't know who Christos or Gabby were. Didn't care. The only thing that mattered to her right now was the scrap of metal she'd conveniently fallen upon. It had torn through her jeans and scratched her thigh, but, blessings of blessings, it could be turned into an excellent weapon. As long as she could stand the heck up. Shaking with exhaustion, she grasped the

jagged metal and dragged herself to her feet, then turned
to face the man with the cloying voice.

Oh crap. She thought it was the red cape that had
made him seem so imposing. She'd been wrong. He was
huge. Gigantic. All of a sudden her piddly piece of metal
didn't seem like much of a defense. Certainly not worth
the tetanus booster she was probably going to have to
have if she survived this encounter.

She looked past him toward Valin. Her hopes for
help from that corner dashed when she saw the Paladin
engaged in battle with the two vampires...and a demon.
Valin wasn't doing so well either. Despite the fact he was
able to do his little ghosting trick, he still bore an alarm-
ing number of bleeding wounds upon his naked body.

Her grip tightened around the shard of metal, brandishing the inadequate weapon like a knife.

"You think to kill me with that?" the black-eyed
man asked on a laugh, drawing her attention back to the
closer threat. "You couldn't. You're weak as a lamb."

And damn him for noticing. With a hiss, Karissa
lunged forward and found the shield wasn't only in front
of her, but it surrounded her.

Frantic, she pounded and slashed at the bubble of
energy that entrapped her. The metal shard skittered
and sparked whenever it met the invisible barrier. Panic
clamped down on her lungs. She began to hyperventi-
late. *Have to get out. Need to get free.*

"Karissa!"

She could hear Valin yelling over the buzzing in her
mind, but she didn't stop.

Trapped trapped trapped trapped.

"Leave her alone, you bastard!"

Pulling on the last of her energy—not sure she could even make the jump if she wanted to—she let it loose, only to find it sapped away into the rolling power of the shield. She whimpered, her vision funneling into a black tunnel.

The man laughed again, closer this time. She couldn't even manage the energy to look.

Her body crumpled, her knees buckling and her head sagging down onto her chest as raking sobs tore through her body.

Too tired to jump. Too tired to fight.

Papa, oh, Papa. I'm so sorry.

She shuddered. Her last thought was that of Papa's mutilated body as she sunk onto the cold pavement.

He's dead.

The thought barely had time to cross Roland's mind before he was plunging off the top of the steel roof of the warehouse, knife singing from his leg sheath, and toward the cloaked merker bending over Karissa's crumpled form. Red fury, red blood. Immortal or not, the merker was a dead man.

Roland slammed into the merker, catching him unprepared. They rolled, fists smashing, fangs slashing, knife and gun sliding out of sleeves. Roland's knife sliced through the tendons of the merker's wrist and the merker's gun dropped before discharging. It didn't stop the creature's other hand though, or the attached claws that popped through his human glamour and ripped a painful slash across Roland's shoulder.

Roland's roar ripped through the alley, cut off the

moment he sunk his canines into the thin flesh around the merker's trachea. Another muffled growl and a yank and the merker's throat was hanging from his body. A Colombian necktie, minus the tongue. The merker's mouth opened in a silent scream, his claws extracting from Roland's flesh as they flew back to grab at the dangling cartilage. A lesser being would be dead, or dying, but virtual immortality was just another perk of being sired by Ganelon. And birthed by a demon. The only way to kill a merker was to cut out their heart, lop off their head, and burn them both—in His light.

The merker would heal, unless Roland could kill it first.

Roland rolled back into a half-crouch and tossed the long-bladed knife from one hand to the other, his gaze following the backpedaling merker. First things first. The heart. He lunged…and was grabbed from behind.

⌇⌇

So cold.

Karissa turned her head, wincing at the grind of gritty pavement against her cheek. Her entire body was twitching, the jerky movements abrading her skin wherever it met blacktop. She didn't care. In this case blacktop was good. It meant no one had kidnapped her while she was unconscious. She was still in the road. And blessed be, alive.

A muffled scream tore her from her momentary optimism. The fight was still on. Trying not to draw attention to herself until she could determine status, she lifted her head just enough to turn her chin toward the noise.

She expected to see Valin, and there he was, struggling with one of the two vampires in a cloud of ash.

The other was noticeably absent, and hope of hopes, the reason for the dust. What she didn't expect to see was the other man playing do-si-do with a demon.

"Roland..." she whispered through her tight throat, watching as he made another thrust with the wicked-looking knife in his hand. The blade was dripping with a black oily substance—demon blood. It would have been another score for the good guys if not for the fact that Roland was similarly dripping—red blood. He was hurt.

Karissa pushed up on her hands and winced as something sharp cut into her palm. The metal shard. Her eyes narrowed on the hideous demon that was digging groves in the pavement with its razor sharp hooves as it danced in for another slice at Roland.

Karissa sucked in a breath, something vital dropped two stories from behind her ribs to below her belly, then let the lungful of used air out again as Roland whirled aside, the demon's clawed hand slashing open space.

A bit of optimism slipped back in. Roland was here. Everything was going to be all right.

Then, out of the corner of her eye, a figure lifted from the sidewalk nearby. She hadn't noticed him before; in the dim light the dark red cloak he wore blended him in with the blood-soaked cement. She felt her heart skip a beat. The night, which seemed warm until that moment, chilled the sweat on her skin, making her shiver.

It was the man with the black eyes, the one who trapped her. He shouldn't have been able to stand. Shouldn't even be alive. He had a friggin' hole in the middle of his chest!

He didn't look at her, his eyes fixed on Roland as he lurched forward first one step, then another.

Uncaring of the sting across her palm, Karissa's fist tightened around the metal and she pulled her legs under her. The world spun.

She could do no more than cry out helplessly as the cloaked man lunged at Roland's unprotected back. In a gravity-defying move, Roland crouched, then sprang up, twisting his body up and over Black Eyes, and landing behind him in an effortless flourish.

Despite the seriousness of the situation, Karissa found the corner of her mouth twitching. The next second her half-smile faded as the cloaked man's head slid from his body, landed with a sickening thud on the ground and rolled to a stop less than three feet away from her hands, its black eyes boring into her.

She hadn't even seen Roland use his knife.

Bile rose in her throat, a scream stuck behind it. The death, the monsters, the constant running, thinking she was safe then the betrayals, more running, more death. Too much.

There was an inhuman roar. A demon's cry.

"Back up, Karissa!" Roland yelled, his boots scuffing as he rushed to engage the remaining enraged demon.

She heard him, noted the clipped tone that bespoke a raised level of anxiety. Still, she could not draw her gaze from the unblinking eyes. She swore there was still something there in the black depths. It saw her.

Dimly, she was aware of Roland still dancing with his demon and at the same time stringing together a series of chants eerily similar in tongue to the one both Logan and Valin had used on her, though different, darker. She started to lift her gaze when the black eyes blinked. They effing blinked! Her jaw dropped open, her eyes riveted on the decapitated head as she desperately tried to convince herself she hadn't seen what she'd seen.

From farther down the road came another inhuman screech. Almost thankful for the distraction, Karissa allowed the instinctive twist of her head. A cloud of ash billowed in the place where Valin and the vampire had been. A second later, a cloud of dark particles separated out, swirling into form a step beyond until only Valin remained.

Valin stood, feet planted wide, arms spread slightly as if ready to tackle something, but with his head half bent and his chest heaving. He was covered in sweat, blood, and grime. He'd killed two vampires, but his battle had not been without personal cost. There was a deep gash across his upper arm, and a wicked wound from his chest down to his groin where it looked like someone had tried to disembowel him—and thankfully failed.

Karissa squirmed. She *was* glad he was alive and that both wounds, though vicious, didn't seem to be life threatening. But she was decidedly uneasy as well. Their momentary camaraderie as they fled was iffy at best.

Valin raised his head, his eyes drifting over her to narrow in on a point to Karissa's left. Her head swiveled back around. The demon was gone. Only Roland stood, his own chest heaving to match the rise and fall of the naked Paladin staring him down.

"Roland," Valin spat the name out like it was something vile that needed to be eradicated.

"Valin," Roland replied more calmly.

"You're supposed to be dead."

Roland nodded, his mouth twisted up into a mocking smile. "Some would say that I am."

Valin tensed. Roland shifted his weight back to the balls of his feet.

Karissa blinked in disbelief. They were both Paladin. They'd just saved each other's assess. They weren't going to fight each other, were they?

In the next second Karissa had her answer. Silent as a hunting cat, Valin rushed forward.

Roland sidestepped Valin's charge. Too easy. Valin, who normally might have been a challenge, was injured and weak with fatigue. Perhaps he should allow his brother Paladin a strike or two for his ego. Something with which to console himself once Roland brought the Paladin down. But one glimpse of the lightening sky, Karissa's trembling body, and the jiggling limbs of the not-yet-dead, headless merker had him pushing aside such feelings of sympathy.

So, as his foot hit pavement, his body twisting out of the way, he also reached out with his arm, snagging the man who'd once fought by his side. The man who'd once called him brother. Given that Valin wanted to kill him, Roland was pretty sure he could count on the fact that those days were definitely over.

With an arm-wrenching twist, he threw the Paladin up against the wall of a nearby building. Knowing Valin would just shift, Roland did the one thing guaranteed to keep him there, the one thing that would also confirm the totality of his lost soul in the Paladin's eyes.

Once, a long time ago when he was initiated into the ranks, Roland went through the ceremony that bound him forever to his fellow Paladin. A ceremony

Valin went through also. A blood ceremony. Using his vampire powers to draw on that blood tie now, Roland forced himself behind Valin's natural defenses, worming his way into the Paladin's mind, and squashing his will to shift.

Valin sucked in a gasp of air, his eyes widening in panic. Fear. It was Roland's only weapon. He would not use the knife he'd pressed up against his former brother's throat. He would not raise a hand to truly harm him. But Valin, and the others, had to understand: They could not kill him, and they would *not* take from him that which was his.

Keeping a firm clamp upon Valin's mind, Roland scratched the blade against the stubble of Valin's five a.m. beard. Amazingly, Valin managed to rein in his panic. His eyes went hollow as his mouth thinned into a line of determination.

The man remained obstinately still. Stubbornly stoic. Roland's grip started to slip.

Well, well. Valin had learned control sometime over the last ninety-four years. Not enough though.

With a deep-throated growl, Roland curled back his upper lips, showing fangs. Valin paled.

A slim hand came down on the elbow of his arm holding the knife. "Roland…don't. This isn't who you are."

Roland wasn't sure what to make of that. He was somewhat surprised Karissa was even willing to admit there might be more to him than his vampire instincts. But he was also angry that she would believe he would actually feed from his brother.

So what if he was considering piercing that stubbled skin. He wouldn't have actually drunk from the vein, and Valin deserved a good scare. The man was desperate with his desire to claim Karissa, like a moth to a flame. The Black Knight was drawn to the light. And Karissa must look like the sun.

Any thought of furthering Valin's lesson was obliterated when Karissa swayed beside him, her fingers digging into his arm.

With a growl, Roland released Valin, the knife quickly disappearing into its sheath on his thigh as he reached out to steady Karissa with his other hand. As soon as he touched her, fire licked up his arm and through his body, burning away his anger and leaving him feeling warm with pleasure. Her head tilted back, her eyes widening in surprise, as if she too felt it.

Valin sucked in breath, pushing away from the building. In a show of strength that was both dangerous and necessary, Roland kept his shoulder to him, not even honoring him with a glance. He did, however, have some last words for his former brother.

"Go, Valin. Run home to Haven. And once you get there, you can tell the others something for me."

There was a distinctive sound of molars grinding, then, "What?"

"Karissa is mine. I will protect her now."

Karissa's lips parted, her lids fluttering as if undecided how to take that. When she bit her lip and didn't say anything, Roland considered it a win.

Air shifted as Valin stepped forward. "You have no right—"

Roland spun around, his red-filled gaze boring into the Paladin. Ruthlessly, he ripped through the man's boundaries again, stabbing a path through his mind.

Valin stumbled back. Just as quickly Roland released his hold over him, leaving the Paladin glaring and rubbing his temples against the nasty headache Roland had given him.

"I have every right. Just as I have the right to kill you for trying to mark her. However, given that we once called each other brother, I will gift you a reprieve. That said, the next man who tries to do so will not be granted such mercy. Brother or not. Clear?"

"Roland, it's almost dawn. We have to go." Karissa's soft words and the tug at his arm broke the glaring face-off. They all looked to the sky, the softening of the oily blackness that said the sun was up and chasing the moon.

Roland glanced over at the merker's headless body. It had regained enough life that it was trying to struggle across the pavement in search of its head. Beside him Karissa gasped.

"What the heck is that thing?"

"Merker," he answered, swinging his gaze back around to Valin. "You might want to gather up the heart and head. Dispose of them properly."

The look Valin threw him said it all: Fuck you. Roland figured that if the Paladin had any energy left he would have tried to emphasize the directive with the appropriate action.

With a sigh Roland turned to Karissa. Despite his words to Valin, it had to be her choice to come with him.

"Ready?" he asked, laying a hand against her abraded cheek. It hurt to see her injured, tired, and still scared. If it would keep her safe, drive away her fears, he'd rip apart a hundred more merkers for her and banish a thousand more demons. Given enough time, he would.

She startled under his touch, dragging her gaze away from the struggling body inching closer and closer to its head. Valin had better get on top of that.

It took a moment for his words to register, but when it did, her eyes flared. Then, with an audible swallow, she nodded her head, stepping closer to him.

He didn't hesitate but wrapped her up in his arms, lifting her to his chest. God, she felt good. Perfect.

"Hold on."

Her arms looped around his neck, her face burying in the crook of his throat and shoulder. He threw a last pointed look at Valin, and then Roland crouched and leapt.

Chapter 15

ROLAND'S HEAVY BOOTS RUNG THROUGH THE EMPTY stairwell. Behind them, the roof door clanged shut and Karissa started in his arms. His fault. The whole way home his anger had built. And as it did she tensed tighter and tighter in his arms. At one point he thought she would demand he put her down, but a quick glimpse to the east had her clinging tighter, urging him on. Yeah, he'd been playing it close. Again. Yet, even though the first pale rays had stained the sky, it didn't hurt. Not really. At least not compared to the pain of the fury already ripping a hole in his chest.

She was his woman, and he hadn't protected her. He never should have left her at Haven. He'd been hurt by her assumptions that he would try to enthrall her, and been unwilling to force her, but he should have, could have, found a way to convince her.

They came to the first landing. A curt command and the door opened. They went along a short hall past the lone penthouse elevator bank, then another door and another curt command. Safety. He'd already changed the codes. No one would be getting in without his permission.

He carried her straight to the bathroom where he dropped her on the closed lid of the toilet and then spun about, twisting on the hot water valve in the sink.

"What possessed you to go hopping across the city,

alone, at night, when you knew those creatures were searching for you?"

Soaking a washcloth in the lukewarm stream, he spun back around. She was perched on the edge of the toilet, eyes wide, face pale, wounds oozing blood. Blood. Her blood. God.

"Damn it, Karissa. You could have been killed!" That the merker had joined forces with both Christos's vamps and Lucifer's demons alarmed him. Those three factions didn't play well together. Chances of things going wrong, orders being ignored…he could have lost her. Just when he'd found her, she could have died.

He bent down, dabbing at the abrasion on her cheek. What he wanted to do was lick the blood off, seal the wound, and heal her beautiful creamy skin. But even that small amount of blood would be enough to form a tie. And though he ached to be bonded to her, it would not be through blood. That sort of tie was completely one-sided. He would not take away her freedom.

Her lips turned down at the corners, endearingly so. "I don't think they want me dead. Or rather, I don't think *he* wants me dead."

"He?" Roland asked carefully, careful not to let his unease spill over on her. How much did she know about the man who hunted her? Other than the basic there-are-monsters-out-there, she seemed all but oblivious to the inner workings of the different factions of evil. At least until now. Perhaps Logan had filled her in.

She shook her head, uncertain. "Before they attacked. I thought I—"

"Thought what?"

"I thought I heard someone talking, in my mind. He

said that they were to catch me without harming me. That he would not tolerate a hair on my head being out of place."

Roland stilled. *He said. They were.* Not someone popping into her mind, then. She'd actually overheard an order. A thought projected from a master to his servant, or in this case, his offspring. Ganelon talking to his merker. "You hear projected thoughts."

"I guess." She blinked, then her chin thrust out. "So?"

Yes, so. She had no idea the amount of power she held. None at all. And it was that power their enemies craved. "You hear projected thoughts, you teleport—anything else, darling?"

"No." She spoke quickly, a blush hitting her cheeks equally as fast. Whether from the endearment or something else, he didn't know.

"No?" He quirked his eyebrow, working on the scratches on her arms and the flecks of pavement embedded in her skin. It looked like she'd tried to take the road with her.

"I—ouch!" She licked her lips then fell silent.

"You what?"

"Nothing. I just…"

Satisfied he'd cleaned the worst, he tossed the bloody washcloth across the bathroom into the basin, then turned back, taking her hand. It was cool and slim. So fragile. What Ganelon would have done to her if he'd managed to abduct her was unthinkable. And Roland wouldn't have been able to save her. With no mark, no blood tie between them, he would never find her in time. The only reason he succeeded this time had been because of Gabriella. But there was no guarantee the young vampire would again be able to throw her master's leash when it was most needed.

Take her now. Mark her. Complete the bond you know is there.

God. He could imagine it now. Full-fledged Technicolor. What would it be like to taste her again? Just a small taste. A kiss drowning in the sweet vanilla honey of her mouth, then a sweet lick at the base of her throat, his hand on her pulsing heart as he took her, possessed her, and forever marked her as his own.

She yanked her hand back. "Stop."

He blinked, taken aback by her abruptness. "I'm sorry." His brow furrowed. He could use his vamp tricks to invade someone's mind, but how was she reading his?

"No, I, it's um, touch. I can hear—no that's not right—I sense intent."

He lifted a brow. "You could sense what I desired just now?"

She raised her head, seeming to look down at him even as she looked up into his eyes. "You wanted to lick my throat while you fucked me."

Fuck her? Hell yeah. But not how she meant. Not so…cold. Roland sat back on his heels, studying her face. A mixture of stubborn determination and unease. She had no idea. Still, after all that had happened, she had no idea she was his mate. And no wonder. It was impossible to think that he, a disgraced Paladin, a vampire, would be granted such a blessing. In a life that already seemed fucked up beyond belief, this was perfectly ironic.

A chuckle rose deep within him, rising until it burst forth in a full-bellied laugh. She bristled, straightening, her chin jutting out regally.

"You deny it?" she asked stiffly.

He broke off the laughter, taking her hand once more. She tried to pull away but he wouldn't let her, all but crushing it within his grip until he'd caught her gaze.

"Yes. I deny it." Her mouth opened in protest, but he cut her off. "What I wished for was to taste you, to possess you, as a Paladin lover would his mate. That, my darling, is a great deal more powerful than a simple fuck."

———

Karissa blinked, trying to escape the intensity of Roland's gaze. Mate. He thought she was his mate?

Yes, Karissa, and so do you.

Ignoring the crazy voice in her head—didn't even want to acknowledge the pulsing thrill running through her nerves—she went into full cross-examination mode.

"Mate." She bit out the word, jerking her hand from his grasp. She couldn't touch him. Not without losing her mind. Okay, so maybe it was a tempting kind of loss. A forget-the-world take-me-I'm-yours kind of crazy. But it was a loss of control nonetheless. Karissa didn't like feeling out of control. Too much of her life was out of control.

"As in you, me," she waved her hand between them, "together forever. As in more of this Neanderthal, beat one's chest, kind of claiming crap all you Paladin seem to buy into?"

He blinked, his eyes shuttering. "You need not worry. It was a fantasy, nothing more."

She watched in silence as he stood up, shrugging off his black T-shirt, and became thoroughly distracted by the rippling muscles. God he was gorgeous.

And mine.

Stop that, Karissa. He's not yours any more than you're his.

He could be, though.

Karissa gave a quick shake of her head, trying to eradicate the illogical, horny slut that seemed to have taken up permanent residence in her psyche. Calm. Logical. That's who she was. Not a dog.

Dog. Heat. Crap, what was it Logan and his father had said about her being in heat?

"As you know, I am not a full Paladin any longer."

What? Not a Paladin? Karissa lifted her gaze. Roland was leaning over the sink, carefully dabbing the blood off a cut on his forearm that had already healed. Oh, right. Honestly, she'd momentarily forgotten about the whole vampire thing. Just like she seemed to keep on forgetting how dangerous he could be.

But not to me.

Wow. That voice was really beginning to insert itself in her unconscious. Because even as she tried to argue, insert some of her well-ingrained logic that said "Keep sharp, be wary," she realized she *did* trust him. She had all along.

Which, ironically, made her more uneasy.

None of this made sense.

She cleared her throat, shifting on her black porcelain perch. Who bought a black toilet anyway? A vampire, that's who. "I wasn't worried."

In the mirror, his eyebrow lifted mockingly. And she knew, *knew*, that he could see right through her.

A rush of heat hit her cheeks. "What the heck is this marking crap anyhow?"

Roland dipped the cloth, squeezed it, then went to work on the trio of scratches on his shoulder. Out of all the wounds, this was the only one that still hadn't closed completely. He repeated the action two more times before he finally answered.

"A mark is an invisible sign that only another Paladin can see. The spell, if you will, not only tells the others that the female is spoken for, but it creates a virtual tether between both the male Paladin who made the mark and the female bearing it."

"A tether?"

He glanced over his shoulder at her. "It allows him to find her no matter where she is. And sometimes it actually allows a pathway between their minds. An intimate knowledge of the other's thoughts and feelings."

She gnawed on her lower lip, remembering Valin's comment about looking forward to seeing into her mind—so he could influence her. Roland's spin seemed a tad more wholesome, but she realized he considered it as such. Guess that went to show that appearances—the vampire vs. Paladin in this case—could be deceiving.

"So basically it's a way for a guy and a gal to get to know each other."

"Somewhat."

She looked at him sharply. Maybe he did know about the whole Jedi mind trick thing.

He sighed, wringing the blood out of the cloth and setting it on the sink. He didn't turn around, but he did meet her eyes in the mirror. "The whole getting-to-know-each-other thing only works when both partners have a certain amount of power. Like a vampire blood-tie, a mark done on an ungifted will create a link that can only be read by the Paladin. It was one of the reasons why a Paladin female is so highly sought after. No matter how much a Paladin might love his human wife, she can never understand the true intimacy of their bond."

Interesting, but if that was the case, then how did Valin figure on controlling her? Wouldn't she have been able to influence him as well? "So what would have happened if Valin, or say Logan, had marked me?"

He finally turned around, planting his hips against the ledge of the counter and folding his arms over his chest. The look he leveled at her was hidden behind multiple layers of walls and made her inherently leery. "Do you want to be bonded to Logan?"

What? Where had he gotten that? She huffed, throwing her hands up in the air. "I don't even know what that is! Marking, and now bonding? What's the difference?"

His lips pulled into a frown as he seemed to mull over his answer before attempting to explain. "Marking is merely a claim, a desire. Like the diamond engagement ring you would wear to show the world you are promised. The Paladin take that promise very seriously and none would interfere with a couple who have gone through the marking ceremony. However, it, like an engagement, can be broken if time shows the pairing is not as compatible as originally thought. A bond…that can never be broken. It takes the pledge of heart, body, and soul and makes it truth. No one can break that bond."

"And mates?"

He hesitated, but then said, "It is said for every Paladin that the Father will one day send down that

Paladin's true mate. The rest—marking, bonding—are merely formal ceremonies to make a pairing valid in the eyes of the others."

"Oh." She sensed he was censoring his answers somewhat, but at the same time she thought all he'd told her was truth. Just as the fantasy she'd glimpsed—and whoa, that had been intense—had struck her as truth. He wanted to be with her, as a Paladin would be with his mate. Did that mean he thought she was his mate? Was that even possible for him anymore?

Yes. Of course it was possible. He may have been irrevocably changed when he was turned, but at his core he was still a Paladin. He might not fight in their ranks anymore, but he fought their war, and he held himself to their codes.

Which meant that he would want the same things they did. He would want the mate, the bond. He wanted her. But was that any different from every other friggin' Paladin she'd met in the last twenty-four hours? Didn't they all want her as their mate?

She realized she was tapping the side of the porcelain toilet and forced herself to stop by neatly folding her hands in her lap. "So that is what you were trying to warn me about. That all those men would want to mark me without even knowing if I was their, um, mate. Kind of a hope-for-the-best strategy."

He nodded, his jaw ticking.

And he'd been trying to protect her. She looked down at her scraped up hands, evidence of her stupidity. She'd not only rejected his help, but then she'd put herself in another deadly situation by running from Haven and forcing him to save her, again. If there were more of those creatures or, God, if more than one Paladin had been there to see him…

Her chest tightened. She had to concentrate hard on breathing deeply. "I'm sorry. I didn't understand. I thought—"

He turned away and set to the task of washing out the bloodstained washcloth. "It's okay. No harm, no foul. You're here. Safe. And unmarked."

Safe *and* unmarked. And that's how she knew it was different with him. Roland would protect her—even from himself. The tension she'd been holding since she'd allowed him to carry her to his apartment flooded out through her feet. In its place spread a tingling warmth, a certainty, a knowledge that this was right. That he was right—for her. He could be hers and she could be his. The potential for the bond was there. Her gut had been trying to tell her from the very beginning, but she'd been too concerned with being logical to believe it. It was confirmed every time he touched her, firing her with greater need. It was there every time he held her with his gaze, the look seeming to sear her to her core. It was there in the way he'd raced to her side to defend her, then cradled her protectively in his arms afterward as he brought her home.

Home. With him she was home. She'd never felt this sort of connection to anyone before and knew instinctively that she never would again. Mates. All they had to do to make that bond true was let it happen. But boy, what a huge leap that was.

And you really are a coward, aren't you, Karissa?

No. No she wasn't.

She stood. Her legs wobbled underneath her. It took

a moment, but with her destination only a few short feet away she was able to shore up her determination and cross until she stood beside him. She felt him tense, but he otherwise ignored her, sudsing and scrubbing that damn washcloth. Looked like the ball was in her court. Fine.

"What if I don't want to be?" she asked, forcing her tone to be even, logical. Logical could be good. True that logic was now based off a boatload of guts and intuition, but what she was about to suggest they do was certainly a reasonable application of their feelings. Right?

His head jerked up, their gazes meeting once more in that damn mirror.

Turn around. Look at me. Can't you see I'm dying of uncertainty here? Her silent plea went unanswered, his eyes measuring her via the impartial barrier of reflective glass.

"You don't want to be safe?"

She narrowed her eyes but could detect no hint of mockery in his tone, so she explained. "No. Unmarked. What if I don't want to be unmarked? What if I want the chance for more?"

The muscle in the corner of his jaw began to tick again, but other than that he showed no hint of emotion. "With Logan?"

Why the heck did he keep bringing up Logan? Like it was her fault his friend had tried to mark her. Damn, the man was impossible. She rolled her eyes, then, laying her hand on his arm, urged him to turn to face her. He turned, but stiffly. And he didn't resist either when she took both his hands and linked her fingers through his. It was a casual gesture, but the intimacy of the suggested link helped give her courage. If she was going to jump in feet first, then she wanted to do it with a lifeline.

"No. With you."

"Karissa…" His fingers tightened around hers, squeezing almost painfully, as if he too needed that lifeline. A quick drop of her shields and she knew she wasn't far off the mark. He was scared to death. And he wanted her. Hot damn he wanted her. Never had she felt someone else's pulsing need as she felt his now.

She smiled, feeling empowered. His touch still brought around that drowning loss of control that she'd felt before, but now she knew it was a two-way street. He felt it too. He'd never been trying to enthrall her; it had been their—what was that he'd called it?— compatibility that had been drawing her to him. She was his mate. And he was hers.

She pulled their linked hands around behind her back, stepping close enough to feel the solid length of his erection through his pants, to shiver with delight as her nipples, even through her bra and shirt, rubbed against his chest. He jerked but didn't pull away, his breath coming in harsh pants as he stared down at her, his eyes glowing red with his hunger.

Oh yeah. She really did like doing that to him.

She licked her lips, letting her eyelids flutter shut then back open, then said in a silky smooth whisper, "Make love to me, Roland."

Chapter 16

PAPERWORK. DAMON HATED PAPERWORK. BAD ENOUGH when it was his paperwork, but now he had to do the front desk's too. He should have waited until tomorrow to kill the schmuck. Then he would have been off and someone else would have pulled the short straw and ended up filling in for the missing front desk officer. Too bad that hadn't been an option.

Damon rubbed his temples, staring blankly down at the report in front of him. Damn his luck. Out of all the precincts to infiltrate in the city, he would get the one with a busybody front desk officer who just happened to have the sight. Anyone else would have merely looked at Damon strangely for "talking to himself" while on his smoke break. But the kid saw the demon, and not only saw but heard the demon too. Which meant he heard the demon tell Damon to keep an ear to the ground for any incidents that might be connected to Christos's renegade vampire who was rumored to know where the woman was hidden.

Damon didn't mind the killing. He did mind the residual consequences. Two weeks. It was going to take two weeks to get the next rookie over here and fully trained on front desk work. In the meantime, Damon was going to have to tough it out.

The doors to the station swung open. Damon looked up from the stack of paperwork to take in the tall blond bearing down on him. She wore pressed khaki pants and a blouse buttoned to the very top. Prim and proper, except for the fact that the blouse was silk and clung to her generous curves. And the high-heeled sandals? Well, fuck me, indeed.

He sat up straighter in his chair. She stopped, looking over and past him as if searching for someone specifically.

"Can I help you?" he asked, calling her attention to him.

She started for the desk. "I'm looking for—" She stumbled, drawing up five feet back, her eyes wide as she stared at him. Damon was used to the reaction. Eyes as dark as his were unusual and he'd been told how arresting they were, but he had another advantage going on: His mother had been a succubus.

"Who were you looking for?" he prompted.

"Detective Ward," she stuttered, nervously pulling her gaze away.

He grunted. Mike Ward was another one of those gifted humans—what was up with them and this station house anyway?—but thankfully his gift wasn't sight and just as thankfully, "Not in right now."

She squared up her shoulders, as if she could draw in courage from the air of the station. "I'd like to report a crime."

"Really," he drawled. "Is that so?" Of course she wanted to report a crime. It was either that or follow up on the status of a case, but since she didn't have the desperate beaten down look in her eyes yet, he figured the later was unlikely. Cases either got solved fairly quickly or not at all. By mid-morning the waiting area would be full of hopeless victims, or relatives of victims who'd come to plead with the detective in charge to do something, anything, to put the man, woman, or monster—ha, if they only knew how true that actually was—behind bars.

"Yes," she said firmly, plunking her cell phone down on the podium desk in front of her. "I have a picture of him too."

"A picture of who, exactly?"

She shuffled from one foot to the other. "I'd rather speak with a detective."

He leaned forward, putting just a touch of mesmerization behind the intensity of his gaze. "I am a detective." He gestured at the desk he sat behind. "Just filling in for the time being."

"Oh…"

Her mouth sure as hell was sexy when it went all slack jawed like that. Maybe working the front desk wouldn't be so bad after all.

"Here." He pulled out a form, gesturing for her to come back around behind the desk with him. "Why don't you show me the picture of this man, and tell me exactly what he did."

"Oh, okay." She moved around, punching buttons on the cell. "Here he is."

Damon looked at the picture. Middle-aged white male. Graying temples but otherwise had a healthy brown head of hair. The man was still relatively handsome but not exactly the type he pictured the curvy, young blond to hang out with. He was smiling though, like he'd voluntarily posed for the picture, which suggested there was some sort of relationship between them.

"So," he nudged the phone, "what did he do?"

"He tried to drug me."

Damon looked up at her sharply, hearing the quiver in her voice. She was pale as a chameleon and trembling.

"Tried?"

"He put something in my drink." She hesitated, rubbing her arms. "A date rape drug."

He narrowed his gaze. If she was telling the truth then her attacker was either really stupid or had been planning on deleting the picture she'd taken after the fact. "So, since you obviously are okay, how do you know that he actually tried to drug you?"

"Because of the witness."

"Witness?"

She nodded. "I went to the bathroom. He was in my seat when I came back. He must have seen Tom slip the drug into the drink because he told me what Tom had done."

"All right…" He grabbed up a report paper and a pen. Damn paperwork. "And this witness's name?"

She didn't reply. He looked up at her. She squirmed.

"I, uh, didn't think to ask. I'd, um, had a bit much to drink." She gave him a rueful smile. "Thinking to ask for details like that was a bit beyond me at that point."

"Including what he looked like?"

"Now *that* I remember. About six feet. Almost black hair down to his chin. And these eyes that looked like dark embers from a fire…" She trailed off, a pretty blush staining her cheeks. "Well, *that* I'm pretty sure I'm not remembering correctly. But they were dark brown, almost black as yours."

Damon's heart started to hammer. Yes. Yes! A do-gooder vampire. There weren't exactly many of those, and if Damon could confirm this woman's savior to be the one and only Fallen Paladin Roland…Well, he wouldn't be sitting at this front desk anymore, that was for sure.

With visions of sitting at his father's right side in his head, he turned toward prying the information he needed out of the idiot blond. And she was an idiot. She'd not only hooked up with a rapist, but didn't even know the man who'd saved her was actually ten times worse. He almost wished he could tell her she had a narrow escape with a vampire, just to see her reaction. Instead he said, "And you didn't worry this second man was part of the scam?"

She shook her head adamantly. "No. He was definitely trying to help me. He told me to take a cab home while he took care of Tom." She gestured back at the picture on the phone.

"Don't suppose you have a picture of the Good Samaritan?"

She narrowed her eyes.

"So we can try and track him down, get him to collaborate your story. Two witnesses could really nail a case like this shut, otherwise it's he said she said."

"Oh." Her face crumpled, the thought of her would-be attacker getting off scot-free obviously distressing.

"You don't have a picture," he guessed.

She shook her head, worrying her lips with her teeth.

"Can you describe him?"

Her eyes lighted. "Better, I was going to go to college for art before I decided to go pre-law. So…I can sketch him."

~~~

Make love to me…

Roland trembled. His body sung even as his heart howled. She said them, the words he'd been longing to hear since the moment she opened those big brown eyes. Yet it was a hollow victory given he could never be enough for her.

She was his mate. But he dared not take her. He knew if he did, it would be at the cost of his control. Eighty-nine years he'd managed to hold onto the pulsing needs of his dark nature. By just being near her he felt that thin thread of control fraying. He dared not risk it snapping.

She was his mate. But he could never allow her to bind herself to him. She owned his heart and his body, but she deserved his soul as well. And of that he had none to give.

She was his mate. He had nothing to offer, except to love her, protect her, and…

"Come," he said, tugging her gently toward the door. His body was raging with the need to pull her closer, to tear her jeans from her, to toss her up on the granite counter by the sink and plunge into her moist heat. But even if he were able to give into his body's needs, that would not be the way or the place to take her. Not for her first time. His Karissa deserved more: wining and dining, flowers and silken sheets. He had none of those but the sheets. Hopefully they would do.

For a moment she hesitated. As if now after the offer was made she was unsure. That uncertainty was both a kick in the gut and a load off his shoulders. If she drew away, he'd let her go. No harm, no foul. Only his mangled heart plopped down in her wake. Then she smiled—a brilliant smile that did nothing but emphasize the light of her soul in comparison to his lack thereof—and squeezing his hands, she twisted around and began to lead him toward his bedroom.

He should tell her this was a bad idea. He should at least remind her of *what* she was giving herself to. But he was a selfish bastard and wanted this one time, this one taste. Regrets could come later.

He was fully in tune with her body and her reactions: the racing of her heart that far outpaced them down the hall, the slightly hysterical quality to her giggle when she tripped on her overtired legs, and the sharp intake of her breath when he caught her, drawing her against his length.

Their gazes met and held. Her eyes, pools of melted chocolate, searched his face expectantly, her lips flushed and plump with her excitement. She wanted to be kissed. He didn't dare. Instead he smiled, freeing his hands from hers and sliding them up to her shoulders. Her head tipped back, her lips parting. He slid a hand up the back of her neck and into her hair, then, with his other hand anchored around her lower back, he pulled her up against him. Using his enhanced strength to ease their fall, he laid her out on the bed.

His body burned where he touched her. Having her here, pinned beneath him, her glistening curls spread out against the sheets? Temptation. And that smile, lips turned up tentatively at the corners, the quick dart of her tongue to wet them? Torture.

"Don't do that."

She blinked and gave another nervous little lick to her lips. "Do what?"

"Gawd, that." He closed his eyes, concentrating on breathing deeply. "Don't lick your lips like that."

"Lick my lips, I didn't—"

"You did," he said, giving her a hard glare.

"Okay," she agreed, then grinned, her white teeth flashing as she wiggled her hips beneath him. "How about that? Can I do that?"

"You're a minx."

"But I'm your minx," she said with another hip grinding wiggle.

"No, you are *ma petite peste*."

Her eyes narrowed, but it also had the desired effect of making her go still. He took advantage of the reprieve and peeled himself off her, shifting to kneel on the bed beside her.

"Where are you—"

He laid a finger over her lips. "Hush. Let me do this my way."

He knew he was asking a lot. His little minx liked to be in control. But he was counting on her innocence making her compliant in this. She was nervous. He could feel it in the slight vibrations that racked her body. Someone with senses less keen than his probably wouldn't have noticed, but he did and trusted that she would let him take the lead.

She sunk back into the bed, forcing herself to relax and let him take control. He rewarded her with a smile and a caress to the side of her face. Holding her gaze, he went to work on her clothing, drawing the seduction out by making sure to caress every inch of skin that he exposed. He started at the hem of her T-shirt, working it up her rib cage a centimeter at a time. Fanning his hand out under the thin cotton fabric, he would catch the hem with his thumb, pulling it a touch farther, then follow an agonizing roll where his knuckles brushed a series of steps up one rib then the next.

In the silence of the apartment, the ragged edge to her breathing became more and more noticeable the farther up her torso he went. Or was that his breathing? Wait. He cocked his head, his hands stilling. Hell. It was both of them. Damn. This was harder than he'd thought.

Fast. Like a Band-Aid. He grabbed the bottom corners of her shirt and slid it up over her breasts, exposing the lacy pink bra beneath that did little to hide the perfect roundness of her breasts. He was fantasizing about feasting on them when her hands slid alongside his. With an eye-popping shimmy, she pulled the shirt from his grip and over her head. His vision went red.

Get it together, Roland. Think of it as a job that has to be done.

Yet he couldn't drag his eyes away. She was beyond perfect. She was too perfect. And innocent. The blackness where his soul used to be would soil her if he touched her.

"I used to think it was silly to pay so much for a frilly bra that no one was going to see. Now I'm glad I did."

He gulped. Taking a series of long deep breaths, he fought back the red haze. He could do this. He would do this.

"Roland?"

Her tone highlighted her uncertainty. And of course she would be. He was staring at her and panting like a convicted rapist. Not the impression he wanted to make.

She was safe with him. He would always protect her. Always. No matter the personal cost.

He forced himself to make eye contact. With a twist of his lip he said, "And the panties? Do they match?"

A mischievous twinkle flashed across her brown eyes. With a smile, she reached behind her back and unsnapped her bra, quickly shrugging it off her shoulders where she grabbed it in both of her hands. Before he knew what she was going to do, she'd looped it behind his neck, pulling herself up so her mouth was a hairbreadth from his.

"Why don't you find out?" she whispered, her breath fanning across his jaw.

Too much. Too close. He needed to stay in control. Which meant keeping her under control.

Rather than kissing her as he knew she expected, he turned his face alongside hers, letting his breath tickle her ear as he whispered his reply. "Why don't I?"

Then with deliberate care, he sat back, grabbing onto her hands. It showed her lack of experience when she hesitantly allowed him to do so. He took the bra from her hands, loosely looping it around her wrists. She gasped and he worried she might panic. But when he urged her back down, positioning her arms over her head in an inherently submissive position, she allowed it.

Good. The bindings wouldn't hold her, but it threw her off her stride and back in the place of seducee rather than seducer.

Still, there was a question in her eyes, that faint bit of uncertainty. Instinct, as much as any decency he might have left, had him needing to drive away even that slight bit of fear.

He reached down, cupping her face, holding her gaze with his own. "One word from you and I stop. Promise."

She nodded, then closed her eyes, her rib cage rising and falling in deep, even measures as she worked to relax.

He frowned, watching her settle into a distinctly meditative state. Hmm. Relaxed was good. Comatose was not. He wanted her screaming in pleasure.

Heart thudding, he skimmed his hands along the outside of her breasts, sliding his palms around to cup them and lift them together. Her nipples peaked beautifully and he raked his thumb over the dusky buds.

Her eyes flew open, as she drew in a sharp breath. Her chest rising and falling created even more friction where his skin met hers.

She arched her back, her bound hands gripping his silk sheets as she lifted her breasts closer to him, as if begging him to feast upon her. Ah, Gawd. He wanted to, damn but he wanted to, but the moment his mouth touched the delicate perfection of her creamy skin it would mark the true beginning of his internal war. Paladin warrior and mate vs. mindless monster. He would not let the monster win.

Releasing her breasts, he trailed his hands down over her ribs, scowling when he was easily able to count each one—his mate needed to eat more. His fingertips moved under the waistband of her jeans.

"Roland."

He wasn't sure if she said his name as a plea for more or as a question. He treated it as both, keeping his explorations to the skin under the rim of her jeans.

"Roland, please, stop teasing me."

He chuckled. A plea then.

"Do you like pretty panties, *mon chaton*?" he asked, working the top button of her jeans and then, with agonizing slowness, pulled down the copper zipper. The label on the inside was red and read "Lucky you." Oh yes indeed. He smiled. Who would have thought his snarling minx would have a sexy, kittenish side too? Or maybe she just liked the fit of this brand of jeans. That wasn't as fun to imagine though.

With exaggerated care, he flipped open the fabric, curling it down as far as he could without actually removing her jeans. A pretty pink bow peeked out at him, the promise of frilly lace underneath. He was indeed a lucky, lucky man.

Unable to resist, he bent down, nuzzling his nose against the silky little bow as he drew in her scent. Flowers and peaches and musk that was all Karissa.

"You're cruel," she told him, and then her hips were wiggling. He reared back to see she'd undone her hands which were now wrapped around the sides of the denim. Needed to stop her, take back control. But instead he watched, his fangs aching to elongate as she worked the tight denim over her ass and started down her smoothly muscled legs.

"And you're impatient," he said, clasping his hands over hers. Pulling her hands off the denim, he lifted them to his mouth, brushing them over his lips in a parody of a kiss. "Lie back down, Karissa. Let me do this."

"What you're doing is taking too long."

He chuckled. "*Oui, ma petite peste*. But let me enjoy this. I promise you will enjoy it too."

"I am. But you're still taking too long."

He shook his head. Stubborn woman. "Lie down."

She obeyed this time. And when he placed her arms out to the side, urging her to cling to his sheets, she did that too.

"Don't move," he said firmly and smiled at the flash in her eyes.

"Only if you hurry," she snapped back.

So be it. He grabbed onto the jeans, quickly plucking them off the rest of her legs, then went back up and started on the panties. Perhaps it was better this way anyway. This way he could concentrate on the task rather than the heady perfume that marked Karissa's arousal. And damn but she was aroused. The panties were practically soaking with her juices.

Okay then. Don't think of that.

When he had her fully naked, he began to make his way back up, following a path of curves and angles up the inside of her calf, across the outer part of her thigh, valiantly not looking at the neat thatch of curls as he traced her hips and dipped in toward her belly. But there he stopped, unable to move on, his gaze caught on the vision of her rising and falling breasts. He glanced through the sloping curve between them and saw her watching him, her mouth parted, her pupils dilated, her lids heavy.

"You are so beautiful."

She blushed, her teeth nipping at her bottom lip. He wanted to be biting that lip. He settled for pressing his lips against the bottom of her rib cage. Better if he stayed away from her mouth...and her neck. What he had planned was going to be hard enough.

Tracing his hands back down the same path as before, he worked his way to her knees. He didn't even have to urge her to lift and spread them before she was doing so. Her desire to speed things was obvious with the ease that she was overriding what must be an instinctive shyness. There were not many twenty-four-year-old virgins out there. Frankly, he wondered how and why this miraculous gift came to be.

Because she's your woman. And only yours.

And right now his woman was laid out like a gift for him to claim. Slipping his hands back up her inner thighs, he stopped inches from the juncture of her legs. There was no avoiding looking at her now, but he made a point of breathing through his mouth. A line of short curls stretched out from the top of her mons downward, the bottom few dewy from her moisture and barely hiding her clit which was already plump with need. And her slit, that gorgeous flower of womanhood, was similarly engorged, the intimate lips swollen and blushed and dripping.

"Perfect." His voice was choked with dangerous desire, the clawing need to rear up and take her, fuck her, bite her, tearing at his control. He pushed it away, concentrating on the faint tremors of her body beneath his hands. She was nervous, but still she wanted this, wanted him. He was determined to give her all that he could.

He bent down, blowing gently. She gasped, her hips lifting to him imploringly.

"Do you like that?" he asked, more to distract himself than because he was unsure.

"God, yes. Please, Roland. I need…"

He lowered his head, brushing his cheek against the inside of her thigh. "What do you need, Karissa?"

She remained silent; he glanced up over her stomach to look at her. Her head was tipped back, her bottom lip gripped tightly between her teeth as she slowly shook her head from side to side.

"What do you need? Do you want me to stop?"

Her head snapped up, her eyes popping open, pupils dilated as if panicked. "God no."

He couldn't help but chuckle, which brought about a narrowing of her eyes and a tensing of her thigh beneath his hands.

"Relax," he whispered, dipping his chin so his hair trailed across the intimate folds. When he lifted his head again, she was wide-eyed once more and practically panting. "Let me love you."

"Yes, please. That is what I need." Her legs drifted back open, her head settling against the sheets.

Gorgeous. And his. For now at least. He turned his focus back to his task, bracing himself. He'd known the scent of her arousal was going to be difficult to tolerate. He'd known the pulsing aphrodisiac flowing through her veins, pooling in her core, was going to be a temptation beyond all others. He hadn't known it was going to be this bad.

He cursed under his breath, concentrating on the sting from where his fangs had scraped the inside of his lips. Monster. Yet he was more. He was her mate. He may have lacked a vital part of his being that should in all rights belong to her, but he could give her this.

He could cherish her.

He lowered his mouth, finally kissing *his* woman. And while she writhed beneath him, whimpering his name as her nails gripped his pristine white sheets, he decided there was nothing more exquisite than her falling apart in his arms.

———ⱳⱳⱳ———

Karissa lay on the bed, her limbs limp, her ears ringing, and her breath coming in short pants. Oh, and she couldn't see. The world was still spinning in a kaleidoscope of sparking colors. Holy crap. If she'd known being with a man could be like that, she would never have waited so damn long. She'd had orgasms before—she was a healthy, modern-day woman and saw nothing wrong with masturbation—but she'd never had one like that. Little death indeed. The French were right.

It's because it was Roland.

Probably. What Roland had done to her had surely been a sin. Nothing should feel that good. And she was a sinner too because she wanted more. She wanted to finish what they'd started. Now.

"Hmmm," she purred, rolling onto her side. She'd felt Roland shift off of her partway through the explosion and expected to find him there, watching her and smiling that smug smile. But he wasn't. The only thing beside her was rumpled sheets and her discarded clothing.

Alarmed, she sat up, quickly scanning the room.

He was gone. As in not here. As in he'd *left* her. After the most spectacular orgasm of her life he'd left. Why?

Maybe he doesn't want you after all.

No, she didn't believe that. The few times she'd been coherent enough to read him she'd gotten the impression of barely checked desire. Which would mean that he should be here, as eager as she was for the next step.

"Roland?" she called tentatively, tilting her head

to listen for his response. It was then she heard it, the shower in the bathroom. Uh, wrong.

She didn't know what the heck he thought he was doing, but that wasn't going to fly.

She wrapped herself in the top sheet and moved from the bed. Her legs held, from anger or rejuvenated by her orgasm, who knew, and she marched into the bathroom.

The air was moist and cold. No steam. Strange. Through the rippled glass she could make out the curve of Roland's back and shoulders, the rippling muscles of his legs and, damn, he had a fine ass. She was so engrossed by his ass that it took her a moment to notice what his hands were doing. One was braced against the tiles in front of him and the other was lowered in front of him, working off a measured beat of movements that went up and down, up and...No effing way. He was jerking off? He could have been inside her right now but instead he was here? Using his hand?

She must have made a noise, a gasp, or a choked cry of hurt and disappointment. Roland's head snapped up, his hand stilling as he twisted to glare over his shoulder at her.

"For Christ's sake, Karissa, go away."

It was impossible to miss his anger. His voice was a rumbling growl of warning. And that wasn't even mentioning the hellfire in his eyes or the wicked curve of his elongated canines. She took a step back, one hand clutching the sheet to her as the other searched for the doorframe.

Coward.

She tried to shake off the condescending inner voice.

Couldn't. It was right. Going got tough and she ran. And here she was. About to run. Again.

Roland had turned his back on her once more, seemingly content with the assurance that she had left or was at least in the process of leaving. Well tough for him. She was done with running.

"Why didn't you…"

His shoulders tensed, the pumping hand dropping to his side and clenching into a fist. An image of that fist pummeling into the demon in the alley came back to her. The demon had staggered under the impact but remained upright. She, on the other hand, could be crushed by that fist.

The cold air in the bathroom froze her vocal cords. She raised her hand, letting the warmth of her palm seep some heat into her throat. Roland wouldn't hurt her. She tried again. "I mean, why did you leave?"

His shoulders lifted and he spun around. He was obscured by the running water and the rippled shower door, but there was no hiding the fact that she'd been right about the state he was in—both his eyes and fangs, and his cock.

She sucked in a breath, forcing her chin up to keep herself from staring. Even distorted by the glass, she could tell he was impressive. Of course, she knew that, having felt his erection pressing against both her belly and her ass on numerous occasions. And just the memories of those moments were enough to send heat pooling down between her thighs.

"If I let myself go, I'm going to bite you."

Karissa blinked. Her first thought was would that be so bad? But she quickly tossed that away. Yeah, it would be bad. Worse than the supposed link the Paladin's marking ceremony might bring, a vampire could flat out control those whose blood he drank. It was a legitimate concern. Yet, for some reason she wasn't concerned.

She took a step forward, her hand unclenching so the sheet dropped to the floor behind her. Completely naked, she closed the distance so she stood inches away and mirrored him through the shower door. "No you won't."

He laughed, running his hands down over his face, wincing when the action cut his canines into his lip.

"Oh yeah?" He smiled an evil, twisted smile that emphasized the bead of blood forming along the wound. "How do you know that?"

"I just do." The fact that he was trying to protect her told her as much. She grasped the door handle, yanking it open, then before he could object, she stepped over the lip and into the cold stream of water.

He didn't attack her, didn't grab her up either, but quickly gave ground, retreating as far as the five-by-five custom tiled shower would let him.

"It's cold in here." She reached out, twisting the knob toward hot. She looked over at him, noting that though his hands were both fisted at his sides he was also panting, his eyes locked on her breasts.

She stepped forward. He trembled, so much so that she thought the only thing keeping him up was the tile at his back. Except his cock. His cock was having no problem standing at attention.

And all of a sudden the shower was too hot, even though the water had yet to make it past lukewarm.

Better to not look there. Not if she wanted to keep her nerve.

She desperately wanted to explore that tantalizing piece of flesh though, so she reached out, her fingers tentative as they closed around his throbbing length. Silken velvet over iron. Not grossly long. Well proportioned for his height. But wide, oh so wide.

He sucked in a sharp breath, his cock jerking in her hand.

"Karissa." It sounded like a plea for mercy.

"Trust me, okay?"

"Isn't that supposed to be the other way around?" Despite what she could tell was an attempt at flippancy, his voice was tight, harsh even.

Their gazes met, his fears laid out for her to see. She didn't even need to read him to know what was going on in that head of his. He was scared to death. Torn between his desire to be with her and his fear of hurting her. Strange how she got more than intent from him. It was as if she could actually read his emotions.

It's because you're mates.

Yes. The truth of that pealed like a bell in her mind. Her mate. She knew it, he knew it. Now she had to convince him that he could trust in that bond.

Holding his gaze, her hand boldly stroking up and down his length, she leaned up on her tiptoes so her lips were close to grazing his chin. "I already trust you. I know you. Body, heart, soul. You won't bite me."

His eyes flared. Across that strange whisper of a bond, she felt a lash of something: anger. Despite her resolve, she still flinched. He took that moment to push off the wall, using the muscular breadth of his body to intimidate as he leaned forward, the features of his face chiseled into hard lines of indifference as he blatantly leered down at her breasts. "See, that just goes to show how little you know. I have no soul, remember?"

Chapter 17

KARISSA BLINKED, STARING INTO THE BANKED EMBERS of Roland's eyes. He honestly believed he had no soul. It was etched in the tight lines of his jaw, the rigid tension in his body, the hollow pain echoing over their bond. His pain was like a sharp knife twisting beneath her breast, ripping another layer away from an already tattered grip on sanity.

It wasn't true.

If he had no soul, then that meant he couldn't be her soul mate, or bond mate, or whatever the heck those Paladin called it. And she knew, in her heart, that that couldn't be true. He was of her. And she was of him. So it took her a while to figure that out, but her body—and that annoying alter ego in her head—had known it the moment she met him.

She shook her head. "No. You're wrong. It's your soul that calls to mine."

He bared his teeth, exposing the impressive set of fangs, probably trying to scare her off. Well, it wasn't happening. It was a good attempt at deception, but he forgot something: She could read him now. Enough to know his intent was to drive her away. Enough to know he did it to protect her. And enough to know that it was killing him to do so.

And then there was another thing that couldn't lie.

She slid down onto her knees, her gaze honing in on

the engorged head of his cock and the beading moisture upon it. Her hand looked slim and fragile around the hard length of pure male. Unnerving, yet thrilling.

"You're a damn foolish woman," he hissed, but he didn't move so much of a muscle to escape or push her away.

Probably. She knew sex, no matter how powerful, wasn't going to convince him that he had a soul, but proving he could trust himself with her might.

Leaning forward, she flashed her tongue out to taste the wet tip of his cock. Tangy sweetness. Not just shower water.

His body shook. There was a loud thud as flesh met tile. She peeked up to see his head tossed back, arms planted on the sides of the shower. One of the tiles had cracked beneath the impact.

Because she'd tasted him. Because she was touching him, pleasuring him. For her he had to fight for control.

She knew she was taking a risk. Despite all her pretty words she knew that if he was worried over his control, then she should be too. But she found she didn't care. Even if he did lose control and bit her, she trusted him. He would never use the vampire dominance over her. He was still too much a Paladin protector for that.

Braver now, she circled the head of his cock with her lips. She had to stretch her mouth awkwardly. How did women do this? She was hopelessly inexperienced in the sex department. She'd seen movies, read romances—including the erotic ones—and even found an old *Joy of Sex* book in Papa's attic that had practically burned her skin off from blushing, but she'd never really thought about the exact technicalities. All she could do was run her tongue around the plump head of his cock and stroke the base with her hand.

Then Roland's hand was there, wrapped in the hair at the back of her scalp and urging her to tip her head just so and taking him in didn't seem like such a strain. With further urging she began to fall into a rhythm that, in less than a minute, had him panting like an overheated animal and his balls curling up at the base of his cock. She knew because her knuckles kept on brushing into them. Interesting.

Somewhere a phone rang, but Karissa didn't care and Roland didn't seem to notice. He was alternating between cursing her out and choking on spine-tingling sex words that always ended with a reverent endearment that included her name.

Her name, whispered across his lips like a prayer, sent a gush of warmth down the inside of her thighs. She wanted to have him inside her, but to get that, she would have to take her mouth off him, and she *didn't* want that. She needn't have worried. The next second had Roland's hand tightening even further on her hair, his hips rocking forward in a sharp thrust, and a guttural scream emerging from his lips and echoing with a roar off the acoustic tiles. Seed poured into the back of her mouth.

God, yes. This was right. This was perfect. And now that she'd proved he could let go without losing control, he'd take her up and bring her back to the bedroom where he would relieve her of her dratted innocence and mark her as his.

The spasms along the length of his cock finally stopped. She tried to shift off him but was stopped by the hand lodged in her hair. She winced at the sting, only now realizing how tightly he'd been holding her. As if just coming to the realization that he'd been holding her fast, his fingers loosened, his hand jerking away.

She tipped her head up, licking her lips that positively tingled from her efforts. No two ways about it. Losing her virginity to him, no matter how careful he was, no matter how ready she was, was going to hurt.

She didn't care.

The phone started ringing again. She gave an absent glance over her shoulder before deciding it should be ignored. Roland wasn't paying it any mind either. Nor was he giving her any attention.

"Roland?" she prompted when he continued to stare at the tiled ceiling.

"Go. Go to the bedroom and get dressed while I answer the phone."

She frowned. The bedroom part sounded fine, she'd even give him a reprieve to answer the phone, but the clothes bit? Uh, no. She had other ideas. Like, oh, finishing what they started. And if the way he was already hardening again was any indication, he wouldn't be averse.

She cupped his balls, then ran the fingers of her other hand along the underside of the rising shaft to the bead of moisture on the tip. "We could ignore it."

His hand lashed out, grabbing her wrist. She gasped, her head snapping back. His eyes were twin pits of glowing embers, his face a mask of rage. Something chilled deep inside her chest.

"I said go." And with that he tossed her hand away, pointedly turning his back on her.

Gathering up her shredded dignity, she left.

~~~

The phone had finally stopped ringing. It had started and stopped twice more while he'd been trying to collect himself. Gawd. He couldn't erase the erotic images. His sweet Karissa shyly taking him in her hand. Gaining confidence quickly. Boldly stroking him. That hot seductive tongue teasing. The Cupid's bow of a mouth opening wide, wrapping around him. Her swanlike neck stretched out, taking him in. He couldn't help it. He'd lost himself. He'd come. Pouring his seed down her throat. And all he could think of now was that he needed to bite it. Taste the heady concoction of her blood that would be spiked with the faintest mark of his seed. Her blood. His seed. His woman.

A series of loud bangs echoed down the hall through the apartment. He practically jumped out of his skin until he realized it was someone pounding on the outer door.

"Shit." He jerked a towel off the rack, wishing it were sandpaper rather than downy soft cotton as he viciously dried himself—and the hard-on that had yet to go the fuck away—off. Only one person would have called repeatedly. Only one person knew where he lived and would dare pound on the door. Calhoun. Bastard better have a damn good reason for coming. Other than to try and collect the lost Paladin female. Because no one—not Calhoun, not the elders, not Ganelon and all his armies—would ever take Karissa away from him. He might not be able to give her all that she deserved, but as long as she chose to stay, he would do all he could to make her happy. And he'd stop at nothing to protect her. Even from himself.

Which meant no more incidents like the shower.

After jerking on his pants, he stalked down the hall where the door, after a simple command from him, opened. Calhoun burst in, his hair frazzled from running his hands through it. "Damn it, Roland. You need to stop fucking screening your calls."

"My, my. I didn't know you were my mother." Roland folded his arms over his chest. "Should I start checking in at regular intervals too?"

Calhoun flashed him a look that spoke volumes. Passing by Roland, he glanced first into the bedroom, then the bath, and continued down toward the great room. "You have to get out of here. Now."

Roland followed him into the open living area, glancing at the clock over the stove. High noon. "Definitely not now."

Calhoun's eyes hardened to burnished steel. "I'm trying to save your life. Valin managed to follow you to this section of town. Right now Bennett is pulling records on every apartment in the area. It's only a matter of time before they find the one that recently underwent some pretty impressive and unusual cosmetic changes."

Roland's stomach dropped forty-nine floors into the basement of the building. Valin had followed him. He'd been so concerned about getting Karissa to safety he hadn't even looked for the telltale shadow of the Black Knight.

Calhoun moved past him into the study, immediately spun around, and pinned him with a hard stare. "Where is Karissa?"

"Here."

Both men turned to find her standing at the end of the hall. She'd pulled on her dirty jeans, but her brown locks were still wet, curled tight and dripping fat droplets on the thin undershirt she'd confiscated from Roland's wardrobe.

Calhoun looked from the wet curls to Roland's naked chest and his own damp black mop. Calhoun's mouth thinned, his knuckles fisting dangerously.

"We were a bit messy after a scuffle with some of Ganelon's runts," Roland offered in an effort to save face. Not his, but Karissa's. All that talk of "I'm yours" aside, Roland doubted she wanted to announce what had happened between them during the last few hours. Not to mention that if—no, when—Karissa came to her senses and left him for a man who could give her what she needed, Logan would be a good candidate. As long as Roland could keep himself from killing his supposed best friend for the very thought of him touching her.

Roland's half-assed explanation did nothing to ease the tension in the room. Logan had gone back to drinking in the sight of Karissa like some forbidden drink, and Karissa, finally realizing what her wet strands were doing to that undershirt, which she wasn't wearing a bra under, had folded her arms across her chest and was pointedly looking anywhere but at the two men in the room.

"Karissa," Logan tried.

Karissa ignored him, moving into the kitchen and flipping through the mostly empty cabinets searching for only-God-knew what. Which reminded him—if he was going to leave his studio for the Paladin to paw through, there were some things he needed to remove first.

"Stay here. I'm going to grab a few things. Then we can go."

"Go?" Karissa spun around, her gaze honing in on him. Brown eyes filled with a mix of hurt and shock. She might as well have stuck a knife in him. Did she think he was sending her back to Haven? Did she really think he was the type of man to get his kicks then kick her out?

An image of her crumpled features as she'd fled the bathroom rose in his mind. Ah, hell. Yeah, she did think that. She didn't understand that for him the tie between sex and feeding was as intricately connected as a two-headed dragon. Just because she'd helped him sate the first need didn't mean that the second would—*poof*—disappear. He was going to have to clear up their misunderstanding ASAP. But not in front of Logan.

He took a step toward her. She flinched. So he stopped, keeping his tone level as he explained. "Valin followed us. We need to find another safe house."

"Oh. Okay." She shivered, rubbed her arms, and then looked down at what she was wearing. "I don't have any other clothes that aren't ruined."

"Don't worry about that. We'll figure something out." Like, say, keeping her naked as much as possible. He couldn't risk letting himself go like he had in the shower again, but coming in a close second would be to have Karissa naked and sated in his bed for however long she would stay. Though maybe he shouldn't. If her doubt of a moment ago was any indication, the shower incident had actually cooled off her determination to be with him. If he had any honor at all he'd let it stand at that. Momentary pleasure aside, it would certainly be easier, and healthier, for her in the long run.

Later. They'd work it out later.

Still feeling like his heart was being ripped out of his chest, Roland stomped down the hall and went into the closet off his bedroom. Popping open a drawer full of controls, he typed in a series of codes that opened a sliding panel. There, perched on a series of shallow shelves and hooks, was his collection of weapons, including his old knife. He hadn't used the blade since he'd been turned. Wouldn't use the blade. It belonged to the Paladin he'd once been, not the monster he'd become. But nor could he let his former brothers have it. He knew, just knew, that if they were to take it and lift it against him, he would lose it. Nothing Calhoun could say, no self-imposed morals he might have left, would be able to stop him from killing.

He was reaching for the ancient steel when the sound of Karissa's name spilling off a man's tongue stopped him. Calhoun, trying to engage her in conversation again and not having much luck judging by the heated reply that came next.

"Don't. Don't touch me, don't talk to me, don't even look at me."

Yeah, like that request was going to be honored. Roland had to empathize with his friend on this account. It was hard not to look at her, not when she was dressed like something out of every man's wet dream. Tight jeans, wet white undershirt.

My undershirt.

Hand shaking, Roland momentarily bypassed the

knife and started loading himself up with weapons, all the while keeping his ears tuned to pick up the conversation in the other room.

"You have every right to be mad," Calhoun was saying. "I should have warned you. I should have told you what your presence would mean to the other Paladin."

That was met with silence. Roland reached for the hilt.

"Karissa, I swear I never meant to hurt you, and I wouldn't have used the mark to harm you either."

Roland's hands fumbled on the ancient blade he'd been strapping onto his thigh. Mark her? Logan had tried to mark her too?

"Only to control me," Karissa snapped back.

"What? Where did you...never mind. It's not important."

Like hell it wasn't important. Why Logan would have tried to mark her was the only important thing right now. Because if it had been for any other reason than her safety...

Apparently Karissa agreed with Roland on the importance issue because she scoffed.

"Karissa, please, I know I failed you when you needed my protection most. I know because of that I've lost your trust, but please listen to what I have to say."

"I'm not going back with you. I'm not going to let you or your father or any man make decisions for me. And I'm certainly not going to give you another chance to try to mark me."

"I wouldn't do that."

"Funny. I don't exactly believe you anymore."

Grabbing up his cloak, Roland closed the panel, not hiding the sound of his approach as he moved back down the hall. "Ready."

Karissa and Logan both swung their heads around. Karissa looked relieved by his timely return. Logan, well, it was hard to read Logan right then. Barring the seemingly heartfelt apology Roland overheard, Logan seemed completely in control. Remote even.

Hard-ass was back.

Good. It will be a fair fight when I take him to task for trying to mark Karissa.

Roland tamped down the thought, at the same time reining in the call for blood. His friend had only tried to do what Roland himself had once suggested. Mark her before the others did. Roland also knew Logan well enough to know his friend, unlike Valin, would not have taken advantage of the mark. Anything more would have been of Karissa's choosing, on Karissa's time frame. Honorable bastard that he was.

And the reason you keep toying with the idea of Karissa being with him someday.

Yeah. Someday. But not as in today. Not for a long number of todays.

Shaking off his conflicting wants and desires, he moved into the hall. Karissa immediately moved closer to his side. He reached up, rubbing a hand down her cheek. "It's going to be okay. You have my vow that I will keep you safe."

Karissa swallowed hard, bobbing her head as if to agree.

Logan watched the exchange with narrowed eyes but wisely didn't say anything.

"Thank you for your aid," Roland told him.

"I can get you guys set up—"

Roland shook his head, cutting Logan off. "No. I have a place in mind."

"Going to tell me where that is?"

"Nope."

Logan's lips thinned, but he eventually nodded.

"What? Not going to argue with me?"

"Nope." Logan dropped his eyes pointedly to the long knife lying against Roland's thigh. "You have the right to protect your own."

―⁓―

Christos looked around the high-rise apartment building, the wind whipping at his silken shirt so it billowed and flattened like a twisted parachute. The blood bond had led him here, courtesy of one Thomas Rhodes. Christos had considered it fate when Ganelon had contacted him, informing him that one of his merkers had found a connection to his wayward creation. Even better was that Thomas had a list of minor priors…and an address. It had been child's play to get one of his human lambs to break into the man's home and scoop him up. And baby's work to overpower his mind, searching out the pathways of the blood bond that linked a lamb to its master. He'd used that pathway to pinpoint the locale of the rebellious vampire who thought himself special enough to severe their ties. Then, no longer needing the human, Christos had disposed of him—whiny bastard that he was. Cried like a big baby, peeing his pants when Christos had sucked the life out of him.

Filled with energy, Christos was ready for the confrontation with the vampire that thought he could escape his rule. The penthouse was an obvious choice and picking his way up the façade of the building via a stepladder of balconies had been easy. More difficult was breaking down the tinted bulletproof glass. Almost impossible was tearing down the lead-lined walls that housed the inner sanctum of the sheep that got away. It took another favor from Ganelon for that, which racked his tab up to a demon on loan, a dead merker, and Thomas Rhodes's location. And now this. When it was over, he was going to be up to his eyeballs in debt. Unless he could actually track down the Paladin woman, then, well then the payoff would be worth it.

So far, though…He closed his eyes, taking in the scents of the vacated apartment.

Empty. The place was fucking empty. Sometime between late that morning when he'd sucked the location and life out of Thomas and that evening when it finally got dark enough to make his move on the place, Roland had left…and taken the woman with him. At least they knew for sure that the woman had been here. And, if the imprints of scents were correct, that she and Roland had left before the virtual army of Paladin had trashed the place for clues.

Seems everyone wanted the girl. Well, he wished the Paladin luck, bad luck. Christos knew Roland well enough to know the tricky vampire would not have left his former brothers any clues. Christos, on the other hand, didn't need luck. He had his own personal ace in the hole.

With a smile pulling his lips practically to his ears, Christos spun about and leapt out into the night.

Chapter 18

IT WAS AN HOUR PAST SUNSET WHEN ROLAND AND Karissa stumbled across the threshold of the safe house. Karissa wasn't sure who was holding who up. It had been a harrowing journey. Being as powerful as he was, Roland could stand a certain amount of sun, but they'd done all they could to reduce it: traveling by subway, then renting a van. He'd ridden in the back, burrowed under a cloak, but he'd still gotten a distinct red cast to his face.

The daytime journey weakened him, no doubt. Her exhaustion was more of a bone-deep wariness. Part of it, she was sure, came from being up and running for more than seventy-five percent of the last couple days. But the other part was purely her sagging spirit. She felt deflated. The roller coaster ride she'd been on since she slid into the vampire's cab ended with a major crash on the final spiral S curve.

Her mate didn't want her.

Three days before, she hadn't even know him, never dreamed she could have such a soul deep connection to another being. But it was there, and to take it away now would be akin to ripping her heart out of her chest. Vital. Life-giving, or deadly.

Her mate didn't want her.

The truth of that had come through the developing link. Every time she had to touch him it was a slap in the face as his anger, his frustration, and his disgust rolled over her.

Her mate didn't want her. And so, as soon as they made it into the slightly sagging structure, the thick pine door swinging shut behind them, he untangled his arm from over her shoulder and lurched a good ten feet away.

Too bad the cabin was so small. Just a simple log structure in the middle of the woods. Light-blocking shades with—she glanced past the cracked door to the right—one windowless bedroom. And one too small bed. Two people would have to be awfully close to share that bed. Like on top of each other close. Or take turns.

Ships passing. To think she'd once wanted that.

"You can have the bed. I need to…" he trailed off, removing the backpack cooler that he'd filled back at his loft. Blood. The backpack was filled with pints of blood.

She swallowed hard, trying not to squirm under his penetrating gaze. It shouldn't bother her. The concept itself—that he used Red Cross discards to sustain himself—didn't. It was simply that she'd been raised to believe there were firm lines between good and evil, and according to Papa, all vampires were evil.

She knew now it wasn't true. The man who owned her soul, who had earned her trust with his honorable nature, was not evil.

I only need to prove it to him.

"You're tired too." She took a step forward, determined to close the gap that had arisen between them, both physically and emotionally. "I'll grab the rest of our stuff from the van and have dinner with you and then we can both—"

"No!" He spat the word like an oath, his eyes flashing red for a moment before receding back to black.

She flinched. She'd closed eight of the ten feet and started to raise her hand to rest it on his arm. Now she dropped it, looking away. Guess his vow to keep her safe had a limitation clause. Keep her safe, as long as he didn't have to touch her.

Without a word she turned around and made her way into the bedroom where she kicked off her shoes and filthy jeans, and then slid into the chilled sheets—alone.

—⁓—

A deep, gut-wrenching moan filled the room, pulling Gabriella from her personal hell and into the real one.

How long had she been out? Judging by the ripping pull in her stomach and the violent shaking of her muscles, it had been long enough to get the worst of the healing process over with. It would slow down now. Her body had used up all of its reserve energy to mend the broken bones, bind back together the ruptured organs, and smooth over the shredded skin. What was left was bone-deep bruising and an all-over fatigue that would keep her lying here on this cold floor until she got the blood she needed to rejuvenate her strength.

Christos was pissed. No, pissed was too tame a word. There were no words to describe the fury with which he'd torn into her flesh. Toward the end, she'd been sure that he'd lost all control, that when she did pass out he'd keep on beating her and that this time, maybe, just maybe, there would be no waking back into the nightmare that was her life. No such luck.

With a groan of agony, she rolled over onto her back

and then lay there, staring at the ceiling and breathing in the stagnant smell of her own blood. She was still in the corner where she'd cowered through the last half of the beating, but at least her room was empty. Christos must have decided there wasn't anything else he could strip her of: information or dignity-wise.

It was now out of her hands. She'd tried. Damn it, she'd tried. And really, she didn't think any of the information he'd extracted from her was enough to matter. Christos already knew the Paladin would be raised into a war frenzy over the female Paladin. Knowing Roland had a thing for her too wasn't all that much more. They still had to catch her. And judging by the snit Christos was in when he came after Gabriella, the woman had somehow managed to slip through his net. She could be anywhere now. With Roland or the Paladin. Either one made her virtually inaccessible.

Gabriella was still lying there when an oppressive blanket of evil settled around the room, making the stagnant air even more difficult to gulp down. She knew that presence: Ganelon. But why would he have lowered himself to come here? Christos was his partner of sorts, but Ganelon held all the power.

Moments later the door opened, Christos entered first, followed by Ganelon and two merkers who took up position inside the door. Great. Did that mean she was going to receive four more beatings instead of one? No. Ganelon would never dirty himself with her blood.

Hence the tagalongs, Gabby.

"Hello, Gabriella." Christos held up a squishy bag of blood, giving it a jiggle.

Her belly rumbled, disgusting her. Why so soon? Christos liked it when she suffered, so long as she eventually recovered. Which, frankly, was just another form of suffering.

She licked her lips, or at least tried. Her tongue was so dry it stuck to the bottom of her mouth. "I'm not taking that."

A mocking brow lifted. "Oh yes you are. You've been quite disobedient of late. Time to prove you're worth the trouble."

Ganelon stepped farther into the room. He wasn't nearly as handsome as Christos, nor did he hold the threatening physique of their third partner, Lucifer. But there was something decidedly intimidating about Ganelon's presence, an emptiness in his eyes, an indifference in the way he looked at her. He was looking at her like that now, like she was so inconsequential as to be invisible and it was work to bring her into focus. "You're sure on this? Glena was not exactly a one-man kind of woman."

"Oh, I'm quite sure," Christos said, twisting a needle onto the IV.

"She looks nothing like him. Even if she is his, it's going to be hard enough for me to pull on my old Paladin ties, what with her blood being removed so many generations."

"Sirens take after their mother. You know that."

"If you're wrong—"

"I'm not." Christos tipped his head to the side, a chilling smile spread across the lower half of his face. "Am I, Gabriella?"

She stared back at him—quite impartially if she did

say so herself—but her hands, which were already trembling, began to convulse against her sides.

Christos laughed, reaching out to grab her arm. She tried to jerk away but the slap of his mind on hers had her going limp. "Oh yes, quite sure."

There was a sharp prick as the needle slipped under the skin of her arm. She couldn't move, couldn't scream.

"There. We'll get you all fixed up, and then…" He leaned closer, pushing her hair off her face. Something hot and wet slipped down her cheek. His grin turned positively evil. "Then I think it's time that we dropped in to see dear old dad. What say you?"

She was back in the park; the imps sniffing out her trail. Her breath hissed in and out of her lungs as she ran on, pressing past the point where her muscles burned, through where her arms became numb, and toward the point where she simply collapsed in a heap on the rotting leaves scattered over the floor of the wood.

Something snapped behind her, a twig. She glanced over her shoulder, saw nothing, and looked forward again, just in time to smack up against a man's broad chest.

Logan! Oh god, Logan. He'd save her. Papa said so.

Only it wasn't Logan, it was Valin, and he was looking at her with that dark hunger that said he didn't give a damn about her, only having her. She tried to pull away, but his arms were locked tight around her. She couldn't get away, couldn't even draw enough air to scream.

Over his shoulder, movement caught her eyes. Roland stood there, watching. Unable to call out she merely pleaded to him with her eyes. Please, save me.

He blinked, then, in a move that had her heart ripping out of her chest, turned and walked away.

———— ᵕᵕ ————

Karissa woke with a start. Her heart wasn't missing but pounded like a jackhammer in her chest. It was only a nightmare. The whole thing. All of it. She was on her back in her small twin-sized bed staring into the oily blackness of the darkened room…

…with a man wrapped around her, his arms like vises, his leg like a hunter's trap, holding her firmly in place. And he was…oh God!

The hard ridge of his erection pressed against her hip had her panicking. She twisted her shoulders, trying to free her arms as her lower body bucked against the weight of his leg. "Let go. Let me go. Letmego!"

Her terror-stricken cries had the opposite of the desired effect and he slipped over top of her instead, pinning her down with a full body embrace.

"Shh. Stop. I'm not going to hurt you."

Not a monster. Not Valin. Roland. Her immediate instinct was to curl up against him and sob into his shoulder, but then she remembered how, for the last twelve hours, he'd done everything in his power to avoid contact with her. She stiffened. Cleared her throat.

"What are you doing in here?"

He grunted, rolling off her and out of the bed. "Want a drink?"

A drink? What the hell. She never drank. But she'd also just had the most effed up nightmare of her adult life.

After a quick trip to the small bathroom attached to the bedroom, she followed Roland into the main part of the cabin. He'd already poured two tumblers half-full of amber liquid and was lounging in one of the two chairs sipping on his.

She grabbed up the second scotch, plopped down in the adjacent chair, and swigged it down.

Bad idea. She choked, barely managing to not sputter the liquid out again.

His eyebrow arched. She could almost see his thoughts. That this was the woman who'd accused him of escaping in alcohol. Yet he didn't say anything as he reached for the bottle on the table and poured out two more fingers worth into her cup.

"Want to talk about it?"

She shook her head. No, she didn't want to talk about her dream. Her near escapes, the monsters chasing her, they didn't matter. What mattered was that, ultimately, she always had to face the monsters alone.

"My mother died in childbirth. And my father, I don't even know who he is." She looked over at Roland, but he was a poster child for relaxation, his ankle crossed over the knee of his other leg, the tumbler in his hand resting at a slight angle on the arm the chair.

"My Aahma died three years later. I don't know how. I was too young to ask and by the time I was old enough I knew better than to force Papa to recount memories that were obviously painful. That left Papa and me. We had only each other, but it was enough."

She stared down at the glass in her hands, her knuckles white against the clouded glass. The temptation to drink the rest of the liquor Roland had poured her was great, and because of that, she pointedly reached over and set it on the small round table that sat between them.

Before she could remove her hand from the glass, Roland's hand was there, closing over her wrist. He'd moved so quickly and silently that she hadn't even seen it.

Lifting her head, she met his gaze; his eyes bored into her steadily, the only sign of his emotion was the slight crease in his brow.

"You don't have to drink that, but I'd like to hear the rest."

She swallowed, her saliva tasting like acid in the back of her mouth. "You know the rest; Papa died."

"How?"

"Because of me."

Something flashed across his face, echoing down through their bond. Pain, understanding. He released her arm, sitting back in his chair. "I'm sure you're wrong. It may only seem that way."

"I led them to our home. I left him there, alone and vulnerable, while I went to work the next day."

"Did you know?"

"That I'd led them there?" She shook her head. "The cab driver was a vampire. I had him drop me off across town and then got another cab. But he must have followed me. Or had someone else do it."

"Why didn't they attack that night then?"

"Papa had the house warded against vampires. They couldn't enter without invitation."

"The wards were keyed to your grandfather?"

She nodded.

He tapped the glass with his finger, the small sound pinging in the quiet cabin.

"What are you thinking?"

"That they must have watched you for a while. Then

gone back to report. Most likely the merkers expected you to be home the next day when they came."

"Merker. That's what you said that thing last night was."

Roland nodded, then as if anticipating her next question, explained. "Merkers are Ganelon's get. The offspring is created when he mates with one of the more powerful demons from hell."

"They're half demon?"

He nodded.

"But Ganelon...wouldn't that make them half Paladin too?"

"They are abominations," he hissed, his lip curling up.

Okay then. She gnawed on her own lip. She had to give him that. That thing last night had been freaky, and demons were just plain bad.

"How do you know it was a merker that killed my papa?" she asked.

"Because I went there."

She sat up straighter. "And?"

"And I could smell them. I was trying to use my gift to show me exactly what had happened but it was a no-go."

"You're a seer?"

"A poor one."

"Why do you say that?"

"Because I see things: past, present, future. But I cannot control what I see, and what I do see, I cannot change."

"Wow. That must suck."

He laughed, a tell-me-about-it laugh emphasized by an Adam's-apple-bobbing swallow of scotch.

She frowned, settling back in the lumpy cushions. "So how does it happen? Do these visions come in dreams or through touch?"

"As I said, I have little control over it. I can ride wide open and get a sense of knowing at times. I've used that to get a reading on my surroundings, get a bead on a person or where bad events might be going down. But that is very limited both in what it tells me and how far away I can read."

"Sounds a bit like my being able to read someone's intent, only I need to touch them."

"A bit, though I don't exactly get a sense of intent, more of a Spidey tingly feeling of awareness rather than a true knowledge."

"Is that how you found me last night?"

"Partly. Once I was in the right part of town I was able to hone in on where something bad was occurring, but it was Gabriella who told me you were still up in South Bronx."

"Gabriella?"

"She's a vampire too. But she's not too fond of her master so she sometimes bats for our team."

Karissa thought of the redheaded teenage vampire that had warned her and Valin before fleeing. "I think I met her."

"She said as much." He stood, grabbed the scotch bottle, and opened one of the narrow cabinets in the kitchen. Discussion over.

Karissa rubbed her palms together. Something he'd said bothered her. "This morning, when I touched you in the bathroom and saw what you were thinking of, was that one of these seeing the future things?"

She couldn't hide the wistfulness in her voice and was disappointed when he shook his head and said, "That was fantasy. Nothing more."

"Oh." She dropped her gaze to her lap. She hadn't bothered to pull back on her jeans and her legs were bare from mid-thigh down. Goose bumps covered her flesh.

The cabinet slammed shut and she jumped. "I haven't had a true seeing since the day I was turned."

Her head snapped back up, her gaze honing in on where Roland was standing, hands planted on the counter, head bowed.

"Tell me."

He slowly turned around and leaned against the counter, his arms folded across his chest. There was something haunting in the way his eyes were staring through her, beyond her. In evenly distributed, unemotional sentences he began to tell her about the night his entire life had changed. The night the last female Paladin had been killed.

"I knew something was off. Back then I could take that sense of knowing and meditate and normally I would come up with a vision. What I saw…" he trailed off, the first catch of emotion stealing his voice. It took him a minute to compose himself before he went on. "I can't project. The women were having a gathering at my mother's house. It was closer than Haven so I didn't warn the others but rushed over. I wasn't prepared for the siren who opened the door. She, uh, ensnared me. In the back of my mind I knew she shouldn't have been there, that the quiet in the manor house was all wrong, but I couldn't—" He shook his head, then thrust his head back so he looked at the cobwebbed ceiling. His throat bobbed as he swallowed tears.

"Roland…" Karissa stood, starting for him, but his head snapped back down, his hard glare nailing her feet where they were.

"I failed them. I was so blinded by false lust that I didn't care about anything but what she wanted. And she wanted what Christos wanted. I let them take my blood, and then when she told me to drink from Christos's vein, I did. All the while they had been dying. Ensnared, I hadn't even heard the screams."

Karissa's heart was breaking for him. She didn't have to touch him to feel the agony eating him from the inside out. It was tearing her apart too.

"Christos made sure I knew, though. They'd saved my sister for last. My pregnant sister. I was in midst of the change, the fire of Christos's blood burning me alive from the inside out, and all I could do was watch helpless as they tore her apart."

Silence descended in the cabin. She wanted to go to him, wrap him in her arms, but she knew instinctively that at this moment he'd reject her offered comfort. Yet she couldn't bring herself to let things go at that.

"I'm sorry."

"For what?"

"For what happened to them and to you. But mostly I'm sorry that you think it's your fault."

His mouth hardened. "It is my fault."

"No. It's not."

"If I'd gone for the others first—"

"They'd still be dead."

His eyes shuttered. "It was my weakness that—"

"We all have weaknesses."

His jaw ticked. Silence. "I've killed. And not only monsters, or men with black souls. I've killed innocents."

"Recently?"

"No," he practically grumbled, a reluctant admittance.

"How long ago?"

He looked away, refusing to meet her gaze, yet he did answer. "Eighty-nine years."

"Eighty-nine—" she snapped her mouth closed. Of course, duh, he was a vampire, only…"Wait. Logan. I thought you two have been friends since before you were turned?"

"We were. If it hadn't been for Calhoun's belief in me, I would have never made it back from that time of darkness. I may not have a soul, but it is because of him that I was able to regain some small measure of my humanity."

She was quiet a moment. Her own emotions regarding Logan were mixed. He'd helped her, but he'd also tried to claim her. Without explaining why, without asking permission. He'd tried to steal her from her mate. Yet, if what Roland was saying were true, then Logan had also saved her mate. She supposed, for that alone, she had to forgive him.

She pulled herself from her thoughts only to notice Roland watching her intently, studying her.

"What?"

"He's a good man," he said softly.

She scowled. Twice now Roland had said things like that. It was as if he were trying to push her away and into Logan's arms. Well it wasn't going to happen, and she didn't want to talk about Logan.

"How old are you?"

"How old?"

"Yes. I mean how old were you when…" She waved helplessly at her neck.

"Ah." He took a deep swallow. "Hmm…let's see.

I'm currently two hundred and fifty-three and I've been like this, oh, about ninety-four years now."

Two hundred and fifty-three! She felt her knees buckling, but then Roland was there, holding her up with a hand under her elbow. She lifted her chin, trying to find a sense of calm in face of his revelation. "Is that...will I?"

This time he actually chuckled before becoming serious once more. "Well, you obviously have Paladin blood in you. So technically you could live thousands of years."

Thousands. Holy crap. Another thought occurred to her. "But you'll live longer. You'll live forever now, won't you?"

Could that be why he didn't want to claim her? Because he didn't want to be tied to a woman who would die and leave him alone again?

"No."

"No what?"

"Yes, it will kill me when you die, but that is not what keeps me from claiming you."

She didn't ask how he knew what she was thinking. She already knew the answer. Their bond, even if unrecognized, was getting stronger. She wondered if he realized it and what he planned to do about it if he was as set against claiming her as he seemed to be. "Then what?"

He sighed, dropping her elbow and taking a step back so he was leaning against the counter again. "You deserve to have options. Being bonded to a man with no soul is not fair to you."

She didn't bother arguing with him on the issue of

his soul, already realizing it was a lost cause. "I've been shown my options, and I've made my decision. I want to be with you. I'll be happy with however long I have left, as long as I'm with you."

"After fifty or so years of hiding from the world, fifty more with no children, no one but me, you might change your mind." He didn't move a millimeter, but she could see the rigid lines etched in his muscles.

"I won't."

"You can't know that. You don't know how lonely this existence can be."

She stepped closer, laying her hands on the counter on either side of his hips. This close she could feel his heat, this close, even without touching, she could sense his desire. Stronger indeed.

"It can't be as lonely as living my life without my s—" she almost said soul, damn, "heart mate."

He looked unconvinced, yet he couldn't hide the want. It wasn't just the bond now; his eyes were starting to glow that deep blood red again. A slight shift of her hips had his erection pressing into her stomach. Oh yes. He needed her as much as she needed him.

"I don't know all the fancy words. I only have myself to give, but…" She raised her hand, meeting his gaze as she placed it on the bottom of his throat. She had no idea what she was doing, but she put all her desire for this to work, for her pleas to be heard, her prayer for a chance to be answered, into her next words. "As you are for me, I am for you. All that I am, I give to you. So that you shall know me, as I shall know thee: body, heart, soul."

Her hand tingled. Roland sucked in a breath, his pupils flaring as the skin under her palm warmed.

All of a sudden it was more than his emotions or even a shadow of his thoughts. *She knew what he was thinking*. And the word racing through his mind over and over again: Impossible.

His shock gave way to joy, then anger. She almost recoiled before she picked up on the reason for that anger: He still didn't think he had a soul. Large pools of liquid formed along the bottom rim of her eyes. Her heart twisted in her chest, her soul howling for its mate. *See me. I'm here. We are one*.

The next instant his anger was replaced by resolve. She could still sense his belief that he had no soul, but he was determined not to disappoint her. At least, not if he could help it.

She began to tremble with anticipation, her senses revved to a hyper-awareness. One of his large hands wrapped around hers over his throat, and an instant later his other was gently circling the base of her neck. Her heart rate spiked; having gone through this twice and not liking the results she was decidedly nervous, but then he was in her mind, shushing her with a gentle caress.

"Amazing," he said aloud. His words were as incredulous as his tentative touch had been, as if he still couldn't believe this bond between them was real.

"It is."

"It shouldn't be. What you did was primitive, a mixing of ceremonies."

She jutted her chin out. "So?"

"So nothing, *mon petite peste*."

"Roland, so help me God, if you don't stop stalling and get on with this."

He started chanting, the words a beautiful flowing of

vowels and consonants similar to Latin, but not. Some of it she recognized from earlier, but she sensed, instinctively, that there was more. Finally, when her body was tingling all over, her very being seeming to lift from her core, he finished with, "All I have, everything I am, is yours. My life for yours. My heart for yours. My soul…"

He swallowed, closing his eyes. She placed a finger over his lips. "Shh…I don't want that anyway. True love would never ask for the sacrifice of another for themselves."

His lids opened, revealing his haunted eyes. "But if I had one, and the need arose, I would have gladly sacrificed it if it meant saving you."

She knew he would. Which is why she thought perhaps it was better that he thought he didn't have one. She'd rather die, rather have her very being extinguished from the very fabric of time, than to have his destroyed.

He growled. "Don't you dare even think that."

"Why not? You think that way."

He bent over, dropping his forehead against hers. "By the Father, Karissa, I can't even promise…I don't have…"

She felt the raging incompetence he experienced. A ripping of his perceived manhood that was soul deep. *Soul* deep. Why couldn't he realize that?

He lifted his head, grabbing onto her shoulders, and stared at her with an intensity that burned into her core. "I can protect you. I can love you and cherish you. That's all I have."

"Then love me. Make love to me and truly make me yours."

Chapter 19

ROLAND STARED DOWN AT HER, HER CHALLENGE ringing in the vaults of his being. Make love to her, and make her his. Yes.

Before any of his personal demons could rear their ugly heads again, he scooped her up and raced with her to the bedroom. She gasped when he dropped her onto the bed and giggled when she bounced, but then went silent, her eyes widening to saucers when, in one motion, he had her shirt ripped off—and not over her head.

"Stay there," he commanded, and went about removing his clothes. He'd taken the weapons off earlier, before sliding into bed with her that first time, so it was quick work to remove his pants and T-shirt. The way she was drinking in his naked body was heady indeed, but he didn't stop to bask. He had to do this quickly. It was the only way he'd survive.

Not too quickly. Otherwise she won't relax and if she doesn't relax…

Right.

He forced himself to slow down, easing over her, and since he wasn't completely gone yet, he gave her what her upturned face demanded: a kiss. It was short and sweet and tender and not nearly enough, but all he dared. Pulling his mouth away, he bent down to another area of her body that was begging for attention, taking and rolling first one peaked nipple, then the other around in his mouth with his tongue.

He'd half expected his canines to elongate while he was doing so, and had been careful to keep his mouth light upon her, but they didn't. There was no blind lust, no driving need to feed, only her sense of wonderful discovery as her body throbbed and tingled under his touch.

Their bond. It was going to be his lifeline.

Emboldened, he deepened the kiss upon her breast until he was suckling the pink disk deep into his mouth. She gasped, her hands coming up to grip at his shoulders, her uneven nails digging into his flesh. He repeated on the other.

Still no desperate bloodlust.

He wrapped one arm around her back, his palm flat as he slid it up along her spine. With the other he lifted her until she was sitting up and perched on one of his knees.

Gawd, she was already dripping wet, the heat of her center pooling on his thigh above his knee. He could feel it, smell it, and when she started to rotate her hips back and forth against him, he went wild with it.

"Stop. Don't do that."

"Why not?" she countered, and then blasted him with a riot of sensations that showed him how exquisite the action of rubbing herself against the coarse hairs on his muscled leg felt.

Holy crap, how did she learn to do that?

"You're doing it too," she teased, nipping at his bottom lip. "I can practically feel the blood boiling in your cock."

"Hell."

"No," she purred. "This is a far, far cry from hell."

He chuckled, nuzzling the curls that had drifted down over her forehead. "I'm going to have to agree with that."

"Now if you had said 'fuck me…'" She emphasized this with another little grind against his leg.

He growled, fighting the red haze trying to overtake his vision. For pure matters of self-preservation he lifted her off him, plopping her down on the cool sheets.

She pouted, her lower lip jutting out. "Now, that's the opposite of what I had in mind."

He couldn't look at her and keep control. So he focused on staring at the rough panels of the walls instead. He knew he was disappointing her so he tried to explain. "Give me a minute. I need to cool off a bit and—"

A finger pressed against his lips. He turned his gaze back to her. Her eyes were soft, filled with understanding. "It's okay, I feel it. We can take our time."

The red haze didn't recede. If anything it got a toehold and latched on. "I'm afraid that won't be enough."

"It will be. And I'll help you." She pressed her lips to his, her tongue darting along the line of his mouth. Pleasure, joy, a sense of rightness flooded into him from her. Yes. When nothing happened to signify that he was about to lose further control, he returned in kind, tracing the plump fullness of her lips.

She moaned, her mouth parting wider. As if it had a mind of its own, his tongue took the chance and plundered, thrusting into her mouth and swiping the velvety softness of her tongue. The sensations became so intense that the world narrowed to this moment, her mouth, their fencing tongues.

Lost. A man could become lost in sensations like these and die happy.

He didn't know how it happened, but he had her stretched out on the bed again, her legs parted wide as he came over her, his mouth still latched onto hers.

Too fast. He was moving too fast.

She made a noise into his mouth, her hips arching up as a jolt of erotic torture coursed over their bond. She needed, she wanted. His cock brushed the inside of her thigh. And oh Gawd, so did he.

She broke her mouth from his, her breasts rising and falling, scraping against the course hairs of his chest with each gasping breath. "Now, Roland. I need you inside me now."

Roland swallowed down his doubt, then took his cock in hand, guiding it into the slick heat of her core. Tight, hot, wet. He breathed in sharply, trying to gain control over the spike of adrenaline that had pierced through his system at the mere thought of plunging into her.

And then he was. Only he didn't make it far, her innocence blocking him with a resounding no.

The sharp scent of copper permeated the air. The gut-wrenching muffle of her pain echoed over their bond even as she tried to hide it from him.

Damn, I hurt her.

Even as he thought it his canines pierced the inside of his lip. Monster.

Hissing through his clenched teeth he tried to force himself to pull back out, leave her be, but the moment he started to withdraw her sharp little nails dug into his back, demanding he stay.

"Karissa…" He swallowed. "I can't."

"Don't go, feels good," she murmured as she squirmed beneath him, as if trying to climb his shaft with her body. Only she couldn't because she was too tight and too small for his overzealous cock.

Must have heard her wrong, he thought she'd said it felt go—

A wave of pleasure slammed into him from their newly formed bond. Oh God. Oh shit! He couldn't take that. He sunk back into her. This time her body allowed it, even welcomed it.

"Oh my God, Roland!" Her eyes went wide. One, two more strokes and he was fully inside her, and her head was tipping back as she made a guttural moan in the back of her throat.

She was so close. Her channel rippling around him. Her heartbeat quickening. Veins pulsing.

Damn. Don't think of that.

The need to come, the need to strike, drink, claim was an addict's pull throbbing with each breath he drew, each gulping swallow of her scent.

Mine!

He sucked in one last breath, then did the only thing he could do. Held it. He was going to do this. He was going to make her come. He was going to be inside of her when she shattered. He was going to be what she needed. Partners. Mates. In bed and out of it. He had to do this—without losing control, without biting her.

She screamed, thrusting up to meet him, and started to convulse around him. Thank God. He let his pent up breath out, ready to leap off her and run before he could lose his last thread of control. The next instant the backlash of her orgasm hit him like a freight train over their link. There was nothing he could do. He came.

—◆—

Roland fingered the mahogany curls spread over his chest. Karissa was draped over him, head on his shoulder as he valiantly kept his head turned away. He couldn't resist the little bit of extra contact though. He loved her hair. So soft. Silky.

He still had the urge to drink from her, but it was fading. He hadn't bitten her. Bitten his own arm, yes, but at least it wasn't her tender skin and frankly, he'd gnaw himself to the bone if it meant he could have a repeat of the experience.

"Hmm." Her breasts rumbled against his chest. "Maybe I should buy you some chain mail. That way you won't hurt yourself."

"Ha, ha. Very funny." However, her jest, more than anything else, took the edge off his hunger. He turned his face toward her and met her brilliant smile. She was smiling, at him. And not just because he'd knocked her socks off, so to speak, but because, for her, he'd done something he was scared to do.

Her pride in him was both ego inflating and embarrassing. And all of a sudden he understood what his father meant when he talked about the bond between Paladin mates being a double-edged sword.

Her brow furrowed, forming an adorable crease across the bridge of her nose. "What was that you did? You know, the words you spoke before. It wasn't the same as the marking ceremony Logan and Valin tried to use."

"No. It was the bonding ceremony." And it should have been done in Haven's Hall. Not in some grimy cabin in the woods with both Ganelon's army and the entire Paladin regiment searching for her and ready to rip her away from him.

"And the equivalent to the rest of us laypeople would be?"

He refocused on her, feeling the nervous tension in her question. "There is no equivalent. Nothing can come close to the binding of a Paladin to his mate."

The crease got bigger. She nibbled her bottom lip. "Can I assume that we're like, um, married now? In a sense, that is, not that I'm trying to force you into—"

He shut her up with a kiss. She was so damn cute when she was flustered. When they broke apart he said, "You are mine, and I am yours. Forever. It's as simple and as profound as that."

"Good. That's good." She smiled, snuggling in tight. Moments later her breath had evened out into a light sleep.

He felt a bit of guilt promising her forever. The truth was he would always be hers. Even after she passed and he continued to live his horrible, immortal existence alone. It would be her, and the memories he had of whatever time they were allowed that he would use to keep from going insane, to stay true to the path of morality she would want him to walk. But when all was said and done, she would eventually move on without him. She may have pledged her heart, body, and soul in this moment, this life, but without a soul of his own to truly bind them together, she would eventually move on. *God* would not condemn one of his children to live eternity alone. Someday, somewhere, either up in heaven or in another life, there would be another man, another mate, for his Karissa. Roland just hoped to hell that when it happened he wouldn't know. Because God help the man who took her from him.

Chapter 20

THE BIRDS WERE SINGING, AND SO WAS KARISSA'S heart. Last night could not have been more perfect, filled with alternate bouts of erotic sex, then languid love-making that was only punctuated with short bursts of sleep when pure exhaustion took over. And waking now with the heat of her lover, her mate, pressed up against her back was like waking to heaven on earth.

The past twelve hours had been a dream. But like all dreams, eventually one woke up as reality reinserted itself. In this case reality was her stomach, which was currently rumbling loud enough to drown out the faint birdsong that seeped through the thick walls of the cabin. As much as she hated it, she was going to have to get up and get some food.

Carefully, she took the heavy arm draped across her middle and tried to lift it over her back to return it to its owner. The arm tightened, and rather than allow her to escape, it pulled her closer. It became obvious right away that Roland hadn't been asleep. His erection was a thick length of iron against the crease of her buttocks.

"Where do you think you're going?" The words rumbled from low in Roland's chest. He slid his hand farther down her belly and then concurrently ground his hips into her ass as he rubbed the tender flesh between her thighs.

Maybe breakfast could wait. Karissa arched her back

to increase the sensations, but again her stomach had other ideas, giving off another loud rumble that overpowered the needy moan.

"Guess that answers that." Roland chuckled, removing the hand that was doing the most delicious things to her. "And no you can't wait. I can feel the hungry beast gnawing through your spine. Come on," he added with a pat on her ass as he shifted off the bed.

She sat up, twisting around and pulling her legs under her as she watched Roland gather up the discarded clothes. Even in the dim light cast from the bedside lamp, his eyes were black as night, no telltale embers. Nor did she feel any burning need to feed through their link. Of course, her own "monster" hunger was such that it might just be overriding his. "Do you, uh, need to feed?"

"No. But I can help you whip something up and sit with you."

She nibbled on her lip, her desire to be with him warring with her desire to have a short reprieve.

Roland stilled in the act of pulling on his pants, his body going impossibly still.

"What?"

"If you want a break from me, all you have to do is ask."

"From you?" Oh crap. He'd gotten another dollop of her thoughts, though only her surface thoughts, otherwise he would not have jumped to such an off-base conclusion. She vehemently shook her head. "I don't want a break, at least not from you. It's just that…"

She broke off, suddenly realizing, to her horror, that what she wanted could seem like a rejection.

"It's just what?" He sat down on the bed, his face shuttered, as if expecting her to fist her hand up and strike him in the gut.

She shrugged her shoulders helplessly. "I, uh, wanted to do it on my own. Make breakfast, that is. It's one of my routines, to make breakfast early in the morning when the birds are singing and the sun is coming up…"

She looked away, unable to watch the tensing of the muscle along his jaw. How could something as simple as a desire to watch the sunrise be such a hurtful thing? But it was. There was no denying the deep ache flowing through their bond.

She shifted, the sheets whispering. "I'm sorry. It's stupid and I don't need—"

His hand touched the bottom of her chin, forcing her gaze up to his. "It's all right, Karissa. You shouldn't have to deny yourself one of life's simple pleasures because of me. I wouldn't want that. And you'd come to resent me if I did."

"No I wouldn't. I can live—"

"Don't. Don't lie to yourself and don't lie to me."

She dashed away a tear. It was no longer just her stomach tearing around behind her ribs. "I hate that I can hurt you like this."

"I'm harder to hurt than that."

"Now who's lying?"

Silence stretched out between them, then eventually he sighed, dropping his hand. "You're right. It hurts. I want to be there with you. But what would hurt more is if you were to deny yourself something that is vital to you because of me."

She gave him a doubtful look.

"Karissa, you are my light. You practically shine with it. If you were to deny yourself the sun, I know you would glow a bit dimmer, and I won't have that for the world." He leaned forward, kissing her forehead. "Go. I'll be here when you're done soaking up your rays."

He reached down, scooping up her panties along with his T-shirt from the floor and offered them both to her. She took them and pulled the shirt over her head, then stood up to shimmy into her panties. Roland watched her the whole time, his hunger a craving that licked at her senses.

"Okay. But I'll hurry."

"You don't have to do that. Stay in the cabin, that's all I ask."

"I'll hurry because…" She leaned over, kissing him with a passion fired by the memories of their numerous lovemaking sessions throughout the night. She finally broke away and had Roland growling in objection. "…I never was good at waiting for dessert."

"I suggest that if you're going to go, you go now…" His eyes raked her over, stuttering over her breasts that she knew were swollen and peaked with desire and the hemline of his shirt that barely covered her ass. "…because I was never good at waiting for dessert either."

He made a play dive for her. Laughing, Karissa skipped out of his reach and exited the room. On the other side she stopped, leaning against the rough pine as she concentrated on evening out both her heart rate and her emotions. She had to bite her lip to keep from crying. *Have to stop this.* Distance had muffled the intimate sense of him being in her mind, but she could still feel his ache.

More composed, she made her way into the small kitchen. They hadn't had the time or inclination to stop for food supplies, but Roland had said there would be some staples where he was bringing her. The staples turned out to be an interesting mix of canned and boxed foods and nothing that appealed to her for breakfast. She did find coffee, though, along with a percolator, and set it to brewing. The sun wasn't out yet, or at least if it was it was hiding behind a thick bank of clouds.

So much for her sunrise.

She pulled out a box of granola bars, snagging out a Nutty-nut Trail, and tore off a bite with her teeth. The food clawed at her esophagus the whole way down, but once it reached her stomach it was welcomed with open arms. When she was done, she turned her attention to the cupboards again, this time searching for powdered creamer and sugar. She'd found the sugar and was pulling a mug down when she noticed that something was different, something off, not right. Her hand dropped back to her side. She tilted her head, listening. Nothing. Uneasy, but not yet alarmed, she reached for Roland and discovered what the "off" thing was. Roland had drifted off, his thoughts so deep in his subconscious that she couldn't sense them without reaching for him.

Huh. This bond thing was going to take some getting used to. It was deeper than anything she'd ever experienced before. In comparison, her ability to sense someone's intent through touch seemed like a baby's first gibbering attempt at true language. Even now, as she pulled back from the dreamlike ebb and flow of his sleep-thoughts, she felt more of a connection with him than any other person she'd ever tried to read. Or ever loved.

"I love Roland." She tried the words out, letting them settle into her conscious. What was between them had happened so fast that she hadn't really thought of it in those terms yet. He was Roland. Her mate. The other half of her soul—or at least the man who was made for her soul. Love was a happy bonus. She did love him too. The way he would tenderly caress the hair back from her cheek, the way his eyes glowed like deep embers when he looked at her with longing, the way he would give anything of himself if it meant keeping her safe, keeping her happy.

She both loved and resented the bond. It made it so his happiness was directly linked to hers and vice versa. And because of that her little morning ritual would never hold the same sort of peace for her. But he was right. She did need the sun. For her it meant warmth, safety, joy.

She poured her coffee, adding a heap of sugar, and moved over to the back door. There was a small deck but she'd promised Roland she wouldn't leave. Instead she opened the door wide, letting the crisp morning air greet her.

Nope. Definitely not going to get her sunrise. At least not for a while. The fog here was dense and would take hours to burn off. Some people might find the soft haze on the world, the feeling of isolation, to be peaceful. Not Karissa. She was a city girl, and to her the shifting mist created an eerie landscape for dangers to hide in.

Something shifted in the fog. She straightened, squinted her eyes. Some animal or something. But whatever it was moved toward the cabin, its movements purposeful but staggering.

Karissa started to step back into the safety of the

cabin, her hand on the door, when a glimpse of red hair stopped her. She took a step forward to get a better look and the figure popped out of the worst of the fog.

The alley. The girl who'd tried to warn them. She was hobbling, and half her face looked beaten. Not beaten but burned; in fact, the blisters were still spreading. *Because she's a vampire.* And if she didn't get out of the light soon she was going to die.

Karissa scrambled across the small deck and down the two steps to the ground, running forward.

The girl threw out her arm, her face contorting past the pain of her injuries. "Why did you come out?...warn Roland." She mumbled something else incoherent. Hurt ear?

Karissa ignored the hand meant to fend her off, wrapping her arm around her. The girl had come to warn Roland. She was not the enemy, though it was obvious she had knowledge of the enemy and was willing to risk everything to try and help them. "We need to get you inside."

The girl groaned under her touch but gave way to her shaking limbs and fell into Karissa's side. Karissa tried to shield her as much as possible from the natural light of day. Cloud cover or not, this slip of a girl was burning to death...slowly.

Urgency nipped at their heels. Though only a hundred feet or so, the cabin seemed miles away. She couldn't jump unless she abandoned the girl. Roland had survived the light there, but his reaction to the little adventure told her all she needed to know. It wasn't safe there for a vampire. If this girl still had ties to the enemy, then she doubted this girl was as strong as Roland.

"Leave me," the girl gasped. "Tell Roland."

"Tell Roland what?"

The girl stiffened, moaning out her despair. Her words finally registered. *They're here.*

It was a trap.

Karissa's gut clenched. She twisted her head around, looking for the threat. Somewhere there rose the sound of laughter.

Oh God.

Roland! Help me!

His body was on fire. Nothing mattered except the acid burning through his veins, the sizzling poison filling his muscles and organs, the blistering disease that boiled up from under his skin.

He writhed on the floor, twisting and convulsing as agony took over his body, held prisoner his breath, stole his very life. It was in the moment of his death that the pain shattered, falling away as if it had merely been some sort of shawl enshrouding him. Then laughter.

He pried open his eyelids, turning his head on the hard marble. A man, tall and GQ handsome, leaned against the scalloped post at the end of the banister. Laughing, clapping.

"Good performance." He pushed off the post, striding like a monarch through his court across the large foyer. "Now, Paladin, I have a show for you."

The man's lips curled back, revealing fangs. Roland's eyes narrowed. If he had any energy left he'd leap up and cut that superior smile off the vampire's face. Just had to get his knife from the sheath on his thigh and...

A woman screamed. Roland's head snapped up. Down the hall, half dragged, half carried by two other vampires was, fuck no, his sister.

"Angeline!" He tried to push up, made it halfway before something brutal and suffocating clamped down on his will. For long seconds he fought for control before crashing back down onto the hard floor to lie there, gasping.

"Roland. What have they done to you?" His sister was sobbing, tears streaming down her face to land with large splats upon her distended belly.

Done? Other than tried to kill him? He'd gone there to warn them. His vision. The blood. He'd arrived and...

It was all a blank fog after that. What happened between then and his waking to agony? He didn't know. Didn't matter. He had to save his sister. He would not allow her to die like she had in his vision.

He reached for his knife but again was met with the searing agony of something, or someone, snuffing out his will.

"Nuh-uh-uh." The GQ vampire crouched down in front of him, waving his index finger back and forth.

"What..." he gasped, unable to continue speaking past his raw throat. He licked his lips, tried to swallow. His tongue, swollen, scraped across something sharp in his mouth. Tentatively he thrust his tongue out again. A line of blood welled on the thick muscle, dripping down his parched throat. The taste of the sweet coppery liquid had his heart racing, his body clenching in need. Alarmed, he looked up toward his sister. Only it wasn't his sister. It was Karissa. Their eyes latched for but a moment before she turned her face away, unable to even meet his gaze.

Vampire. Monster. She should *reject him.*

"*Kill her.*" *The order was given negligently, as if the life of the woman the man had ordered dead didn't matter.*

"*You bastard!*" *Roland roared, lunging for the man before him. He made it to his knees before his master's will slashed like a knife into his brain and sent him sprawling, again.*

Karissa. Not Karissa too.

A hand touched his shoulder, forcing him onto his back.

Roland glared at the man with all of his hatred in his eyes, even as his treacherous body gave up, sinking like a pool of mercury into the floor.

"*That's right, Paladin. I own you now.*"

…I own you now.

I own you.

…own *you.*

Roland woke on a defiant roar. No. It was not true. He'd broken that bond. His sister was dead, but Karissa wasn't. Karissa was out in the kitchen having her break-fast and to prove it all he had to do was reach out with his mind and…nothing. He bolted upright in the bed. Why couldn't he feel her? Possibly because the bond was so new?

He threw off the tangled blankets and charged for the door. Belatedly he remembered that Karissa had wanted to open the blinds. He spun around, grabbing up his pants and yanking out another T-shirt from the drawer. His cloak was out in the main roam, but he'd be all right as long as it was only a quick peek.

He moved back to the door, cracked it open. "Karissa?"

No answer. The cabin was dim despite the open blinds. The blinds weren't the only thing open. Through the back door that was swung all the way open on its hinges he could see the morning steeped in fog.

Karissa must have gone out on the back deck. Shit. He'd told her to stay in the cabin.

With his gut clenched up in a ball, he jerked his cloak off the hook by the front door and raced out the back door. Even through the fog he could feel the singe of the morning sun, but he didn't let that stop him from barreling down the steps into the yard.

Karissa's signature of passage was an even brighter burn. He felt the residual path of her concerned flight toward the woods, the spark of confusion, and then, here, he crouched down to touch the dewy grass, an ugly stain of fear. The fear is where her path ended. There was nothing after that last powerful emotion. It was as if she had disappeared, or…No. He would not think like that. He'd know if she were dead. He'd feel the ripping out of their bond. She had, however, stopped here. And wherever she was now, she was unconscious.

Forcing down his panic, he stood, spinning around as he scanned the woods. What, or who, had drawn her past the safety of the cabin? As much as he wanted to kill whoever it was who'd tricked her and taken her from him, he was sincerely hoping it was that bastard Valin.

A twig snapped behind him. Roland spun back around, his slim hope vaporizing at the sight of the creature that stepped out of the woods.

Gabriella lay on the floor of the van, her burnt cheek pressed tight against the rubber mats on the floor and her eyes squeezed as tight as she could get them. She hurt. God, she hurt. She wasn't powerful enough to withstand daylight, even clouded daylight, and she hadn't been given nearly enough blood before to allow her body to regenerate with any sort of speed now.

<<*You don't have to be thirsty, my pet.*>> Christos's voice was another violation within the vaults of her mind. <<*Food is but a bite away.*>>

She screamed, trying to drive him out. Christos thought he was so fucking funny. The moment Ganelon's merkers had tossed her and Roland's woman into the van, Christos had gone all parental on her: clucking his tongue, smoothing back her hair from her burnt face. And then he dragged the woman closer, sliced a shallow slit in her wrist, and raised it to Gabriella's mouth.

"Drink. My gift to you for a job well done. You will be the first to drink of the prophesied one's blood and break the bonds of dark and light."

Yeah, not happening. One, Gabriella didn't know what he was talking about with all that prophecy crap. And two, she hadn't drunk directly from a vein yet and wasn't about to start now. If Christos wanted her to drink from Roland's woman, he was going to have to take the woman's blood and pump it into her directly.

"My, my, Gabriella." A thick finger coated in blood tapped her nose, then traced a path around the edges of her split and cracked mouth. "What splendid ideas you have."

Gabriella groaned, trying to turn her head away from temptation. If he touched her lips…

He leaned in close, his breath rasping across her agonized skin, that finger coated in the promise of heavenly bliss circling dangerously closer. "I think we shall do just that."

No, no. Not Roland's woman. Had she not betrayed them enough?

I'm sorry, Daddy. I'm so sorry...

And then the finger dipped into her mouth.

Chapter 21

A DEMON AND A MERKER. ROLAND STARED AT THE TWO creatures that were trying to cut him off from the cabin and shook his head.

Ganelon must be stupid. Roland had already been up against these odds and won.

Two more demons appeared out of the fading fog behind their buddies.

All right, he took a step backward, *maybe not so stupid*.

"Sorry, boys. Sun's up. Not my time to play." With that he leapt and landed with a heavy crash on the back deck. The ancient boarding gave and smashed, the jagged edges tore at his flesh as his leg fell through.

Fuck. He dragged his leg out of the splintered boards, stumbled into the cabin, and slammed the door behind him, twisting the dead bolt. It wasn't going to stop them, but it might slow them down.

Grabbing his phone off the counter on the way to the bedroom—and his arsenal of weapons—he punched in the first speed dial on his cell. It rang. Rang again. He slammed the bedroom door shut. "Come on, Logan." Rang once more. Finally, as he began pushing the dresser across the floor to block the door, the call was picked up, a gruff voice biting out a "What."

A glass-shattering scream—literally—blew out every single window in the outer room. So much for the locked door.

"What the hell was that?" Logan demanded.

"Hey there, Logan. Roland here." He yanked open a drawer, grabbed out a 9mm, and stuffed it into the back of his pants, then reached for the satchel of throwing stars. "I've changed my mind about needing that help."

———

Logan lowered his phone, lifting his gaze. Alexander was watching him, his face unreadable. Roland in trouble. Karissa taken. And Logan was stuck here under guard as he awaited his sentence.

"Did you catch that?" He eyed the huge warrior. Paladin hearing was a touch above human levels, and war zones tended to be noisy anyway. War zone. Roland hadn't had to say what he was up against. If they'd taken Karissa from him and he was calling Logan for help then his vampire friend—who could handle just about anything—was facing some serious opposition.

Alexander nodded. "The elders must be told."

Yes. The other Paladin would race to Karissa's aid. As was right. But not one of them would race to help Roland.

"You can tell the others. I'm going to help Roland." He braced himself for the argument, his body flowing into a fighting stance: feet planted apart slightly greater than the width of his shoulders, arms low and at his sides, but ready to flash out and attack or defend. Too bad he'd been stripped of his weapons. Traitors, or vampire lovers, weren't allowed weapons.

Alexander drew his knife, flipping the blade around so it lay across his forearm, hilt extended. "You'll want a weapon."

Hesitatingly, he reached out, his hand closing around the carved hilt. "Thanks."

"No need for thanks. Paladin stand by one another."

That was a far cry from the uproar of outrage that had occurred when Valin squealed and told the others that Roland, the man Logan had been ordered to kill ninety-four years ago, was alive and well...and in possession of *their* Paladin female.

"Even when that Paladin is a vampire?"

"No matter what."

Logan parked behind the blackened carcass of a van in the driveway, his gut clenching as he stepped out of the car and took in the state of the cabin beyond it. It was half burnt out too—gaping holes where the door and windows used to be, and where they never were. His eyes honed in on a ragged hole in the wall and the overturned bed that had been tossed halfway out of it.

Shit. There wasn't an inch of the place that wasn't being bathed in sunlight.

"Roland..." Heedless of his own danger, he ran forward into the cabin, frantically tossing aside the mess of charred furniture and blasted in logs from the wall. Not that he had hopes of distinguishing wood ash from vampire ash, but Roland was strong enough to survive a bit of indirect light—assuming he'd found cover in time.

When his search of the main part revealed nothing, he yanked the bedroom door that was already hanging on its hinges the rest of the way off, heaving it aside. A tangled lump lay sprawled out under the mattress, the top of the body crushed under a dresser.

"Roland!"

He was pushing through the debris of the room when the body shifted, jerking in an inhuman motion. An arm pushed out from under the remains of a shattered drawer. Burned.

"Took you long enough."

Logan jerked his head around. The voice hadn't come from the body, but past the body, beyond the overturned dresser, and behind a paneled door.

He started shifting things away. First the mattress. The merker was missing a leg too, though it was trying to regenerate. "Shit, Roland. I hope to hell that you have the heart and head."

"My present to you, buddy. A thanks for coming to visit."

Logan tossed off the dresser that was barring the bathroom door from opening. The merker tried to stagger up but Logan pulled the knife Alexander had given him and hamstrung its other leg before pinning its arm to the floor.

The bathroom door cracked open. A large, lumpy bundle was shoved out. Logan took the towel, noting the blisters on his friend's arm. "That arm doesn't look so good."

"You should see my face."

"What can I get for you?"

"There is, or least was, a cooler in the kitchen. Inside are a dozen pints of blood. Two should do. Oh, and a blanket or something. My cloak got singed during the fireball volley."

"Fireballs?"

"That merker is a pyro."

"Not for much longer. Hold on. I'll take care of this and see if we can't find you some breakfast."

"Thanks," Roland said, pulling the door closed.

Taking a quick pause, he channeled his gift into the merker's heart and brain until the pulpy flesh charred and condensed into ash. Satisfied, Logan grabbed up his knife from the merker's now dead body and made his way into the main part of the cabin. He had to toss a few things aside—a couple burnt-through cushions and the charred countertop that had been dislodged from the cabinets, but he found the cooler, which was singed but amazingly whole. He opened it and grabbed out a bag. The blood was warm but hopefully would still do.

He moved back into the bedroom, rapped on the bathroom door, and passed the pint through when it cracked open. A moment later there was the distinctive sound of swallowing. Funny how he'd watched it enough now that it didn't bother him a bit.

"What happened?" He didn't need to clarify. Roland would understand what he was asking.

"I was sleeping. Having a fucking nightmare actually. I think Christos must have been near. He can't control me, but in a sleep state he must have been able to invade my thoughts. The dream…" there was a pause, an audible gulp, "it was Karissa instead of my sister."

"Can you, um, track her?"

"I feel a directional pull, but I can't reach her."

"Good enough. I'll put the middle seat down. You can ride in the trunk and with the blanket you should be protected enough to give me directions."

It took some maneuvering, but Logan got Roland in the car without singeing him further. They'd been driving for a short while before Roland spoke, his voice cracked and warbled as if it too had been burned by the sun. "It's been over an hour. They've had her for over an hour."

"We're going to get her back. Alexander told the others. Every single Paladin is out searching for her."

"And I thank every one of them for their help. But they won't be taking her home with them when this is over."

Logan thought there were a few who would honor the bond between Roland and Karissa, but not everyone. The Paladin were fighting a losing battle. More often than not they found themselves running rather than fighting. With every new generation of Paladin, and the dilution of their gene pool, they'd have to run more and more. There wasn't a Paladin alive, even Logan, who wasn't frustrated by that fact. He took a quick glimpse in the rearview mirror but saw nothing in the dark space between the two raised seats. "I'm assuming you marked her given that you can sense her now."

"I didn't bite her, if that is what you're asking."

"I didn't figure you would. I only wanted to know how complete the bonding process was."

"Why do you care? Wondering if you can break it so you can mark her instead?"

"I can't mark her." He glanced back in rearview mirror. This time there were two points of glowing red embers glaring out at him from the recesses of the dark trunk. "She's my sister."

Those eyes blinked. "Your sister."

"Half sister. Guess Dad was lonely enough to take up with a human."

"A human with a trace of Paladin blood though."

Logan glanced in the mirror again.

"Her grandfather was clairvoyant, remember? That's normally a good sign that there is Paladin blood in the gene pool. And given how much power Karissa holds…"

"Right." Logan's hands tightened around the wheel. Power. The double-edged blade for their females. It made them so desirable that idiot brothers lost their heads. "Regardless. My point is that I'm asking because she is my sister, not because I wish to mark her." Nope, his hopes of ever finding a mate were slimmer than no-way-in-hell. His feelings were torn on whether Karissa and Roland should be together. He wanted them to be happy, he truly did, but with no chance of offspring between them? It was just another nail in the coffin of the Paladin order.

"It's a full bond."

He lifted his gaze from the road. "Body, heart, and soul?"

The red orbs extinguished. Whether Roland had turned his head away, closed his eyes, or whether the question had snuffed the fire out, Logan didn't know. He'd say he didn't care, but he did. In the same way he cared when he'd stood before the twisted monster who'd once been his best friend, with orders to kill, and had hesitated.

"For me there is no other. If Karissa were to choose to leave, I would let her. I would ask, however, that you ensure that I will not have to be here if she were to decide to bond with another."

And that's why Logan hesitated all those years ago. Monster or not, Roland had more heart, more honor, than any other man Logan knew.

He shook his head, meeting Roland's gaze in the mirror. "I won't kill you."

"If she leaves, I'll already be dead."

The conviction behind Roland's words were enough to convince Logan. Somehow, someway, their bond was real. And if the bond was real, then Logan would do everything in his power to protect them both. "I won't kill you."

"Logan."

"I won't have to. I've seen the way my sister looks at you. Karissa would never leave you." Not by choice.

"How go the proceedings?"

Christos's skin itched under the seeming innocuous question. Look who finally decided to show up. Three hours late. Not that he expected less from Mr. High and Mighty himself. Where Ganelon was concerned, it was the peons of the world who did all the dirty work. And in Ganelon's eyes, everyone but perhaps himself and the lord of the underworld, Lucifer, were peons. Including Christos. *Find the girl, Christos. Bring her to us, Christos. Use your men to distract the Paladin, Christos.* Do this, do that, give, give, give.

Christos was getting damn sick of giving without receiving something in return.

"It goes slowly," he replied, sliding the needle out from under bruised skin. Another vein blown. They were taking too much, too fast. The yield was going to be nowhere near what they wanted it to be. Instead of performing a futile search for an uncollapsed vein, he set the needle down, turning to face the man who was supposed to be his partner. Christos realized that he totally deluded himself on that front. As evidenced by the fiasco in the van earlier.

His blood practically burned at the memory. Guinea pig. He'd been reduced to nothing less than a guinea pig. Testing the girl's blood on Gabriella should have been enough, but no, Ganelon had wanted to be sure that the blood would work on a vampire who did not possess some of the goody-two-shoes Paladin genes.

The skin under his left eye began to twitch, remembering the stunning prick of the needle in the back of his neck. Too bad Ganelon hadn't done it. Paranoid bastard that he was, he hadn't even been there, ordering one of his merkers to do the deed. Not that he shouldn't have been leery of double-crossing Christos. The merker who'd been following his liege's orders was still, at this moment, trying to regenerate all the pieces that Christos had cut off of him. It hadn't nearly been enough to sooth his anger.

But Ganelon was here now. And without his escort.

"Really, Christos? Do you truly believe you have a chance against me?"

"You're not all powerful. And you can die."

"Not all powerful, no." Ganelon's mouth curled up, his eyes drifting past Christos's shoulder. "But he is."

Christos spun around and fell to his knees. Lucifer. He was the perfect example of what a god should look like, if evil had rotted him from the inside out, which it had. Oily skin slid over herculean muscles, ink-stained eyes acted as windows into a twisted soul. He towered on the other side of table where the girl lay, his slanted eyes bearing down on Christos as if he was looking upon scum.

"Christos, come here." Lucifer's voice turned the simple command into a seduction, one Christos could not resist. Limbs trembling uncontrollably, he half knee-walked, half crawled around the table toward the fallen angel.

Wings, as black as the deepest abyss, snapped out and encircled Christos. Christos choked. No air. No sense of time or space. Only the suffocation of Lucifer's dark presence as it filtered through him, absorbing his essence.

Just when Christos thought he could take no more, that he would cease to exist here and now, Lucifer hissed, snapping his wings back. "Her blood has changed you."

Christos bowed his head, muscles shivering from pure exhaustion and fear shriveling him to the size of a bug. He'd upset his master. "Yes, my lord."

"It has made you both stronger and weaker."

"Yes, my lord."

Lucifer stepped away, circling the table. "Pick your darkest, most trusted followers. No more than ten. And give them her blood."

"But my lord, we have enough for far more than that," Ganelon said from across the room.

"No." Lucifer flared his wings out, the black webbing snapping. "Ten. No more." He turned his gaze back to Christos. "And make sure their hearts are as dark as they come."

"And the woman?" Ganelon's voice was as cold as ice, but he did not contradict Lucifer.

Lucifer turned back to the table, one clawed hand reaching out to stroke the woman's pale cheek. "They come for her."

"What should we do?"

"Let them come." He dragged the clawed hand up over her forehead. She gasped, her eyes popping open, her mouth twisted in a silent cry of agony. Lucifer smiled. "By then she will be dead."

Chapter 22

THEY WERE GOING UNERRINGLY WESTWARD NOW. AT first the directional pull had switched around, first west, then south, then all of a sudden northwest, before turning west again. The roads weren't helping. More than once they found that they'd gone down a road only to end up going in a direction they didn't want to go. When following a changing trail, GPS and maps were worse than worthless. Now, however, the aching tug of his and Karissa's bond had steadied out. The ever-increasing throb in his veins evidence of the closing distance.

"Crap. We have company," Logan said from the front seat, punctuating the announcement with another string of curses.

Roland scooted closer to the folded down opening. "Merker? Demons?" Like him, the vamps would have had to take cover during the day. Even Christos would be reduced to hiding in shadow under the bright afternoon sun.

"No. Valin. He's following us."

Crap was right. "Windows rolled up, right?"

"I don't think that—" even as Logan said it a fine dusting of particles sifted through the air vents of the car, settling into the passenger seat. The dark particles solidified until Valin sat there, casually picking something—dried blood?—out from under his fingernails.

Roland couldn't stop the rumble that rose in his

throat. Where this particular Paladin was concerned, he was far from unbiased. They had a history to begin with and that was before Valin had tried to mark *his* woman. Nope. Roland's feelings for the bastard weren't exactly stable.

"What, Logan, did you get a dog?" Valin asked.

"Go away, Valin," Logan commanded dispassionately.

Valin twisted around in the seat, smiling back at Roland. A false smile. "Hey there, Roland. You look surprisingly good for someone who's supposed to be dead. Though, maybe a little pinkish. Too much sun?"

"Fuck you."

Valin chuckled, turning back around in the seat. "Westward on." He clucked his tongue. "Hmm. You guys were acting like blind mice running round in a maze there for a while. Now you're not." He cocked his head, tapping his lips as if in thought. "Gee, if I didn't know better, I'd think you must have a way to track her. Like some sort of bond, a blood bond maybe…Did your dog bite her, Logan?"

"Valin…" Logan warned, but Valin ignored him.

"Talk about reaching above one's station."

"Possibly, but at least what Karissa and I have is a true bond, not some hyped up pairing. What sort of Paladin doesn't even feel his partner's need when she's dying?"

Valin went deathly silent, his pain a palpable stain in the recycled air of the vehicle. Logan didn't say anything; he didn't have to. His eyes skewering Roland's through the rearview mirror said it all: You fucking asshole. Not that Roland needed the chastisement. The moment the words had crossed his lips he'd wished he could take them back. Valin and Angeline may never have been true mates, but they had been friends, and that bond had been enough that when they had been paired in hopes of rejuvenating the failing Paladin line, they'd managed to conceive a child. A child lost before it could ever be held by its father.

"I'm sorry. That was," he cleared his throat, "uncalled for. And I, of all people, have no right to judge." Valin and Angeline's bond may not have been strong enough for the Paladin to feel his mate's impending doom, but Roland had actually been there—and been unable to do anything as Christos had her throat slit. Because he was weak. Because he'd succumbed to temptation and been made slave to a master vamp. It didn't matter that a few years later he clawed his way back to freedom; the fact that it happened at all just proved Valin right: Roland wasn't good enough for Karissa. The only way he could make up for the defect now was to find her and save her.

"What are the other Paladin doing?" This came from Logan. Trust him to break an awkward silence and drive things back on track.

"Why don't you ask your father? I'm sure you could reach him, even at this distance."

Logan glared at him.

Valin laughed, returning to his earlier sarcastic glee-fulness, though there was a hint of hollowness in the malice, as if he derived no pleasure from it now. "So the prodigal son fears running into the father. Yet at the same time hopes he can help him on his quest."

Logan's hands tightened around the wheel. "You know, I really don't like you, Valin."

"Ah, and here I thought we were best friends."

Logan glanced upward, the equivalent of rolling his

eyes. "Which is why I'm going to give you one more chance to tell me why you're in this car. And if it is for any reason other than to help us, then I suggest you get the fuck out before I unleash my 'dog' and sic him on you."

Valin took a good minute to answer, his interest seeming completely preoccupied with the cleaning and buffing of his nails. Roland was about to take himself off his leash when the Paladin finally opened his mouth.

"Your father has assembled the others. I was sent to follow you and have been checking in regularly with updates. And before you both get your boxers in a wad, it was done with the assumption that Roland here had a way of tracking her. Good assumption, huh?" He lifted his head, his eyes meeting Roland's in the mirror.

"I did not bite her. We are bonded. And before you ask, she initiated the ceremony that bonded us."

Valin whistled, shaking his head. "I so want to be in the room when you tell Senior that."

Roland's eyes narrowed. "You seem awfully amused by that when you yourself tried to mark her."

Valin shrugged. "Can't blame a man for trying. A woman like that? Your Karissa is just bursting with light."

And Valin always had a thing for the light. It was as if the darkness that was the power of his gift forced him to seek out other sources of light to balance itself out. It might very well be true too. Roland's sister had been a healer, using the light to cure wounds of the soul and burn demon poison from the blood. If she had lived, Roland always wondered if she could have saved him. But she hadn't, because both Roland and the others had failed her that day.

Turning his thoughts away from bleak memories, he

forced himself into the equally bleak present. Though, at least this time he had a chance of doing something about it. "So are the Paladin coming after me? Or are they after saving Karissa?"

"Both. But they'll save staking you until after you find Karissa for them."

"They do and they might very well incapacitate her."

"You wouldn't be the first vampire Senior's staked to 'protect' his daughter."

Logan snapped his head around. "What do you mean? Father told me he hadn't had contact with her since he'd hidden her at birth."

"Oh, didn't Daddy get that far before locking you up?"

Logan's jaw ticked. "No," he drawled. "So what didn't my father tell me about?"

"About Karissa's mother, of course." Valin's eyes twinkled, obviously enjoying being the holder of unknown information. "I can't believe he didn't tell you what she was."

"You mean that she had Paladin blood?"

"Well, duh, anyone with a brain could figure that out. I meant the other thing."

"What other thing?"

"Wow, Daddy doesn't trust you with much, does he? Then again," Valin glanced at Roland, "maybe his lack of trust is justified."

Roland took one look at Logan, who looked like he was about to leap across the seat, driving or not, and decided he better intervene—the car was handy, but not if it was crumpled into a scrap of metal. "Valin, I suggest you stop fucking with us."

Valin twisted around so he could play to the other

half of his audience. "Well, you know she's his half sister. And obviously her mother had some diluted Paladin blood in her for her daughter to have been born with such strong gifts."

He nodded. "Yes. What I don't understand is why Calhoun Senior didn't bring the mother under the protection of Haven."

"Because first off, she was human. And secondly it wasn't a true bond, merely a pairing—and you know how some Paladin feel about that."

Roland flinched but nodded. "But when she turned up pregnant?"

"By then it was too late."

"How so?"

"By then Ganelon had found her. He figured the best way to torture Elder Calhoun was not to have her killed, but to have Christos—"

"Turn her. Shit." Roland fought to suck in air in the tight space of the trunk. The thought of Christos drinking from Karissa's vein, the thought of him forcing his tainted blood upon her was too much. He couldn't think, couldn't breathe past the panic that hit him like a freight train in his chest.

Not Karissa. Karissa could not survive without the light. It would kill her as assuredly as ripping off her limbs and bleeding her out would.

"Roland. Roland!" Logan's sharp tone had Roland lifting his head. Their gazes met in the mirror, Logan's blue-gray eyes fired with steel. "They're not going to turn her."

Sick acid burned in the back of Roland's throat, but he managed to press the panic down enough to speak.

"Why not? What better way to stick it to the Paladin than to compromise the last female."

Valin scoffed. "She's already compromised if she's bonded to you."

Red coated Roland's vision, his fangs pressing into his gums. "My taint does not pass to her," he hissed. He would not have the Paladin turning on Karissa because of the man she'd bonded to.

"Geez, Roland, paranoid?" Valin shook his head. "I wasn't saying that she wouldn't be a Paladin, merely that as long as she remains with you, the Paladin line will remain as it is. Stagnant.'

I.e., There would be no offspring. A pang of guilt had his gut twisting.

"How's it feel, bub? Being the death of an entire race?"

Like shit, but that didn't cap Roland's anger. Valin was having way too much fun driving the stake home. "Don't let the air conditioning belt hit you on the way out."

Valin shrugged. "Logan's right though. They aren't going to turn her."

"How do you know?"

"Because I, unlike a certain scolded child, was in the hall when Logan Senior explained why he tried to hide her instead of bringing her in."

"Why?"

"Because of your dad, Rolly."

"What does my dad have to do with any of this?" Roland didn't like talking about his dad. The man he'd loved, the man he could never live up to, the man who'd gone to his grave with the belief that his son was a monster.

"Come now, your dad was an even more powerful clairvoyant than you, right?"

"So?"

"So, he made a prediction."

"About?"

"About Karissa, of course."

———∿∿∿———

Karissa sucked in the dank air. She knew if she could look at herself in the mirror right now that her eyes would be fully dilated and her face paler than chalk. What was that thing?

Too dark. There was a portable spotlight set up in the corner bathing light on what appeared to be a hollowed out cavern, but not a drop spilled upon the creature hovering over her. All she got was a sense of vast size that was only defined by the blackness of the creature's edges. Human in body shape, but with a presence of evil about it that sucked the hope right out of her. And it had touched her.

She'd woken on a scream. A bone-deep knowledge that having brushed against such evil she might never be at home in the light again. That she was somehow tainted and if it continued to touch her it would be at the cost of her soul.

Evil. Her mind had recoiled from its purity. All thought had focused on an escape which she knew was unachievable. The evil held her, cutting her off from all sense of reality.

Evil. She was going to shatter under its pressure. When Roland eventually found her, and she knew he would, it would be to find a broken body, alive but devoid of any sense of mind or soul.

Evil. It wrapped her up, spiraling her down into

darkness until there was nothing else. This was her existence. This was her life. This was—and then…then it was gone.

―᷈᷈᷈―

Karissa tore back into the real world on a gasp, her eyes blinking against the blinding light around her. She tried to lift her hand to wipe her eyes but couldn't lift her arms past the burning cut of rope bindings.

Where was she? What happened? The last thing she remembered was stepping outside the cabin to…

Oh crap. The girl. Bait for the trap. How stupid, stupid, stupid could she be?

"She's awake."

Karissa sucked in a breath, sweat beading and instantly chilling on her skin. She shivered. She knew that voice. It was the last thing she'd heard after the pleased laughter, before her world had gone dark. She twisted her head. Still in the cave. The monster was gone but now there were two men, neither of whom looked like a white knight.

"What shall we do with her?" the first man, the scary, handsome one said.

The second man absently waved his hand. "Do as you wish. We have the blood we need."

"For ten chosen." His lips curled back, revealing long pointed fangs. "Do you wonder why only ten? Do you wonder why the ten should be mine alone?"

Eyes narrowed. "It is your children who cannot breach the light."

The vampire nodded. "Conceived by the light and born in darkness, the child's blood shall give the dark lord's children the ability to breach the two worlds." He smiled. "Worlds. Not day and night. Why just mine? Do you think he's afraid? Or do you think, perhaps, that he likes me better?"

"Just do as you've been told." The other man spun around, grabbing up a handful of vials and stiffly marching out of the room.

The vampire laughed, leaning down over Karissa. "Guess it's just you and me, pet."

"What," Karissa croaked, wet her cracked lips, and tried again, "What do you want?"

"Want? Why, for you to scream." He lifted a wicked looking instrument in front of her. Scalpel. Oh crap. "Scream, darling. Call your mate's name."

He lowered the blade and pierced her skin. Karissa screamed.

Chapter 23

ROLAND JERKED UP SO FAST HE RAPPED HIS HEAD ON the lid of the trunk. "Crap." He grabbed the top of his head, even as he tried to hone in on the frantic thought that had him jumping out of his pants.

"What? What's wrong?" Logan asked.

"She's awake. Goddamn bastards. They're hurting her." He closed his eyes, following the residual stain of fear and pain that had jarred him from the silent tension in the car. *Where are you, baby? Tell me where you are.*

Roland?

Her essence clung to him, like nails digging into his insides. He could feel her panic and the throbbing agony that was her body.

Karissa, God. I'm coming for you, honey. I'm coming.

No…don't. The nails slipped free, her mental presence trying to push away.

Karissa! he screamed, grasping onto her with all his might. *Don't you dare leave me!*

Can't come here…Trap. He wants you.

Who, baby? Who wants me?

The second he asked, her mind provided the answer: a blurred image of a man with high cheekbones and a chiseled face. Christos. Placing the knowledge aside, he forced himself to look past the object of his eternal hatred and onto the room beyond. Not a room, but some sort of unnatural cavern. Whatever the light source was it bounced off the reflective stone in the background creating an eye-blinking mix of light and shadow.

Christos leaned in closer, clucking his tongue over something. Searing pain tore over their link, obliterating the image.

Karissa! Roland rode out Karissa's pain, trying to take it in but knowing he couldn't. All he could do was share it. He felt her slipping, her mind shutting down as the torture, heaped upon whatever else she'd already been put through, became too much. Good. If she was unconscious they'd leave her alone. *Please, Father, make them leave her alone.*

Hold on, mon chaton. With all that he was, he reached out to her, soothing her into her slumber. *I'm coming.*

And when he got there, Christos was going to die.

It was Logan's question, a solid minute of silence later, that broke him from the haze of residual pain and anger. "Where is she?"

He looked up, meeting his friend's questioning gaze in the mirror. He cleared his throat, swallowing blood. Damn, he'd bitten himself again. "It looks like some sort of mining operation. The cavern she's in has been dug out somewhat, but the entrance has railroad ties that suggest it leads back into a man-made tunnel."

"Coal mines," Valin said from the passenger seat.

"What?"

"We're well into Pennsylvania. There are a bunch of abandoned coal mines in the western part of the state. It's the perfect place for an army of vampires and demons to hide out." Valin shook his head. "Fuck. Of all the luck."

"What?"

"Have you ever driven through the back roads of western Pennsylvania?"

"No."

"They suck. And they don't go in a straight line. The closest mine I know of is probably going to take us another two or three hours to drive to."

Roland's blood chilled to ice. "She doesn't have two or three hours."

Silence sucked up the tension in the car. Roland worked on taking deep breaths, working through his fear. Valin was right. The road they were on now was running northwest along a ridge of mountains on their left, but that was after having gone north for a while after having originally been going southwest. It was more than infuriating. Every single time they switched directions it seemed like the distance between them and Karissa was increasing, not decreasing. Overall that wasn't true, but as the crow flew, he knew they could have been there by now. If it hadn't been daylight outside, even if he could have been blessed with some frigging rain, he could have used his vamp tricks to be across the many mountain ridges that were forcing them off their path.

His hands fisted, cutting and digging, cutting and digging until the scent of his own blood permeated the air around him. The pain, barely a shadow of what he'd felt coming from Karissa over their link, eased his churning guts and allowed him to think more clearly. He couldn't go out. Logan couldn't magically transport their car over the massive ridge on their left, but there was someone…"Go, Valin. You're the only one who can get to her in time."

"And if she's not at the first mine? Or the second?

There are dozens of these mines in the general direction you're suggesting."

"Damn you. Does the fact she's a Paladin mean nothing to you? Do you hate me so much you'd let her die because of our bond? Please. You have to try."

Valin tapped the dashboard, his mouth twisted as he contemplated. Roland was about ready to beg again, or, perhaps more likely, reach through the seats, grab him, then pummel him until he agreed when the bastard finally spoke.

"Pull over, Logan."

Logan looked sharply at Valin but pulled off onto the shoulder.

Valin threw open his door, marching out of sight around the car. A second later there was a pop and the trunk lifted, sunlight bathing the previously dark haven. Roland hissed, pulling his blanket over as much of himself as possible. From the front Logan swore as he bolted out of the car. Valin started to reach inside the trunk.

"What the hell do you think you're doing?" Logan demanded, slapping Valin's hand away and lunging for the tailgate.

Valin raised an arm, preventing Logan from closing the trunk again, and stood with his other arm outstretched toward Roland. "Come on, vamp. I'll cloak you."

"What?"

"Do you want to save your woman?"

"Fuck you. You know I do." Even with Logan and Valin's body shadowing him, his skin was burning. A slow tingle and sizzle that meant he was already lobster quality wherever his skin was still exposed.

"Then get out. I'll cloak you."

Valin fell out of the Shade, forming with a cloud of particles into his human form beside Roland. He reached up, swiping the sheet of instantaneous wet locks out of his face and tossed them over his shoulder.

"Rain. I hate rain."

"I love it," Roland said from where he crouched down beside the Paladin. Not only did the rain make it possible for him to be out in the open while it was still day, but it did wonders to cool the heated skin on his face and hands. Even with Valin cloaking him, he was able to feel the sizzle of the sun on his face. Of course, in order to see where he needed to "leap" to next, Valin had to thin the veil of darkness he created for Roland to see through.

"Yeah, but rain is harder to sift through. Makes traveling in the Shade difficult."

"Kind of sucks."

"Not to mention this is a cold rain. I think my balls are trying to hide somewhere in the vicinity of my small intestine."

Without a word, Roland pulled Valin's T-shirt and jeans from his rolled up blanket and passed them to Valin, then donned the blanket again as an added precaution. Knowing his luck, the rain would break and the clouds would miraculously part in a beam of heavenly light. Bad for the two vamps standing a few meters back in the mine shaft, but worse for Roland crouching out here.

Valin yanked on a pant leg, then the other, as he nodded at the vamps. "Think anyone will notice if they go missing?"

"They're Christos's, so yeah."

Valin sighed, planting his hands on his hips despite the fact he'd yet to zip up. "That sucks."

"Finish getting dressed so we can go kick some ass, would you?"

"Why?" Valin started pulling the pants off again. "I'm just going to have to take them off again."

Roland twisted around to look at him head-on. Valin winked. "How would you like to be invisible?"

Of course. When Valin was in his particle form, he was all but impossible to see, unless he let you see him. It was probably safe to assume the same went for anything within Valin's circumference of influence—like the vampire he'd encircled. "Invisibility is handy. But not if it means slicking up with you again."

"Ah, poor Roland, your masculinity being threatened by hanging with me?"

"Shit no."

Valin's lips curled up saying, "Suck it up, vamp," just before he twisted into darkness.

——————

Gabriella screamed a soundless scream, straining against the thick leather and metal manacles that kept her anchored to the granite wall. She was fully healed. Had all her strength back, and yet, for the life of her, she couldn't break through a couple measly bindings. What the hell?

Most of the van ride was a blur. The agony the sun wrought on her was enough to blur the edges of her memory. She remembered Christos sliding the bloody finger in her mouth. And though she'd instinctively

swallowed, she remembered that she'd somehow managed to resist leaping onto the curly-haired woman and
sucking her dry. She also remembered how a little while
later, as they'd driven out of the fog, how the van had
pulled over, the back doors cracking open, and Christos
ordering she be tossed outside into the full effects of the
burning sun.

She'd screamed, clawing at the doorframe, then
crawled on hands and knees across the ground as she
searched for a bush or something. Her already taxed
body hadn't been able to take the stress and she'd
passed out—and woken here. Perfectly healed, perfectly healthy. Someone must have picked her up off
the ground before she could burn to a crisp and fed her
the blood she needed to heal. Who that was, why, or
whose blood she'd been given, she didn't know. Didn't
care. Only thing that mattered was getting free, finding Roland's woman, and getting them both out of this
mess. Problem was, the only thing she knew how to
do was the second. Whether she'd had a mere drop
or a full IV bag of Curls's blood, Gabriella now had
the ability to track the woman down. Blood called to
blood. Gabriella, Roland, and Curls were now as tight
as family.

She only hoped that she'd be given the time to make
that Disney dream come true.

—⁂—

"I think you might want to tell busybody Calhoun
about this," Roland whispered into the Paladin's ear
as he shifted to get a better look into the huge cavern before them. Filled to bursting with vampire,

merker, and demon, he was shocked to see that no bloodshed had occurred. The three groups, though on the same side, were not known to play nice without their masters there to keep them chained. Roland had spotted Ganelon right away among the masses, and as Lucifer's right-hand man, he could probably control both merker and demon, but Christos was blatantly absent. Not good. Roland liked his enemies close, and not knowing where the troublemaking vampire was, was driving him nuts.

Close. The vampires would not amass unless Christos was around to call them to order.

Valin shook his head. "Can't. Distance, time in the Shade. The connection is lost. He obviously can't locate me now, and I can't seem to get a bead past all this rock to fix it."

The corners of Roland's mouth pulled tight. "The other Paladin need to know what they will be facing if they come here."

His only answer was an extreme sort of silence.

He squeezed Valin's shoulder. "I want you to head back to the surface. Hopefully it's just these walls interfering with your projections and you'll be able to warn them." He looked back down into the cavern. "I'll find Karissa and bring her out."

"You're good, Roland. But without me here to cloak you, you're not invisible."

"True." Roland pulled his old Paladin blade from the sheath on his thigh, the etched metal glinting in the faint light. "But with this I don't have to be."

Valin eyed him, eyed the blade. "You know, I think our problem always was that we are both cocky bastards."

"Probably."

"All right." Valin stood. "I'll meet you topside. But if you're not out in twenty minutes, I'm coming back in after you."

Roland watched Valin sift, the curl of dark cloud zipping back up the tunnel as the Paladin's words echoed in his mind. Twenty minutes, and Valin and the other Paladin would come in after him. Why didn't that make Roland feel any better?

—⁓—

Valin was almost to the entrance of the mines before he finally drew a bead on Calhoun. Only it wasn't Senior, but the son. Good. Might be easier that way. Logan would know how to arrange the help of the other Paladin without the end result being a knife stuck in Roland's heart. And damn if Valin wasn't starting to wonder if all that animosity they'd shared in the past was a situational thing rather than a true dislike.

No worries. Something to ponder later...if Roland found his bond mate and they got them both out. Because if that didn't happen, then Roland would not be anyone that Valin would want to know.

Valin settled his mind and tapped up against Logan's shields. There was a moment of wary hesitation, but then the other Paladin opened a pathway.

<<Hey, where's Daddy?>> Valin asked.

Logan ignored that. <<Did you find her?>>

<<Found the place, at least. It's crawling with vamps, demons, and merkers.>>

<<Crap. It's a trap.>>

<<Did you expect anything less?>> Spine tingling,

Valin shifted back into a side tunnel. There was a distinctive scuffle of booted feet, then, "What do you think about this prophecy crap?"

A second voice answered, "I think it's just that—crap."

<<*Where is Roland?*>> Logan asked through the link.

"Sure you're not just saying that because you weren't chosen to receive the gift?" from the first.

The other grunted in reply. Valin took that as a maybe. Trying to keep his mental voice tight and direct he "whispered" a reply to Logan. <<*He's gone in to find Karissa.*>>

There was a slight hesitation before Logan replied, equally quiet and direct. <<*Where are you?*>>

<<*By the entrance talking to you.*>>

Logan's fury needed no medium. It was like acid in a raw wound as he mentally hissed, <<*Get in there and help him!*>>

The conversational vamps walked past the opening where Valin hid. Thank the Father they weren't merker, otherwise they might have overheard his little mental conversation with Logan, or at least known it was going on and that someone who shouldn't be there was. The way things were starting to buzz, it was going to be short of impossible to get both Roland and Karissa out. He could only spread himself so far, especially when moving. <<*You going to contact Daddy and bring the others?*>>

<<*Yeah.*>>

<<*All right.*>> Valin cut off the connection, dissipating back into the Shade.

Roland slunk into the oddly shaped cavern, his eyes honed in on the figure on the makeshift table, but his other senses—both vamp and Paladin ones—searched the dim corners. It was hard to concentrate on a possible trap though when Karissa lay on that table. Unconscious, barely breathing, and stained with her own blood. His very being howled with fury, but he remained silent as he finished the sweep for enemies with his eyes as well.

Confident they were alone, he raced across the room, his hands immediately going to the bindings that held her arms obscenely out to the side. Bruised arms. Cuts. Wounds that suggested she'd been poked multiple times with a needle. And her torso—someone had taken a blade to her there as well, her shirt slashed open where the sharp metal had bitten into her in long, jagged streaks before being wedged beneath the lowest rib.

"Karissa," he choked on her name. No, it was tears he was choking on. He was crying. He'd found Karissa, but it was too late. He didn't need to be a healer to know that it was too late.

Chapter 24

<<*No! Not that way!*>> THE PROJECTED THOUGHT had Valin stumbling out of the Shade and almost reforming in his human form. It was sheer survival instinct that had him clinging to the self he used to skip along the particles of air.

What the hell was that? The mind voice had been feminine in nature, but he was quite sure it hadn't been Karissa. And since there were no other female Paladin, that left merker.

Great. They knew he was here now, unless this one was alone. In which case, given the properties of the stone around them, the merker probably hadn't warned anyone else. She probably only called out because she'd overheard part of his conversation with Logan and, not able to find him, was now trying to lure him to her.

Well, wasn't this her lucky day. Valin was in the mood to oblige. Only he wasn't about to roll over and play dead.

Reversing direction, he headed back closer to the surface, sending out a well-shielded probe. The merker tried to grasp on but slipped off, her frustration evident in the smack of the rebound. Temper, temper. It did give him a direction though. The next time another tunnel intersected he veered off. This tunnel was heading upward and within moments he was slithering through a set of plank wood that boarded up the opening to the tunnel.

Once through, he stopped, taking in the dilapidated building. It was a warehouse of sorts, and inside were the rusted out remains of more than one coal car. There was also something else in the room, namely the woman who'd been bashing at his shields. She was chained up along the far wall, a gag stuffed into her mouth, but she was not defeated. Her eyes flashed with fire as she jerked at the leather and steel manacles around her wrists. There was something odd about her, besides the fact that she was not a merker. Something in the tilt of her eyes that reminded him of someone.

Even though she couldn't know for sure he was there—he was still in the Shade—he felt another brush of her mind as she tried to penetrate his shields. He wasn't that great a fool. Still, she had him deathly curious. Who was she? And why was she chained up here in this building?

He slipped closer to her, then coalesced into his human form. Her eyes widened, the black pupils all but obliterating the emerald green irises. Before he could decide whether it was the abruptness of his appearance, or the fact that he was naked, the pupils constricted back to normal.

Tough cookie.

He reached up, pulled the gag out of her mouth.

She worked her jaw and swallowed. "Thank you." She jerked at the manacles. "Now let me out of these."

His gaze traveled to the manacles. "Why? So you can feed on me?" He'd seen her pretty fangs when he'd pulled the gag out. "Any vampire worth their salt could get out of those. Fact that you can't says you must be hungry."

Her eyes narrowed. "I'm not hungry. But if I were, I certainly wouldn't want blood from the likes of you."

"The likes of me?"

"You're one of the Paladin bastards who like to turn their backs on their own. I wouldn't lap at your vein if you were the last red-blooded creature in the world."

He folded his arms across his chest. Forget the cookie. There was nothing sweet about this one. He took another long look at her, studying her from head to toe before returning to her face. What was it about her eyes?

She jerked her bindings again, screeching an inhuman shriek. "Come on! The woman doesn't have much time left."

His arms dropped to his sides. "What woman?"

"The Paladin woman, you idiot! She's dying."

"How do you know?"

She turned her face away, mouth pinched, forehead bunched up. A wave of heat spread through Valin. As if of its own accord, his hand shot out, latching around her throat. "Did you feed off her?"

"Not by choice," she gasped through his bruising stranglehold.

Her eyes darted to the side. He followed her gaze to the discarded IV bag that lay empty and wrinkled upon the dirt floor. Ah, crap. So Roland wasn't the only vamp out there who didn't like his status in life. He looked back at her again, took in the softness of her skin, the slightness of her adolescent curves. The poor girl couldn't have been much past puberty when she was turned.

He dropped his hand, suddenly feeling sick to his stomach. How many others had treated her thusly? Had she experienced anything other than abuse from those she interacted with? Judging by the fact that she had to be force-fed, he somehow doubted it.

He cleared his throat. He couldn't let his sympathy for this child-vampire get to him. "Tell me about the woman."

She looked back up, caught his gaze. "She's dying. I can find her for you but only if you'll let me go."

"Roland is here. He can find her. And he certainly doesn't need you to do it."

—⁓—

With his hand trembling, Roland fought with the restraints, the buckles jingling and rattling. The moment she was free he had her in his arms and was lowering her off the vile table onto the ground.

"Karissa," he said, caressing both her forehead and her mind. There was no response. She was so deep he couldn't reach her.

Because she was dying.

No! She couldn't die. He couldn't lose her. It wasn't that he couldn't imagine life without her; it was that he could. He would not survive her death. His body would, but his heart, his humanity would not. He'd thought himself a monster before, but it would be no comparison to what he would become if she died.

He had to turn her. Yes. He would turn her. As a vampire she'd have exceptional healing powers. And she wouldn't die. But that was after the change was completed. He would have to be careful. She'd already lost so much blood and he knew the moment the first drop of her blood touched his palate he'd want more. But he didn't need more than a drop. Just enough to make her part of him so the conversion would work.

Conversion. What a cold clinical word. He was about to convert his mate into a vampire. Because he was selfish. Because to lose her now, and live himself, would be to exist in an eternity of living hell.

Mine!

Lifting her arm, he scrapped the calloused pad of his thumb across the fleshy part of her lower arm, reopening one of the many jagged wounds. The coppery scent drew his fangs out, saliva slicking the back of his throat. Even now, with Karissa's life in the balance of his control, his monster rattled the cage, demanding to be let loose. Only the light skip of her pulse—too far apart, too light—allowed him to keep the lock turned.

"Forgive me, Karissa."

"This is the one?" Alexander asked, strapping the blade that Logan had returned to him onto his outer thigh.

"This is it." Logan glanced over his shoulder at the small group of a dozen or so Paladin who were busy gearing up. He still didn't have his knife, or his sword, but he supposed it didn't matter. He was backup, not to be on the front lines. Anything got to him and he was to release "the bomb." Or whenever his father ordered it. Yup, Calhoun Senior was back in charge. And though he was allowing his son to participate, he was not happy with Logan.

Alexander shifted closer, using his large body as if to shield something. Logan looked down into man's massive hands and sucked in a breath. His knife.

"How did you..." he started to ask then stopped. Alexander had defied Calhoun Senior, breaking through the elder's shielding in order to retrieve the blade.

Alexander shrugged. "I thought you might need this."

"Thanks." Logan took the blade, quickly stuffing it under his jacket. He wouldn't wear it openly and get the other Paladin in trouble. At least not before there were other distractions for his father's wrath to focus on—like Ganelon and his army.

Alexander jerked his head toward the mass of Paladin. "Every single one of those men has lost a loved one or friend to a vampire at some point."

"We've all lost friends to vampires. Merkers and demons too."

"Yes, but those men won't hesitate to follow through on the order you failed to carry out."

"How about you?" Logan asked. Alexander had shown more than once that he might sympathize with Logan where Roland was concerned, but then again, his actions could be purely practical in nature. Let Logan loose, let him find the vampire who could lead the Paladin to Karissa. And looky here. Here they were.

"I lost my cousin to Christos. But Roland was once a Paladin. If you say there is still some of the man I once called my brother, then I am willing to give him a chance."

A chance. That was better than most of these men would give Roland. "You know why my father allowed me to come."

"I do." Alexander shifted, his gaze flicking to the other Paladin and back again. "I can absorb the energy given off during projected thought, if you think you can reach Valin again."

"You would do that?" To shield his communication with Valin, be part of a conspiracy to warn Roland—a known enemy—would put Alexander in the holding cell with him when they got back. Logan had always known that when push came to shove he'd stand up for his fallen brother, but knowing what Roland could be if the vampire in him ever slipped into full control, Logan would not ask the same sacrifice of another. Roland may still have a Paladin heart, but he was a vampire. A creature of the dark. Alexander had to be sure.

"Just do it. Before your father wonders what we're talking about over here and wanders over."

"All right. Here it goes." Logan centered himself, closing his eyes to better direct his thoughts. Yes, he could communicate no matter where he was or what he was doing, but it was easier when he removed the outside distractions, and since the tunnels themselves seemed to have a buffering quality, the fewer distractions, the better. He just hoped Valin hadn't gone so deep that he couldn't reach him. Two minutes. How far could the Paladin have gotten? In his shadow form, probably far enough.

So he was surprised when moments after he'd started his sweep for the Paladin's presence that he found him. No more than a few hundred yards away.

<<*Valin. Where the hell are you? You couldn't have found Roland and Karissa and gotten back yet.*>>

<<*I'm still in here. I ran into a bit of a complication.*>>

<<*I'll give you another complication. We're here and getting ready to party.*>>

<<*Who's we?*>>

<<Me, my father, and about a dozen other Paladin.>>

<<I told you that it was a trap. You come down in here and you're going to be swarmed.>>

Logan looked at his father, the stoic faces of the Paladin who'd volunteered. Every single one of them were hoping that despite the fact that Karissa had run off with Roland, that they still had chance at a pairing. He couldn't fault them. If she wasn't his sister, he'd be hoping that too. Besides, that was something to worry about later. After Karissa was rescued. Nothing was going to stop these men from going after the first female Paladin in almost a century. Not Christos, Ganelon, Lucifer, or one former Paladin-turned-vampire.

<<Yeah. I don't think they care about that. I have a group of wannabe heroes here.>>

<<Shit.>>

<<No, my friend. The word is fuck, as in fucked. Remember, my father's here too. Only reason I'm not back in lockup is that he's decided I can be useful: As backup.>>

There was a long drawn out silence; he felt the click as understanding registered and knew Valin was probably swearing like a sailor aloud.

Logan turned his back to the other Paladin, as if that would further hide the insubordination he was performing. *<<You have to find Roland. You have to cloak him.>>*

───

Gabriella narrowed her gaze on the Paladin pacing a five-by-five swath out of the warehouse's dirt floor. She recognized him as the Paladin who was with Curls in the alley the night before. It was just as obvious he hadn't placed her yet. Not surprising, she looked a lot different without the hooker getup and the man's attention had been elsewhere at the time. Just as it was now.

The Paladin was communicating with someone— she'd felt the brush of minds like an itch at the back of her head—and ended the conversation with a string of swear words that had even her cheeks heating. Or maybe that was the fact that he was blatantly naked and didn't seem to give a damn. She wished she could say the same. But it would be untrue. The Paladin, and all his jangles, were more than fine.

He stopped pacing, his gaze making a direct hit on her scoping one. She resisted the urge to blush and turn her head away. So what? She'd been caught staring. A man dances around naked in front of a girl, he's got to expect to be turned into eye candy. It took her a moment to realize there was no amusement in his gaze, only speculation.

"What? What's wrong?"

"That was Logan. He's another—"

"Pretty boy." She scoffed. "Yeah, I know him." The Paladin narrowed his eyes. She shrugged, or tried to. Her arms were burning from their twisted up angle. "He hangs with Roland. Our paths cross sometimes."

He shook his head, chuckling.

"What's so funny?"

"Senior is really not going to like that his son's consorting with the enemy."

Her lips curled back as she jerked at the manacles. Had the idiot not noticed that they were in a warehouse full of windows? A slight break in the storm outside and she would be just another pile of ash in this place. "Do I look like the fucking enemy?"

"Well, yeah."

She tossed her hair and rapped her head against the wall. *Crap. Drop the attitude, Gabby. And stop showing your fangs. Calm. Reasonable.* "So what did Logan say?"

"He wants me to find Roland, ASAP."

"Why?" She asked warily. The man seemed to be friends with Logan, who was friends with Roland, so that was good. Also good was the fact that he hadn't immediately staked her. But that didn't mean that he could be trusted.

"He's hoping I can protect him. Logan is about to release his gift."

Gabriella's skin iced over, goose bumps rising on her flesh. She really needed to get this Paladin to set her free. If Logan released his gift it would pour through those windows and bathe this place in light. *Changed your mind about that death wish, Gabby?* The answer was, yeah, she had. She hadn't felt a single tickle in her mind since Christos had given her the woman's blood. It was like she was cut off from the others. No longer part of Christos's web. If it was the woman's blood that had done that for her...

"Oh crap. Is Logan's gift powerful enough to reach down into the caverns?"

"Honey, if he releases 'the bomb' every single inch in a ten-mile radius will light up like a Christmas tree. Including the nooks and crannies."

"Oh, no." Gabriella jerked at her chains, panic rattling the air in her lungs. Why the hell was the Paladin just standing there! "Go, you fool! You need to find him and help him!"

———≈———

One swallow, two.

More!

With a roar of defiance, Roland tore his mouth from Karissa's arm, the pure taste of Karissa's sweet blood sliding down his throat. Flowers, sunshine, spring. Karissa's soul. And he was going to condemn her to darkness. In the back of his mind, the part of him that was still human wept at his selfishness, but he couldn't fight both his nature and the bond. Karissa was his. He couldn't lose her.

Trembling, he lifted his arm up to his mouth, tearing into the tender flesh of his inner wrist until blood ran through the coarse hair down the back of his arm toward his elbow. All he had to do was lower his arm and let the blood drip into her slack mouth. The moment his prepared blood touched the back of her throat, she would swallow. It was part of the necessity of taking her blood first. Her own blood, now a part of his, would call to her and coax her to take it in. It also allowed the body to process the vampire blood as if it were her own.

He dropped his arm. An inch. Two.

Someone clapped, the smack of hands obscene in the reverence of this moment, the echo off the walls like mocking laughter. Roland spun around, his body between Karissa and the back of the cavern where the sound originated.

"Christos." Hatred pooled like molten lead in his

stomach as he came face-to-face with the monster who'd made him. It was this man, with his charming smile and urbane haircut, who was responsible for all of Roland's misery.

"I knew you'd come." Christos's gaze skirted past Roland to where Karissa lay on the floor, then away again, as if dismissing the dying woman as inconsequential. Just like Angeline. "You and your Paladin brothers. All heart."

Standing slowly, Roland slid his knife from the sheath on his thigh. "Well, Christos, since you don't seem to be using yours, you won't mind when I extract it from your body, will you?"

———※———

Gabriella ran down the corridors, the puff of shadow keeping pace around her. How odd. She wasn't sure she liked running through a perpetual black cloud, but if it did what he said it did—hid her from the others and protected her just in case Logan got trigger-happy—she could deal. She still couldn't believe the Paladin had let her go. Though, maybe she shouldn't be that surprised. She'd told him she could find the woman, and since Roland would be looking for Curls, then it was safe to assume she could lead the Paladin to them both.

They were getting close. She could feel it in the throb of her pulse. Maybe a hundred yards or so, all they had to do was find a way around the thick wall of stone between them and wherever the woman lay.

They rounded the corner and came to a split in the tunnel. She ground to a halt. The dark cloud shifted around her, eager to be off again. She studied the two choices before her. The left tunnel seemed to veer too sharply, almost doubling back on the direction they'd come in. Right, then.

Fifty feet later she realized she'd made a mistake. With a muttered curse, she spun around, heading back to the other tunnel. This one was decidedly narrower, and steeper. She slipped on a patch of slick algae, almost went down, but the cloud around her solidified just enough to catch her and prop her back up.

"Thanks." She gasped in a couple deep breaths. The air down here was thicker. Harder to breathe. What would it be like for a human?

With the new worry to propel her forward, she started picking her way down the steep incline. A sound rose. A scuffle of feet, followed by a grunt. Hand running along the wall, she skidded around the corner and found herself wobbling a couple dozen feet above an irregular cavern. In the center, all but floating over the uneven footing, Roland and Christos were engaged in a battle that looked more like an intricate dance than a fight.

Gabriella's pulse hammered, her palms itching as sweat broke out on them. She glanced back at the two men on the ground about three or so stories below. Roland spun around and back, defying gravity as he landed a roundhouse kick to Christos's solar plexus. Christos grunted, grabbing onto the foot as he started to fall backward and twisted it sharply. An obscene snap echoed through the cavern.

Ah, hell.

Gabriella crouched, braced, and then leapt. Darkness embraced her, easing her down onto the ground. She hissed, annoyed at being slowed down. Didn't the fool know she could jump five times that distance without real harm?

The moment the dark cloud dissipated she was running toward the two men rolling upon the floor. Christos was going to die. Here. Now. Today. By her hand.

Christos managed to scramble up from the fray, one hand dangling uselessly from a half-severed wrist. His gaze lifted, then met hers. A smile curled back his lips.

<<*Gabby, how nice for you to join us.*>>

His mind voice slashed into her senses. She smashed to her knees onto the hard ground as she fought the man who tried to sink his claws into her will.

No. Not going to happen.

With an enraged scream she pushed back, ripping him from her mind. It tore, carving out a chunk of herself as she did. Needed to go. Like blight on a tree, this bond between master and slave *had to end*.

Searing lightning. A brilliant flash of white. And then it was gone.

She tried to lift her head but couldn't. The world was a black hole of pain.

You are not going to pass out, Gabby.

Her entire body shook as she wobbled on her knees. Her heart skittered from one rhythm to the next as if it were a drummer on crack.

Then hands were there, clasping onto her shoulders and holding her steady. "Easy there, cookie."

She snapped her head up, baring her fangs. The movement sent a blinding slash of agony through the base of her skull, but when it started to recede, so did the dark tunnel vision. She couldn't decide if the sight of the naked Paladin before her, smiling with his devil-may-care attitude, was welcome or not. She was just glad the extreme weakness was starting to dissipate.

She jerked her shoulders, trying to scramble up. He held firm.

"Let go. I have to help Roland with Christos!"

"I think he's got it under control." Valin stood, linking his arm around her back and helping her up.

Roland stood panting over Christos, eyes red as he stared down at the gaping hole in the vampire's chest. A few yards away Christos's head lay on the ground, the eyes unblinking and dimmed with death.

Gabriella's mouth turned down at the corners, disappointment lying like lead in her chest. "Rats."

"What?" Valin asked.

"I wanted to do that."

A hand came up, tucking a sweaty tendril behind her ear. "You fought your own fight with him and won."

"Did I?" She frowned down at Christos's shell. Had she won her internal battle before or after Roland had lopped off the vampire's head?

She might have asked but just then Roland shook himself and spun around, racing to the back corner of the cavern. He skidded to his knees, lifting something off the floor to cradle it in his arms.

Curls.

"By the Father." Valin all but dropped Gabriella as he raced across the room. Gabriella remained where she was, swaying as she stared at the dark pool of blood that the woman had been laying in. Dying. Or dead. No. Not dead. She wouldn't have felt the connection if the woman were dead. But she'd obviously knocked and had one foot through death's door.

"Why haven't you converted her?" Gabriella screamed as she stumbled after Valin.

Roland reverently bent down, kissing her pale forehead. "She would not want to live like this. I cannot take her light."

A sick wedge lodged deep in Gabriella's gut. If the woman died, Roland would be lost. If Roland were lost then so would she be. It was his defiance that inspired her. The belief that enough of his blood had made it into her to counteract the double whammy of her mother's genetics and her vampire nature. It didn't matter that Christos was dead; if anything that was just a score on the game board for evil. Without Roland to look up to, without Christos to pin all her hatred on? She'd fall. She knew she would.

Squaring her shoulders, she brushed by Valin who'd stopped and was staring like a shell-shocked idiot down at the dying woman. "You fool. Either you do it, or I will."

Roland twisted his head around, his face mottled into a look of inhuman emotion as he bared his teeth at her. "I won't turn her into what we are. I won't turn her into something evil."

Gabriella jerked back as if slapped. Roland's well-placed thrust to her heart was greater than anything Christos could ever have inflicted. "Am I evil? Are you? Truly? Are we?"

A hand slipped into the crook of her elbow, pulling her away from Roland and into the solid weight of a man's steadfastness. "Listen to her, Roland. Don't let another Paladin die."

"Isn't this," Roland gestured at himself, "another sort of death for a Paladin?"

Valin's jaw set, but his gaze was accepting as he reached out and clasped Roland on the shoulder. "I may not like you, but you will always be my brother."

Gabriella sucked in her breath, watching the filmstrip of emotions flash across Roland's face.

Valin's hand tightened, giving Roland a shake. "Do it."

Roland looked from Valin back to Karissa. Gabriella gnawed her lip, holding on to her breath. He had to do it. She wasn't sure how she knew, but she did: They both needed this woman.

With a growl, Roland lowered the woman back to her bed of blood. In a movement too quick for the eye, he reopened a scabbed wound on his wrist and pressed it to Karissa's lips.

Gabriella watched, waiting for the slack lips to tremble, the throat to bob, for the teeth to grasp on. Nothing.

"Karissa…" Roland pleaded, stroking her throat.

Alarmed, Gabriella shook off Valin's grip and moved to flank him. Maybe the woman was too far under? She pressed her finger against the pale throat, her gut sinking as she waited one second, two, three…No pulse.

Chapter 25

KARISSA! HER NAME WAS A HOWLING SCREAM OF AGONY, a soul-piercing cry of grief. Her soul answered, tried to reach out, tried to soothe. And couldn't. She was in the abyss and falling.

She didn't want to die. Didn't want to leave Roland. God. She cried out, tried to grasp onto something, anything. But there was no lifeline here.

Something slid past her lips. Her mouth filled with something hot and sweet and slick, adding to the drowning sensation. A coaxing word. A plea. She swallowed.

The world came alive.

With a gasp, her eyes flew open. "Roland?" She choked on the thick liquid pooling in her throat and turned her head. Roland hushed her, pulling her up against his chest. She tried to grasp his shirt but failed. "Why? Told you. Trap. Shouldn't 've come."

"Because I love you." He pushed back her hair. "Forgive me."

Forgive him? For what? She was about to ask when pain hit her like a fist in the gut. No, not a fist, a fireball. She burned.

Roland ran, cradling Karissa through the agonizing burn of her blood, anchoring her through the shredding of her being. Her pain was his pain. He could only hope that his guilt—like a knife in his gut—didn't feedback to her. What had he done? Had he saved her only to kill her?

"The damn stone walls. I can't reach Logan." Valin's cursed words were a reminder that even now he might not have saved her. There was only so long Logan could stall. The moment he and the other Paladin entered the cave and came across the army Ganelon had prepared would be the moment Elder Calhoun would demand his son release the full power of his gift. Even Logan knew that the loss of his friend, a vampire, was far outweighed by the deaths of a hundred vampires.

But it was not worth Karissa's life. Or the life of the brave young woman who'd helped Valin find them. He glanced sideways at Gabriella, who ran beside him, her face contorted in worry as she watched Karissa writhe in his arms. With each of Karissa's agonizing moans, with each spiked gasp, the redheaded vampire flinched. As if she felt it too. Why?

"And you can't, what was it you called it? Cloak us?" Gabby asked, her question directed to Valin's back as he ran before them. He'd chosen to remain in human form a while in hopes of reaching through the thick stone walls to contact Logan. So far, no luck.

"I can't cover all three of you. One for sure, maybe two. Not three."

Roland doubted the Paladin could even do two, at least not with any sort of assurance. All it took was one small hole, one thin area, and Logan's light would burn through. "Our only chance is getting topside so Valin can let Logan know and he can give us time to get away."

Gabriella skidded to a stop. Roland almost tripped

trying to keep up with the abrupt movement. "Gabby, what's wrong?"

Valin spun around, his eyes widening in alarm when he saw they'd all stopped. "What are you doing? We have to get out of here, now!"

She shook her head, starting back down the path behind her. "I'm fast. I might be able to go deep enough, find a spot to hide."

"Gabriella..." Roland took a step forward, heart torn in two directions. He always knew she was a brave girl, but he didn't want her to sacrifice herself. Not for him, at least. Karissa, yes, but not him. His mouth firmed. "Valin, take Karissa."

Valin ignored him, he was too busy bearing down on Gabriella, his face hardened into cold fury, as if he would grab her, toss her over his shoulder, and spank her like he would a recalcitrant child. "I already told you that wasn't possible."

"You said you can shield two." And with that Gabby spun around, running back into the cave.

—∿∿∿—

Valin roared, his body vibrating as he stared back down the tunnel through which the girl had fled. What was the stupid chit thinking? He took a step downward and stopped, belatedly remembering that smacking some sense into the girl was not his only concern here.

He turned back around, his shoulders sagging a bit as he looked at Roland and the female shuddering in his arms. In his defense, Roland looked as pissed as he did.

"Does she do this sort of foolish crap often?" He tried for the joke, forcing himself to turn back up the tunnel.

Roland's hand shot out, grabbing him and forcing him to stop. "What?" he asked.

"Go after her. You can't reach Logan from down here anyway."

"And you two?" Valin shook his head. "My loyalty does not lie with some foolish vampire child who doesn't listen to reason."

But it did. For some asinine reason it did. Maybe it was seeing her up in that dilapidated warehouse, a cloud-break away from extinction, yet possessing the bravery to try and send him after Roland and the woman rather than trying to bargain for her life.

"Once Karissa and I reach the surface, I'll make sure Logan sees us. He'll do what he can to hold them off while we get away."

"And what if Logan is already in the tunnels?"

"If he was already in the tunnels, we'd hear the fighting, or we'd be fried crisp by now."

Valin wavered, his body leaning forward then back as his loyalties tore at him. One girl. A vampire at that. He shook Roland's grip off, then started forward. He needed to get Roland and Karissa safely to the surface so that Logan would know to call the retreat.

A growl rumbled deep in his throat and he spun back around. Two steps and he faced Roland again. "This doesn't mean I like you." Then clasping his hand around the vampire's head, Valin pulled Roland's forehead to his. "Welcome back, brother. Now hurry, because I'm going to be really pissed if I come out of here and you're not around to settle the debts you've piled up here."

"Understood."

—⁓—

"Roland?" Karissa stirred in his arms, her sweet voice like a rainbow of light in this world of darkness. Her shuddering had stopped a few minutes before and he had hope that she'd come around soon. He hadn't known how hard it would hit him though. She was alive. Because he'd turned her. Would she forgive him when she realized what he'd done?

He tipped his head down, brushing a kiss over her forehead and soaking up her scent. Still flowery, with a soft hint of musk that was all Karissa. His pulse accelerated, blood pumping to regions that were not needed for running, while in the vaults of his mind his primal beast screamed out: *Mine!*

How could so much be the same, while so much had changed?

"Roland. Something's different. I feel strange." Her fingers dug into his chest, her panic evident in her voice.

"Hush, love. We're almost there." He didn't tell her that as soon as they were, they'd have to run again. Two vampires would never be accepted by the men he once called brothers. Valin and Logan were the anomalies in that equation. And Roland knew that when he converted her. And condemned her.

Later. He'd worry about that later. When he had her far away from here. Someplace safe. Then he'd tell her. And if it would make it better, he'd even offer his knife to her and let her end the life of the monster who'd turned her. He cried at the thought of losing her so finitely. With no soul he would never see her again. But if it would ease her pain—a pain he'd caused when he'd let his selfish monster rule him—then he'd help her drive the knife home to his treacherous heart.

A shift in the air, a slight brightening of the near blackness. They were close. First get them out of here. Contact Logan. Then run like hell to safety. He just prayed that the cloud cover held.

He pushed himself harder, knowing every second counted. Every instant. But the moment he rounded the last bend he knew he was wrong. They hadn't heard the fighting because it wasn't in the tunnels, it was outside. The moment he crested the rising floor and caught sight of the violent battle creating those noises, his heart sunk even further.

Holy fuck. How was he ever going to find Logan in all of this?

—∿∿—

Logan roared, slicing into another merker and sending a pulse of light inside it. He had purposely separated himself from his father and was ignoring the ever-increasing brutality of the slaps on his mind. He'd close the trigger-happy bastard completely off if he could do it without closing himself from any possible communications from Valin.

"Come on, Valin. What is taking you so long?" he asked of the air and jumped a bit when the Paladin fighting beside him answered.

"He might be dead."

Alexander's answer to the rhetorical question was not appreciated. If Valin was dead, then none of the sacrifices they were making up here were worth it. More than one Paladin was wounded. The moment one went down for good it was all over. Logan would have to release the bomb. He'd sacrifice everything of himself for Roland, but he would not ask that sacrifice of another brother.

Merker down, Logan spun about and sunk his blade into the back of the vampire that Alexander had been fighting. His aim was true and the blade sunk into the heart. No need for light with this one; a direct hit to the heart with a Paladin blade was akin to staking the creature with blessed wood.

"Thanks."

"You're slipping, Alexander," he said, wiping away the sweat and drizzle from his face.

"Nah. Just thought I'd let you have some fun too. Besides, I'm a demon man, myself."

"You're too kind."

Alexander's grin faded. "Uh-oh. Here he comes."

Logan spun around to see his father advancing down on him, his own knife coated in blood and fury etched into his face. "Why haven't you released the light? Are you trying to kill your brothers?"

Logan's jaw ticked. "I'm trying to *save* my brother."

His father came to a halt before him with a huff, tossing an annoyed glance at the newest enemy that charged at them. But Alexander was there and moved to intercept, allowing the elder—thanks for nothing, Alex—to focus his ire on his son. "Roland is no longer your brother. The only thing that matters now is saving the others. If you won't do it for them, do it for your sister."

"Why do you think I'm holding off? It is for my sister, you fool. She is bonded and mated to Roland. If I call the light and kill him, it will be akin to killing her."

His father gave a sharp shake of his head. "She cannot be bonded to that...thing."

"She is. I swear it on my Paladin soul."

Calhoun Senior's mouth worked, his irritation palpable in the air between them. "Roland has no soul."

"I don't believe that."

"You. And how many centuries have you lived? How many true bonds have you seen? Three centuries? A half-dozen bonds maybe? Most of those when you were still a youngling? I've been here for over a millennium. I've seen hundreds. I will give you that it's possible he could have been her mate, but what they have now is but an echo of what could have been. It's not true."

Logan shook his head.

"Look around, Logan. Are you willing to risk the lives of twelve Paladin on one man's misplaced belief?"

Logan raised his gaze past his father. In general the Paladin were holding their own. If they could just keep this up a few more minutes it would give Roland a fighting chance—

Just then there was a loud blast. A shape, formed of shadow and evil, rose from out of the depths of the mine, reforming into a towering mass of claws and fangs and chiseled hooves. Demon. Master demon.

"Oh, crap." Time had just run out.

Chapter 26

ROLAND STUMBLED AS THE MUDDY GROUND SHOOK beneath his feet. His senses were screaming in a way they hadn't in ninety-four years.

"Roland? What's wrong?" Karissa gripped his arm, her body trembling from the after-effects of the change. He wasn't sure how much of that was true weakness, and how much was the sensory cocktail of her new abilities. The smells, the increased vision, the pulse of life around them. He knew what she felt. Knew that it called to her, making her hungry. He had to get her away from here and to someplace where he could help her deal with her new instincts.

"Nothing. Just a weird feeling."

He started forward again, picking up speed as Karissa was able to keep up. They were trying to skirt the outer edges of the battle and slip behind the ridge that the Paladin had taken their high ground on. He'd given up on finding Logan, but he didn't dare start leaping around until they were past the danger zone. There was at least one Paladin out there with a rifle picking off the vamps doing aerobatic tricks.

A vast roar rose above the clashing sounds of the battle just as another hit to his senses slapped Roland in the back of his skull. He stumbled forward, his arm shooting out to smack into the ground just as the vision overtook him.

Logan stared into his father's firm gaze, then back to the vile monster that had risen out of the mouth of the tunnel. A creature of shadow and evil possibilities brought here from Lucifer's realm to form into a creature of chaos and suffering. Off to the side Alexander was already holding back a merker, but like all his brothers, his mouth had now begun to move in an endless chant that would be their only defense against the master demon that had been thrown into the middle of the fray.

Logan's eyes closed, his hands fisting. "I hope to hell you're cloaking him, Valin."

Then he opened his eyes, lifting his arms up toward the heavens, and called down the light.

"Roland!" Karissa screamed.

Roland's eyes snapped open. He was lying on his back looking up into Karissa's pale face. Her eyes were wide, her brow knit with fear as she glanced from him toward the battle raging to the north of them. He turned his head. Everything was in slow motion, the demon hanging in midair as it smashed up against the Paladin's line of defense, the low roar of violent death. This was it. His vision. What he'd seen was an instant away.

And Karissa was out in the open.

With a roar he leapt up, tackling Karissa and taking her to the ground. She screamed in alarm, her cry muffled against his chest as he tried to gather up all her arms and legs and tuck them firmly under himself. He couldn't cloak her in darkness, but perhaps his body would last long enough to shield her. Please, God. Please.

The burn hit him at the same moment that light blazed in the sky. He closed his eyes, squeezing out the moisture as he tucked his head closer, kissing the soft curls of Karissa's hair. So sweet. So soft. So perfect. If this was his last thought, his last sensation, his last moment, he was glad that it was with her. *My heart, my body, for you. I love you.*

Roland…She wiggled beneath him.

Ah, Gawd. Even now, even while he burned to death above her, he wanted her.

Only he wasn't burning. The burn had turned into a radiant warmth that seeped into his body, spreading out through his limbs.

"Roland. Let me up."

He shook his head, squeezing her tighter underneath him. He didn't understand why he wasn't dead yet, but it would only be a matter of time. As a master vampire he was strong, but not enough to resist the light of heaven.

"Roland! Open your eyes."

Hands clasped onto the side of his face. Alarmed that she'd managed to free her arms enough to expose herself thusly, his lids snapped open. Karissa smiled up at him, her pretty, bowed lips curved up enough to reveal her pointy little fangs. Damn they were sexy. He wanted her to bite him. Mark him. Claim him.

He shook his head, tossing away those thoughts. Strange what he chose to focus on when he was dying.

"You're not dying, silly." She jerked her head toward the battlefield. "But they are."

He looked over the valley and saw the charred remains as they floated to the ground. At the same time the unnatural light dissipated, only so did the clouds, leaving the valley bathed in sunlight.

And still he didn't burn.

His eyes flashed to Karissa. She still smiled.
Completely unharmed by the rays of the sun. "How?"

He shook his head. Didn't matter how. Somehow he
was alive and so was Karissa. But though Christos's
vampires were dead and Lucifer's demons similarly
banished, there were still a couple dozen merkers to
contend with. And if there was one thing Roland had
always been good at, it was dismembering a merker.
And with Karissa's ability to transport their vulnerable remains into His light? Well, they now made the
perfect team.

"Come on. I think the others could use our help."

Karissa scrambled up the mountainside beside Roland,
cursing her weakness. Being turned into a vampire may
have given her body the ability to heal enough to function, but it did nothing to alleviate the pure exhaustion
that the trauma of the last twelve hours had rendered.

She stumbled another few feet, tripping over both
root and brush. Only Roland's firm grip on her waist
kept her upright and running. She'd tell him to go on
without her, except for the fact that she never wanted
to do without him again. Nope, she'd already made that
mistake once. From now on they were joined at the hip.
Well, not literally. She had insisted he put her down
when it became apparent that he too was tiring from
the whole ordeal. A decision she was regretting now
with her bare feet and only his thin T-shirt to cover her
against the branches and twigs that grabbed at her.

"Where are we going?" she demanded when her knee
tried to buckle out from under her.

He glanced over his shoulder at her, then pulled her in tighter. "Let me carry you."

"No. I just want to know where we are going."

"Top of the ridge. The Paladin are good, but there were a couple dozen merkers who will have survived Logan's little bomb."

"Why are we running?"

"Don't want to let them have all the fun."

She planted her feet, forcing him to stop. "No. I mean why are we running? Why not jump?"

"Because there's also a trigger-happy Paladin with a rifle. No offense, I don't like healing large caliber holes through my head. That shit can really fuck with your mind."

She rolled her eyes. "You're not hearing me. I can see the edge of the cliff over there, so I can jump us to it. That can't be far from the ridge."

His eyes widened. He smiled. Then his mouth was descending onto hers. She hardly had time to acclimate to the heady taste of his tongue as it pierced and plundered her mouth and the throb of their simultaneous heartbeats, before he was pulling away. "You're brilliant."

She winked. "Just keep that thought in mind and we'll never have a fight as long as we live. Which, I've been told, could be a long, long while."

He laughed, grabbing onto her hand. "Let's go, *mon chaton*."

She turned her attention to the cliff, concentrating on setting her will on a spot that was just a touch back from the ledge, though slightly above. They'd fall when they came out of the netherplanes, but it would be only a couple of feet, and far better than finding themselves encased in granite rock.

When she was sure she had a bead on the extraction location, she pulled them both into the netherplane, brilliant light flashing as they traveled the couple hundred yards in an instant. They hit the end and popped back out, falling with a grunt and thud to the ground.

She started to turn around to see where they were, but Roland quickly grabbed her up, pulling her into a nearby set of bushes.

"What?" She tried to crane her head around. "What is it?"

"Crap, Logan. Can't you stay out of trouble when I'm not around?"

Roland set her down carefully, his hand reaching down to the wicked looking knife strapped onto his thigh. She followed his gaze to where he was looking and gasped when she saw that Logan wasn't more than a dozen yards away, struggling with two imposing looking men who she guessed were merkers. As she watched, the fight drew close enough to hear the heavy panting of the creatures and the undertone of Paladin swearing.

"Stay here," Roland commanded, then dove into the fray, his knife carving chunks out of the merker who'd been lunging toward Logan's back.

Karissa couldn't keep up with the movements and found her gaze pulled to another battle going on a few yards away. The red-haired giant she'd met back at the hall—heck if she couldn't remember his name—was back-to-back with a man who looked alarmingly like Logan. They were both muttering some strange sort of chant, their blades flashing a defensive pattern against the clawed attack of a blackened demon that had some-how managed to survive the blazing light of a few minutes before.

She forced her attention back to Roland and Logan. She couldn't do much, other than maybe bare her fangs and bite one of the two merkers. But she could be ready to distract if needed.

Good thing it wasn't needed. The two men had obvi-ously worked together in the past. They didn't rely on standing back-to-back, but the merry dance they led the two merkers on as they played with their prey was impres-sive to watch. They taunted, they parried, each swipe of their deadly knives wearing their opponents down, rais-ing their frustration levels, and inviting them to make a mistake. It happened fast. A merker lunged at Logan as Roland swiped the head off the second merker he'd just spun behind. Logan's knife pierced into the first merker's chest cavity. The creature screamed as fire pulsed down Logan's blade as he focused his gift into the knife. Then Roland was there, ignoring the blind stumbling of the other merker as he sank his hand into the creature's hair, pulled its head back, then sliced through its neck.

"Thanks." Logan yanked his knife from the creature's heart and plugged it into the eye socket of the skull Roland held.

"This clears up our scoreboard again. All debts are paid," Roland said, then casually reached out to grab the fumbling body of the second merker and tossed it to the ground. She watched as Roland placed his foot on the merker's chest, but she had to turn her head away when it became obvious he planned to carve the creature's heart from its chest.

She looked back at the red-haired Paladin and the Logan look-alike to see how they were faring. The demon was gone and they were both bent over, arms resting on their knees as they tried to catch their breath. She'd seen that man before. Where? The other man in the study at Haven?

His head lifted, his gaze locking onto hers. She didn't know why, but her heart started hammering in double-time.

The man pushed up. "Logan, take care of that other merker. Alexander." The man made a cutting motion at Roland.

Karissa sucked in a breath, watching as the giant red-haired Paladin straightened, took a step forward, then halted, lowering his knife.

"What are you doing?" the man demanded, his anger obvious that the red giant would disobey him.

"Karissa, I believe you've already met Elder Calhoun." Roland came up behind her, leaning down to whisper the next bit close to her ear. "He has a thing against vampires."

"Is that so?" She bared her fangs at the man who she was now sure had reamed Logan out in the study. "I guess that means he won't be interested in pairing me off anymore."

The man's eyes widened, the blood draining from his face. His nostrils pinched as he snapped his gaze to Roland. "What have you done to my daughter, you bastard!"

Her eyes flew back to Roland, shock causing her vision to blur for a moment.

"Oh yeah. And he's your father. Though he never told anyone. Not even Logan."

Holy crap. A flash of light in the corner of her eye told her that the man was stalking toward them, knife in hand. She hissed, placing herself between Roland and her...nope, she couldn't even think it. A real father wouldn't have abandoned her the moment she was born. A real father wouldn't have clinically talked about pairing her off. "You stay away from us."

The man hesitated, his face inhumanly cold as he stared at her. No, not cold. Disappointed. Well, too bad. That made two of them.

His grip firmed on his knife, his face set into lines of determination as he started forward once more. Roland sucked in a breath, one arm reaching in front of her in an attempt to put her behind him again.

"Stop that," she snapped. "What's he going to do? Drive that knife through me to get to you?"

Then Logan was there, stepping between his father and them both. "Not unless he plans to go through me first."

"Get out of the way, fool."

"Why? So you can kill her like you did her mother?" Karissa gasped, her hand flying to her mouth.

The man's eyes flitted to her then narrowed back on Logan. "Her mother died the moment she was bitten. As now has my daughter."

"That's my sister you're talking about, old man. I've been a sucky brother until now, but I'm going to make up for it. You're not to harm her. Or her bond mate."

"They can't be bond mates. They have no souls."

Karissa shook her head, old wounds and new wounds spreading out and melding together. In an instant, she was made an orphan—again.

"Uh, hate to interrupt this riveting family reunion, but—"

They all looked to where Alexander was pointing at the decapitated body crawling across the forest floor toward its blinking head.

Roland grunted, stepping away from Karissa to grab up the head by the hair, the creature's heart still beating in his other hand. "Can you send these to His realm?" he asked, holding them out to her.

She recoiled from the sight of them. "I don't know what you're talking about."

"The place of light."

She looked up at Roland's face. "That's His realm?"

The corner of his mouth quirked up. "Where did you think you were going, *mon chaton*?"

"I had no idea. I called it the netherplane."

He shook his head. "Doesn't matter. The important thing is that the light of that realm will burn away the presence of pure evil. Can you either send this there or bring them there and come back?"

She looked down at the bloody heart and the dangling head he was holding out to her. "I'm not touching those things."

"How about you bring me there, then. Works either way."

"As long as I don't have to touch them." She stepped forward, laying her hands on his upper arms, but pointedly keeping a large amount of space between them. She didn't want to accidently touch his bloody trophies either. Then she concentrated, shifting her being and everything she touched into that "other" place which was here and nowhere at the same time. The moment they passed through the line of here and now and there, the heart started shriveling in Roland's hand, and then the head. She shuddered. Sparks popped within the skull, the bright white light of…His…planes burning the brain out through the eye sockets.

"Good enough," Roland prompted when the skull stopped sizzling.

With a nod, she popped them out of the plane and back to the same place they'd been before. It took a moment for her eyes to adjust to the dimmer light, but when she did, it was to find Logan smiling and Elder Calhoun standing mouth agape as he stared at the empty skull and the ashes in Roland's hand where the heart had once been.

"You can get rid of those now," she told Roland.

With a shrug, he turned his hand over, ashes spilling onto the ground. The skull he tossed over at her father's feet, the empty eye sockets staring up at the stubborn Elder.

"Isn't that interesting?" Alexander asked, folding his arms across his chest. "Correct me if I'm wrong, Elder, but doesn't that prove that both Roland and Karissa here can't be evil?"

Karissa slid her arms around Roland. "Of course Roland's not evil. He's my soul mate."

―⁓―

"I think that's the last of them." Roland brushed the ashes off his hands, tossing the merker's empty skull onto the pile of others. It thunked up against another, making a sound reminiscent of a hollow drum. Karissa visibly shuddered.

"Thank God." She gestured at the pile. "I mean, can I just say *eww*? That's just gross, really gross."

Roland smiled, shaking his head. "I adore you."

"Good." She stepped up into him, linking her arms around his back. "Because you're stuck with me. Especially now. And just so you know, there will be no biting of necks other than each other's."

Biting necks. He was hit by yet another pang of guilt, the one of many that he'd been having since the moment he'd sunk his teeth into her down in that cavern. She seemed to be taking it all in stride but he wondered how long it would be before the full import would hit her. He only hoped she'd still want him when it did.

He squeezed her tighter. "I'm sorry, Karissa. I never would have turned you, I just couldn't…"

She squirmed, freeing an arm so she could place her finger over his mouth. "Hush. You did what you had to. And I for one am glad. I'm not sure my soul would have survived waiting an eternity for you to join me."

"But it would have been an eternity in heaven."

"You big fool. You are my heaven." She snuggled in closer, her sweet scent drifting into his senses and turning him hard. "Why else do you think He made sure I found my way to you?"

Maybe she was right. But damn, he couldn't help feeling that he'd stolen something from her.

Karissa pulled back, her eyes narrowed as she grabbed onto his hand, placing it over her heart. "Can't you feel it, Roland? It beats for you."

She took the same hand, slid it down her front until the heel of his hand was settled over the pulsing heat of her core. He sucked in a sharp breath, his cock throbbing in rhythm against his leather pants.

"And this," she rubbed his hand over her mons, a soft moan parting her lips, "this throbs for you."

Holy fuck, she was killing him. "Oh yes, *mon petite peste*, I can feel that. And if you don't stop doing that, I'm going to conveniently forget we're less than a dozen yards from both your father and your brother."

She smiled. Her small hand slid around his, linking through his fingers as she pulled it behind her back, jerking him as close as humanly possible.

"And this…"

He felt the caress on his mind, the slight shift as he was pulled with her to the edges of His realm. The blinding white light was as stunning as always, but all he felt was a sense of ease.

"Why would He allow us this, if not to show that within us both lies a soul in His keeping?"

"Do you really believe that?"

"Of course I believe that. I believed it before." She lifted their linked hands up, kissing his knuckles as she dropped them back into the real world. "The sunlight might be a miracle, but His place is truth. And the truth is, even when you feared you'd fallen, you were still welcome there. Remember your loft? The first time we met?"

He did. Now that she brought it up, he recalled that first time she dragged him through the other plane. He'd been terrified and shocked that he'd survived breaching a barrier he'd thought off limits to the likes of him. Yet, he'd come out whole at the other end.

"It's about time you showed up. I was about to send a search party in for your body!"

Logan's voice brought Roland out of his ponderings.

He twisted Karissa around, his gaze honing in on the Paladin who had re-formed on the edge of the ridge.

"Huh. I think I'm starting to get used to that," Karissa said.

"What?" Roland asked, studying the taut pull of the skin around the Paladin's nose and mouth. His pulse accelerated, not liking what the seriousness of the look suggested.

"Valin. Poofing out of the air like that." She bit her lip, gnawing on the plump flesh. "And really, he's not half bad to look at naked."

He blinked down at her, a bit taken aback by her laid-back attitude until he remembered that she wasn't aware enough back in the tunnel to remember who Valin had chased after.

"What the heck?" Valin exclaimed.

Roland looked back up to find the Paladin staring at him and Karissa, shocked.

"Remember that vision Roland's dad had?" Logan asked, dragging his T-shirt off to hand it to Valin.

Valin nodded, then took the T-shirt and pulled it over his head all the while keeping his incredulous gaze on the pair of vampires "lounging" in the sun.

"Seems Roland's dad was right," Logan explained. "Karissa is the child of light. Literally. One sip of her blood and presto. A vamp can stand the light of day. Though not His light. Suckers still fry in that." Logan's gaze turned back to Roland and Karissa. "Unless they have enough of a soul left to still be His, I guess."

"Gabriella?" Roland asked.

"I couldn't find her, and then the light…" Valin's gaze drifted back to the entrance to the mines.

Roland's heart howled. It shouldn't hurt this bad, the

kid had been more annoying than anything else. But damn, she'd been plucky. And over the years he'd come to think of her as his.

Karissa squeezed his hand, offering comfort. "I'm sorry, Roland."

Valin looked back at them, down at their linked hands. His head snapped back up. "She drank Karissa's blood. So she *could* be alive, right?"

Roland sucked in a sharp breath. Gabriella had taken Karissa's vein? Impossible. The girl would rather die than give in to her nature. "Gabby did what?"

"I found her chained up in one of the warehouses. There was an IV bag next to her. She said she could find Karissa and the indication was that she'd been given some of Karissa's blood."

The tightness in Roland's chest eased. He squeezed Karissa closer into his side. "Then she's okay. The light won't hurt her now." Because of Karissa. Another gift. Another miracle. And another affirmation that Ganelon and Christos had had no idea what his father's vision had actually meant. He tipped his head down and brushed his lips against her temple. "Thank you."

Karissa turned her face up, her lips pulled in the most delectable pout. "Is that the best you can do?"

"No. Not nearly." He leaned down and took her mouth, kissing her with everything he had to give: his body, heart, and soul.

Coming Soon…

Book Two in the Paladin Warriors Series

LOGAN'S AND ALEXANDER'S BOOTED FEET THUNDERED down the littered sidewalk as they worked to catch up with the distant figure stumbling along on four-inch heels.

She was good. Or rather *it* was good. Three times the succubus had slipped through their net, starting the chase all over again. It had taken him a while to figure it out, not being familiar with all the side streets in this seedy part of town, but Logan had come to realize something over the last two blocks: they were being led in one very big, very maze-like circle.

She's playing with us. Or this is a trap.

Flashing his hand up in the universal symbol for stop, Logan eased into the shadows of a basement apartment stairwell. Alexander followed, eerily soundless as he shifted into stealth mode.

"What's up?" Alex asked, voicing his confusion in a hushed whisper.

"Hold on. I'm going to try and contact Valin." He closed his eyes, centering himself and reached out on the other plane. Calling Valin when the Paladin was ghosting was never easy and rarely fruitful, but sometimes if he did it just right, a light caress across the other plane… <<*Valin?*>>

<<*You guys all tuckered out?*>>

Valin's voice, clear as a bell, had Logan jerking his head back into the rusted iron railing that flanked the stairs leading up to the first level. He rubbed the already sore lump, silently cursing the other Paladin.

Deciding his injury was nothing more than hurt pride, Logan got to the point. <<*What is the succubus doing?*>>

<<*Not sure. When you guys backed off, she ducked into an abandoned building. I'm perched on the roof, covering the exits.*>>

Logan figured the minx would do something like that. This proved that she was playing them. If she'd really wanted to get away, she would've bolted at the first opportunity. The question now was how far she was willing to take their little game. And whether they could turn the tables somehow.

<<*I want you to draw back. I think she's sensing you.*>>

<<*Really...*>>

Logan could feel the doubt in Valin's thought. Understandable. When Valin was doing his ghost thing, no one knew he was there. He was invisible to any sort of mind-gifts, undetectable to any paranormal creature's nose, and unseen by even the most keen-sighted vampires. Yet each time Valin had drawn near she'd bolted. Once or twice could be coincidence, but three times?

<<*I have a theory I want to test. Draw back a few blocks and wait for my signal to join in. Alexander and I are going to do a little bait and hook.*>>

He felt Valin's internal shrug, <<*Your skin,*>> then he was gone, ghosting again.

Logan turned to Alex, who had an expectant look on his face. "Valin is going to drop back and then you and

I are going to split up. Not far, just enough to give her a chance."

"A chance to what?"

"To come after one of us."

Alexander scoffed, shaking his head. "You think she'd be that stupid?"

"Not really, no. But she's not acting normal. I think she has an ulterior motive here."

"Like what?"

"I'm not sure, but she certainly seems to be trying to lead us somewhere."

"And you want to try and lead her?"

"Exactly." Logan jerked his head toward the sidewalk. "Two blocks down parallel streets. Then we'll meet back up."

Logan took off.

He had just passed the first major intersection and was creeping up on the next when he heard the sound of a scuffle. Swearing, he bolted toward the side street, following the source of the disturbance. Muscles burning, he rounded the corner just in time to see the spandex-clad backside of their succubus take off down a side street.

Alex was crouched against the brick wall of another apartment building. He jerked his head in the direction the succubus had fled. "Go. I'll be…right…behind you. Just need to…get my breath."

Logan squinted down at the bent-over warrior. Alex's skin favored the color of a freshly peeled cucumber and he was still making gasping, hissing noises through his clenched teeth, but there was no blood. Nope, the only thing that seemed to be wrong with the big guy—based on the awkward vertical fetal position of his body and protective cup of his hands—was some injured pride.

Guess it was going around tonight.

"Catch up when you can."

With a grunt from Alex, which Logan took as assent, Logan went after the creature. As soon as Logan rounded the corner and bolted into the side street their little minx had ducked into, he was greeted with an expected sight. The narrow street was empty.

He took a tentative step forward. A whisper of sound had him twisting, but not before a blast of pain erupted across the back of his head, his brain flaring with light as someone—no, something—stabbed into his mind.

Logan slammed up a barrier of mental shields, but they did nothing to counteract the effects of the first, unexpected attack. His ears rang. And when he blinked it was to the sight of his hands gripping the gritty pavement. Talk about bringing him low. The succubus, or someone with her, was proficient with mind-gifts.

Not cool.

When the pain finally subsided enough for Logan to lift his head, he was alone in the alley. Which meant she was out there. With Alexander. And Valin was incommunicado.

<<God damn it, Valin. Where the hell are you?>>

Logan pushed himself to his feet, stumbling around the corner. Ahead of him, illuminated by a lone streetlamp, Alexander struggled with the succubus. Not even half the size of him, the little minx was putting up an awesome fight, her small fists landing faster than humanly possible, each one eliciting a grunt from the large warrior. Then all of a sudden she stopped fighting, her well-aimed punches turning to floppy hand slaps, her silent efforts of escape broken by small whimpers of fear and pain.

WTF?

Alex doubled over, allowing the succubus to bolt again.

Shit, shit, shit. This bitch was too damn good. No way was she just a succubus. Not with her ability to take down Alexander. Not with her ability to stab into Logan's mind.

With a push of speed, Logan roared, his sights zeroing in on the succubus as she whimpered and scrambled up the street.

He had no idea what happened next. One second he was sprinting down the sidewalk and the next, he tripped. His hands flew out, absorbing the worst of the fall, but not enough to stop the umph of pain as he smashed into the unforgiving pavement.

Tonight was really not his night. What had he tripped on? His own feet?

"Hey, asshole. Why don't you pick on someone your own size?" A woman's voice lashed out.

Nope. Not his feet. Goddammit. He did not want to have to deal with a Good Samaritan civvy right now.

He rolled over, ready to spin a story, and came face to nozzle against a can of pepper spray. Better than a gun, he supposed. Still, one little squeeze and he'd be worse than useless for the foreseeable future. And given the trembling state of the hand that was holding the bottle…

He lifted his gaze, following the trembling hand up the shaking arm to the shivering halo of blond curls that framed the most stunning set of wide blue eyes.

Angel.

Startled by the force of the thought, he shook it away. Pretty, yes. An angel…no. More like an inconvenient pain in his ass.

He took a deep breath, closing his eyes and drawing in a deep breath. Why, oh why, couldn't he catch a break tonight?

～～～

Rachael stumbled back holding her can of pepper spray out like a gun as the man slowly and silently stood, brushing his black leather pants off as he looked her over. His eyes singed her like hot pokers of flame as they traced every inch of what her mom would have called a power suit. His perusal, executed with a disdainful twist of his lip, was probably meant to send her scurrying away, but that's not the effect it had on her. All of a sudden and inexplicably, she felt naked. Her clothing completely stripped away. The power suit that had faced down numerous power-hungry board members and allowed her to steamroll over more than one grumpy old know-it-all charity organizer, felt less like armor and more like a negligee under this man's shadowed gaze.

A very, very skimpy, might-as-well-not-be-there negligee.

Ignoring the rising heat in her cheeks, Rachael planted her feet, tipping her chin up defiantly. No perv was going to make her blush and slink off like a cowed dog.

When his perusal of her finally ended, the man folded his arms across his chest. A vast improvement from attacking her, she supposed. Maybe she wouldn't be raped and murdered tonight.

Certifiable, Rach. Positively certifiable.

"And that would be you?" His voice, a rich aristo-cratic tenor, did not match his seedy-bar clothing or his actions of a short while ago. She was so puzzled by this juxtaposition that it took a moment for his words to register.

What had she said? Oh yeah, pick on someone his own size. Stupid, that. Rachael was pretty tall, standing at five foot eleven in her heels, but this man was still a head taller than her, and the man stalking up behind him was almost twice that.

What she should have done was trip the bastard up and then turned tail and run. The problem was that as she'd drawn closer to the struggle between the giant and the woman, she'd realized the woman wasn't a woman at all. She'd been nothing more than a teen. Fifteen, six-teen at best. The thought of two grown men, two mas-sive grown men, preying on someone less than half their age and half their size had filled her with such righteous anger that she'd just had to speak her mind.

And now her tongue was going to make her just another violent crime statistic.

Mike and Damon were going to be so pissed at her. At least the girl had gotten away.

Use your brains, Rach. You can't fight them, but you might still have a chance if you play it cool.

She shifted the bottle farther behind her back. She wasn't completely stupid, after all. Brandishing an empty vodka bottle at these two men would be akin to waving a red flag in front of a bull. Bad enough she'd tripped one and threatened him with some pepper spray.

She took a step back, lowering the pepper spray to

her side, though not removing her finger from the trigger. "I'll just, um, be going now."

"I'm afraid we can't do that." This came from the big man as he shifted out into the street, ready to block off her escape.

Rachael followed his movement, assessing him for possible weakness. He was younger than she'd first thought, probably close to her own twenty-four, and looked almost boyish with his unruly red hair and a dash of light freckles spreading across a set of cheekbones that could only have come from some Scottish Highlander's gene pool. On another day, in another place, he might have looked more like a big teddy bear than anything else. But not now. Not with that distinctively pissed-off expression twisting his features into a scowl.

She swallowed hard, her mind rapidly running in circles as she tried to think of a way out. All she could come up with was: stall.

"You can't do what?" she asked in her best bubble-headed blond voice.

Pretty boy gone slumming took a step toward her, chipping away at the distance she'd opened up with her retreat. "Let you go."

Guess the time for talk was over. She twisted, bringing up the pepper spray and plunging down on the trigger with her thumb. The big man dodged but some of the spray must have hit home because he roared, his massive forearm rising in front of his face. A flash of movement warned Rachael and, with a screech worthy of a B-movie actress, she swung the heavy liquor bottle from behind her back, aiming for the general region of her other assailant's head.

He did something with his hand, a negligible wave, and the bottle went sailing. The next moment his body slammed into hers, his arms encircling her like a wrestler.

She struggled, curling her hands pinned between his rock-solid chest and her own breasts into claws. Her screams for aid reverberating off the buildings.

"Hush. Hush."

No way. She was not going to go down like some meek lamb.

Only she did. His words, so soothing, not only slipped like a blanket of calm over her body, but slipped into her very being, easing her panic. Silence descended as she melted into his hold.

What the hell is this? What is he doing to me?

Hypnotist. It was the only explanation for this lax, out-of-body feeling she was experiencing.

"Look at me."

Obstinately, she tried to turn her face to the side. And found she couldn't. Her own body betrayed her, her head tipping back, her gaze lifting...

His eyes. Like silver. But not cold. Molten like a turbulent sky just before a summer storm.

She was slipping under his spell and knew it. Worse, she didn't care.

"That's it."

His voice lapped over her like a warm wave. Her body shuddered, warmth seeping in wherever his hands touched her. And his eyes. God those eyes.

Those eyes flared. Pupils expanding. Great pools of black trimmed with silver.

And then everything went white.

The Storm That Is Sterling

by Lisa Renee Jones

―〜〜―

He's her best weapon...

Sterling Jeter has remarkable powers as the result of a secret experiment to create a breed of super soldiers. Now he has to use everything he's got to help beautiful, brilliant Rebecca Burns, the only astrobiologist alive who can save humanity from a super-enhanced, deadly street drug.

Sterling and Rebecca's teenage romance was interrupted, and now they're virtually strangers. But the heat and attraction are still there, and even entrapment by an evil enemy can't stop them from picking up their mutual passion right where they left off...

―〜〜―

Praise for **The Legend of Michael***:*

"Jones launches a new series with this thrilling story of love and determination in a society on the brink of war... Readers will be hooked." —*RT Book Reviews*, 4 stars

"Awesome series...plenty of action and romance to keep you glued to your seat...An auto-buy for me." —*Night Owl Romance*, Reviewer Top Pick

For more Lisa Renee Jones, visit:

www.sourcebooks.com

Demons Like It Hot

by Sidney Ayers

If you can't stand the heat, get out of hell's kitchen.

A Recipe for Disaster...

Matthias Ambrose is a demon mercenary who never took
sides, until his attraction to the spunky caterer he was hired
to kidnap leads him to almost botch a job for the first time
in eight hundred years. Now he must protect her from his
former clients, but even an ice-cold demon like Matthias
struggles to resist her fiery charms.

Or the Perfect Ingredients for Passion...

Completely engrossed with planning menus and prepping
recipes for her shot at cooking show fame, star caterer Serah
SanGermano refuses to believe she's on a fast track to Hades.
But how's she supposed to stick to the kitchen if she can't
stand the heat of her gorgeous demonic bodyguard?

As a diabolical plot to destroy humanity unfolds and all hell
breaks loose in Serah's kitchen, she and Matthias find themselves knee-deep in demons and up to their eyeballs in love...

King of Darkness

by Elisabeth Staab

Eternal commitment is not on her agenda...

Scorned by the vampire community for her lack of power, Isabel Anthony lives a carefree existence masquerading as human—although, drifting through the debauched human nightlife, she prefers the patrons' blood to other indulgences. But when she meets the sexy, arrogant king of the vampires, this party-girl's life turns dark and dangerous.

But time's running out for the King of Vampires

Dead-set on finding the prophesied mate who will unlock his fiery powers, Thad Morgan must find his queen before their race is destroyed. Their enemies are gaining ground, and Thad needs his powers to unite his subjects. But when his search leads him to the defiant Isabel, he wonders if fate has gotten it seriously wrong...

For more Elisabeth Staab books, visit:

www.sourcebooks.com

Hold Me If You Can

by Stephanie Rowe

———

Without her passions, she has no magic…

It's unfortunate for Natalie that Nigel Aquarian is so compelling. With his inner demons, his unbridled heat, and his "I will conquer you" looks, he calls to her in exactly the way that nearly killed her.

But losing control means losing her life…

That he's an immortal warrior and that her powers rise from intense passions would seem to make them a match made in heaven. But unless they embrace their greatest fears, they'll play out their final match in hell.

With a unique voice that critics say "carves out her very own niche—call it paranormal romance adventure comedy," Stephanie Rowe delivers an irresistible pair of desperadoes dancing on the edge of self-control and pure temptation.

———

For more Stephanie Rowe books, visit:

www.sourcebooks.com

A Demon Does It Better

by Linda Wisdom

A madhouse is no place for a curious witch...

After more than a century, Doctor Lili Carter, witch healer extraordinaire, has returned to San Francisco and taken a job at Crying Souls Hospital and Asylum, where strange and sinister things are happening. Patients are disappearing, and Lili want to know why.

And doubly dangerous for a demon...

Lili finds herself undeniably attracted to perhaps the most mysterious patient of all—a dangerously demented and seriously sexy demon named Jared. What's behind this gorgeous chameleon demon's bizarre disappearances?

Before long Lili and Jared are investigating each other—and creating a whole new kind of magic.

Praise for Linda Wisdom:

"Humor, danger, and steamy sex make for an exciting read." —*RT Book Reviews*, 4 stars

For more Linda Wisdom books, visit:

www.sourcebooks.com

The Lord of Illusion

by Kathryne Kennedy

—◊—

He'll do anything to save her…

Rebel Lord Drystan Hawkes dreams of fighting for England's freedom. He gets his chance when he finds a clue to opening the magical portal to Elfhame, and he must race to find the slave girl who holds the key to the mystery. But even as Drystan rescues Camille Ashton from the palace of Lord Roden, it becomes unclear exactly who is saving whom…

For the fate of humankind lies with Camille…

Enslaved for years in a realm where illusion and glamour reign, Camille has learned to trust nothing and no one. But she's truly spellbound when she meets Drystan, a man different from any she's ever known, and the force of their passion may yet be strong enough to banish the elven lords from this world forever…

—◊—

Praise for Kathryne Kennedy's
The Fire Lord's Lover:

"Enthralling…a passionate love story."
—*RT Book Reviews*, 4½ stars

For more Kathryne Kennedy books, visit:

www.sourcebooks.com

Stud

by Cheryl Brooks

―――――

They're galaxies apart…

Even for a Zetithian, Tarq Zulveidione's sexual prowess is legendary. Believing it's all he's good for, Tarq sets out to perpetuate his threatened species by offering his services to women across the galaxy…

But one force can bring them together

Lucinda Force is the sensitive dark horse in a self-absorbed family, repeatedly told that no man will ever want such a plain woman. Lucy longs for romance, but is resigned to her loveless lot in life—until Tarq walks through the door of her father's restaurant on Talus Five…

―――――

Praise for Cheryl Brooks's **Virgin**:

"This one is all about the heat." —*Publishers Weekly*

For more Cheryl Brooks books, visit:

www.sourcebooks.com

Assassins in Love

by Kris DeLake

To kiss him? Or to kill him?

Misha's mission is to get Rikki, a rogue assassin who hates organizations and always does it *her* way, to join the Guild or give up her guns. He completely underestimated the effect she would have on him…and what heat and chaos they could bring to each other…

"A fast, edgy, and passionate story."—Mary Jo Putney, *New York Times* bestselling author

For more Kris DeLake books, visit:

www.sourcebooks.com

Untouched

by Sara Humphreys

She may appear to have it all, but inside she harbors a crippling secret...

Kerry Smithson's modeling career assures her that she will be admired from afar—which is what she wants, for human touch sparks blinding pain and mind-numbing visions.

Dante is a dream-walking shapeshifter—an Amoveo, who must find his destined mate or lose his power forever. Now that he has found Kerry, nothing could have prepared him for the challenge of keeping her safe. And it may be altogether impossible for Dante to protect his own heart when Kerry touches his soul...

For more of the Amoveo Legend series, visit:
www.sourcebooks.com

About the Author

Daphne Award–winning author Tes Hilaire started creating whole new worlds to escape Upstate New York's harsh winters before finally fleeing to sultry North Carolina. Her stories are edgy, exciting, and bring a hint of dark fantasy to paranormal romance. And no one ever has to shovel snow. For more information visit www.teshilaire.com.